CHALLENGING THE FIRES OF CHAOS

THE LEGACY OF ZYANTHIA BOOK FOUR

CHANTELLE GRIFFIN

Published by Chantelle Griffin in 2019

Interior layout by Chantelle Griffin
www.chantellegriffin.com

Cover artwork by Matthew K. Hoddy
www.spacepyrates.com

Catalogue-in-Publication details available
from the National Library of Australia

paperback ISBN: 978-0-6487305-0-7

Also available in ebook
ebook ISBN: 978-0-6487305-1-4

For my sister

For all that has been before, for all the pain and sorrow, may you rise above them all. For the path less travelled brings hardship, adventure and triumph.

THE ZYANTHIAN REGION, TORDOREN

CHAPTER ONE

Facing the consequences

No matter how much Saranon tried the taste of blood would not leave. It had been days since her half-brother had challenged her. She smiled at the thought of humiliating him. The victory had been sweet even if she had lost her temper. It had been worth every moment. Her mess of brown hair blew across her face in the wind. Somehow it always managed to break free of the tie. She blew it out of the way and the great black dragon crashed onto the deck mid-flight. She jumped clear swinging over the balcony, clinging to the narrow ledge. 'Kat,' she shouted in disgust.

The dragon moved his large frame overhead as he nimbly sat beside her. His deep dark eyes remained level with hers. A flight of dragon riders swept across the edge of the Menna Range. The dragon nudged her and she clambered up before being squashed. He bolted into the air picking up speed and she clung on. He swooped down without slowing and she shouted at him. Instead the dragon sped up skimming dangerously close to the ground. Saranon shouted again, but he would not listen. Kat began to rise skyward and she let go. For a brief moment she was air born. She flung her arms wide catching the breeze. Then fell, sensing the world Tordoren below. Yet she refrained from using sorcery as the wind caught her. A great whoosh reached upward as a bellowing gust of wizardry softened the blow.

She landed on the damp mossy ground and Mitch ran over. His shadow loomed blocking the sun. He towered over her at the ready with every muscle in his neck showing. Mitch glared at her as she brushed off the dirt. 'You were supposed to stay at the Temple.' He said.

It was difficult to take him seriously with those soft brown eyes. The former guard still had a hard edge, but she ignored it. 'It was getting stuffy,' she retorted.

Before he could respond. The great black marmoz dragon thudded into the side of the mountain. Katholomu was at home in Alveron.

She had stolen the dragon more than year ago, when his rider had attacked Odana Temple. The dragon only listened to her when it suited him. He was watching the dragon riders, daring them to fly closer. The Menna Range was home to the Otturin sorcerer clan. They were renowned for training dragons. Odana Temple had once been theirs, before it was abandoned during the Dreshan Occupation. The temple rose above the mountain and ran deep beneath the rocky ground. Mitch stayed by her side. The temple pass was calm and deceptive. The road that let through was one of the most volatile. Travellers would often disappear or be found days later with tales of horrible creatures.

She stared with intrigue. As several figures in the distance made their way from the pass to the Menna Range. One turned looking straight at her. 'You are asking for trouble.' Mitch said and she waved.

Katholomu glared at her as though she had committed an offence. She wondered if he ever thought of returning to the Otturin. The clan that had trained him and attacked Odana Temple. She watched as a dragon rider broke from the flock, skimming close to the pass. Kat tensed, it was the only warning before he heaved his full weight into the side the dragon. Both dragons and the rider tumbled in a haphazard motion to the ground. The great black dragon growled with his back arched. Mitch grabbed her by the shoulder before she could run toward them. A searing pain ran along her sore muscles and she glared at him. The rider was tall and slim. His dark robes were dishevelled, but his manner was cool and calm. He raised his arms to Katholomu. 'Let go.' She said to the wizard, but Mitch held on with a firm grip.

The dragon lifted his full bulk forward and ploughed in the shield of sorcery. The sorcerer flew backward and she began to laugh until the dragon honed in. The Otturin glared at her and lashed out with his sorcery. To her amazement Mitch strode in front of the volatile dragon. He twisted the Otturin's arm in a firm grip. 'You can let go,' she said in an amused tone.

Mitch now held both her and the Otturin with the dragon growling overhead. She recognised the dragon rider, he had flown Kat toward the Temple. 'You!' She shouted and tried to wrestle free. 'That's him,' she said to the wizard.

She managed to shove the Otturin to the ground and Mitch lifted her in the air. They both fell as the Otturin attacked, Mitch clamped him to the dirt. At least she was free. 'Who are you?' She asked.

The dragon answered, 'Kail.'

Saranon tried to hide her surprise, 'He only says one word, 'Coward'. Is that what your name means?'

She pranced around as Mitch strained to keep Kail from lashing out. 'You hurt my friends.' She said.

The dragon placed the weight of his paw down on the Otturin and Mitch made a hasty retreat. 'I don't like people that hurt my friends.' She said.

The dragon began to move and crush his prey. 'He belongs to me.' Kail sputtered.

'I think Katholomu is done listening.' She responded.

'The clan is coming,' Mitch said. 'You have done enough.'

She pretended to ignore him as the Otturin sorcerers approached from the Menna Range. 'You owe Kat an apology.' She waited for Kail to speak.

He was still trying to wriggle free, but the dragon had him pinned. He reached out with his sorcery and pulled her toward him. The dragon fell back in surprise. The

Otturin clan had reached them and Kail followed with the utmost obedience. The great dragon stood by her side. It was the first time he had ever adhered to her command. She wondered how long it would last. The beast looked down at her with a piercing cold gaze. At least they had one thing in common, they both disliked Kail.

The frustration played in her mind as she followed Mitch. The silence only broke when they reached the temple. The solid formation of the monumental structure provided its own climate. With the warmth of the central core emanating from beneath. She should have dealt with the sorcerer while she had the chance. Saranon glared at Mitch. His face was cold and unforgiving. The expression told her the matter was done, but it only enraged her. 'I had him,' she seethed.

The wizard stood firm, 'You were meant to stay here.'

His words opened a verbal tirade as she shouted at him. 'I had that pathetic weasel, if it wasn't for you...'

His expression changed and she turned to see a crowd watching. Shaun approached them. His broad shoulders and stocky build looked out of place among the guards. He eyed Mitch with a keen interest, 'Did you run into trouble?'

'Kail,' she said. 'The sorcerer went for my dragon.'

'Is that all?' He asked.

She almost exploded in anger, 'Do you care nothing for what they did?'

'The matter is settled,' he said.

The calm air shown by the wizards was infuriating as

she struggled to contain her rage. 'How can you…' She shouted and stormed off letting the thought trail.

Her mind was a blur and she was getting nowhere. She was expected to forget that the Otturin attacked the temple. It did not sit easy on her mind.

The breeze was cool and she closed her eyes, leaning back against the wall. The image replayed in her head. Shaun had been focused on Mitch, but why? Then it dawned on her, the wizard was her hilazen. She never did understand the strange rules that wizards bestowed on their own. She peered around the corner to find Mitch. His expression was caught between wanting to say something, then he let it be. 'It would be best if you forgot Kail.' He said.

She could feel the firm gaze of his stare and the coldness that ran underneath. It was not the first time they had argued, but he always remained calm. The irritation plagued her. As she swung from the balustrade sliding down the narrow staircase. There were many ways to find the dragon pens. An angry dragon required an easy escape route, yet that did not bother her. At Odana the pens opened to the morning sun, capturing the warmth of the day. Noise scattered through the large open arches holding up the mountainous keep. Clara ran up to greet her and they almost collided. Her face as red as her bright fiery hair. 'Kat,' she said in a huff, trying to catch her breath.

The commotion reached her as she glanced across the broken stalls. Two young dragons were cowering in the corner and a voice boomed orders. She dashed through the maze of people clearing up the mess. There was no sign of

Katholomu. 'He's gone to the Menna Range.' Clara said.

'How do you know?' The sight of the great beast in the distant sky answered her question.

Her heart sank. 'If father finds out we're in trouble,' Clara spoke.

'Quick,' she said scrambling onto the nearest dragon.

Holdvar would not budge without his wizard. Where was Mitch? She tried again and the great beast's muscles held like stone. She had no luck with dragons and they were losing time.

She scurried down into the heart of the Keep. The wizard had to be somewhere. She ran ahead through the winding corridors careful not to knock anyone over. The tight corners made it almost impossible. She caught someone's shoulder and spun around as Anthony held her. The last time she had seen him, it had been when she stomped on him. Anthony wore the uniform of a Alveronian soldier, but he was not much older than she. His rugged tone softened as he let go. 'Where are you headed?' He asked in steady tone.

'I lost my wizard,' she said.

'Really?' He exclaimed.

'Really,' she retorted before running off.

Sometimes wizards could be no help. Before she was able to ask again he had left. Was it so hard to find Mitch? He had warned her not to go near the Otturin, but that did not apply to the dragon. She extended her sorcery through the Keep in the hope of finding him. The only noise that returned was the low dull hum of the central core below.

She rushed down the stairs, the thick round columns ebbed out from the solid walls. Not many people ventured underneath the habitable area. It was said the spirits of the people trapped during the Dreshan Occupation still remained. Silent whispers filled the void. She could sense movement, but the sound failed to filter through the air. Saranon ran into the opening between the columns. A group of wizards huddled round. Shaun, the gruff old man had his back turned to her. He turned to face her and she caught sight of Mitch. He was huddled near the floor. It took all her strength to hold back her sorcery and not send Shaun flying across the room. 'That's my wizard,' she shouted into the silence. 'My wizard.'

She stood her ground facing the one who blocked her path. It was all she could do to stay calm. All she wanted to do was rush forward and take Mitch with her. Yet there was a shield of wizardry holding her back.

She fought her way through, yet the shield held tight. 'Let him go,' she was losing patience.

The shield began to weaken and she took a chance. Saranon plunged in, shoving the wizard to the side. A searing pain wrapped around her when she gripped Mitch, but refused to let go. He returned her hold. They ran toward the stairs before she gathered her thoughts. Shouts echoed spiralling upward. The stench from the dragon pens hit them. Mitch leaped onto Holdvar and the dragon lunged forward with a sprint. Pounding his paws hard against the ground. She clung tight as the great beast swayed, his whole body flying into the sky. The air rushed in a wild motion as she gripped close to stay on. A steady beat of the wings gave a calm rhythm. She gazed ahead to the Menna Range, looming ever closer along the horizon.

'I thought you wanted to avoid the Otturin,' she said.

'I asked you to avoid them,' he replied.

She was unsure how this was any different, but kept the thought silent. They swept above the open pass and onto the rising mountains. The air grew thin as every breath made her head feel light. Mitch drove the beast down into a gliding circle as an explosion arced through the air. No one noticed as they landed. The few Otturin were scattered around the raging inferno. Engulfing a building that had once contained dragons. The former occupants gathered among the valley providing an ideal coverage.

Saranon stayed beside a flock of juvenile dragons while gazing across the darkening sky. The blaze lit up the night with an ominous crackle and she turned. Kail stood so close and the anger she felt earlier diminished. His eyes were haunting in the uneven light. While his face showed nothing but exhaustion. Without thinking she gripped his hand, a small welcome gesture. Smoke gathered from the dying blaze sweeping overhead. A great rush of air broke as Katholomu swooped low. She began to shout at the beast and Kail laughed. Another dragon swooped down from the sky, it was identical. She glared at the sorcerer and he only smiled. 'Katholomu,' she shouted.

Both dragons responded. 'Is this some sort of trick?' She asked.

'I swear there is no trick,' Kail replied.

The smirk stayed on his face far too long, 'You can take Kat if you know which one.'

She glared at him and the smirk turned into an open laugh. 'All right, one is Kat's brother.'

'Really?' She asked in amazement and he nodded. 'I should be able to tell them apart.'

'Yes, you should,' he lingered on the final word to her annoyance.

'Do you enjoy being irritating?' She asked.

He snorted with laughter, 'Only to you.'

The dragons began to stir, they both eyed her. There was a glint of amusement as they synchronised their movement. A breeze swept through and she saw the scarring across the other dragon's shoulder. She stifled a gasp, ' What happened?'

'Gormeron survived the Dreshans,' he replied.

The great beast lowered his head and nuzzled her. The tension left his muscles as he sank to the ground. Kat remained close, not wanting to leave his brother. 'You had better come inside,' Kail spoke with a great reluctance.

It was the most affection he had shown and Saranon treated it with suspicion. The charred walls stood well, but the contents had been obliterated. This did not worry the dragons who curled up on the remnants. No one was surprised that a fire had taken hold in the dragon pens. 'You have no idea how to look after Katholomu,' he said.

The cold remark hit home and she glared at him. 'You bite so easy,' he added.

'So do you,' she retorted and he smiled.

'Kat stays with me,' she said.

'Then why don't you take him,' he taunted.

Saranon gazed out into the night, the dragon was going nowhere. 'He's sleeping,' she replied.

Kail burst out laughing, tears rolling down his cheeks. She began to feel her face go red. 'You can stay here until Kat wakes,' he said.

She managed to hold back her anger. Long enough for Mitch to interrupt, 'We accept your gracious hospitality.'

She glared at him, it was going to be a long night. The air carried with it the many rumbles and growls from the hoards of dragons. A thud shook the building. She shouted at Katholomu before realising where they were. Kail gave her a disapproving glance. Before Gormeron hit the building with a resounding thud. She peered over the balcony as both stared back, daring her to say something. 'Did you teach them to do that?' She asked Kail.

'No,' he replied in a sullen tone.

'How did you end up with that?' She pointed at Kat.

'I am a first grade rider,' he answered.

'I was not questioning your ability,' she mused, eyeing him up and down. 'I meant the dragon.'

He let out a sigh of frustration. No answer was forthcoming, but his shoulders relaxed. The dragons slept below and the hour was getting late. Smoke lingered in the air. It was a small reprieve as the occupants were busy settling the dragons.

As she prepared for the night Mitch leaned over. 'I'll take the first watch,' he said.

Saranon was about to protest, but the wizard had been through much. There remained an uneasy feeling from being so close to the Otturin. 'Stay out of trouble,' she replied.

His composure relaxed but he kept an eye on her. Her dreams were filled with dragons, so many of them. Mitch woke her and it was still dark. She peered out to see the moonlight and movement caught her eye. Dragons and their riders filled the sky. There had been a time when she would have given anything to be the one flying on a majestic beast. Saranon gazed, longing to be in the sky rather than stuck on the ground.

The sleeping wizard was the only reason why she fought the urge to climb out the window. That and the fact that she had lost sight of Katholomu. The morning light burst across the mountain range filling the room with warmth. She almost tripped over the wizard who was still half asleep and ran downstairs. Gormeron greeted her. The dragon's scars stretched across the surface of his thick skin. His head lowered and she could not resist the temptation. Shouts rang out as they took to the sky. A sense of exhilaration came over her and she ignored the protests. Gormeron had a graceful peace hidden underneath the rough surface. His movement turned into one fluid motion as he raced for the sky.

The fine shrill of air rushed past the dragon's wings, chilling her face as they went. The elegant beast spiralled before descending to the ground. Her head spun with excitement and she waited as the beast lowered his shoulders.

Katholomu greeted her, his tail curled in a relaxed pose. As Saranon slid away a silence fell. She stood between the two great dragons. Kat moved first, bowing his head in recognition. She reached out and the dragon stepped away. He eyed her, daring her to come closer. 'Would you rather stay here?' She asked.

The giant beast purred and she glared at him. Kail grinned with satisfaction savouring the moment. Mitch patted her on the shoulder, 'We need to go.'

There was a finality in his voice that made her hesitate. The Otturin went about their day as though she and Mitch did not exist. The familiar warm glow of the lay-line enveloped them. She took the lead through the shortcut. The silence surrounding her compounded by the absence of her dragon. Odana Temple loomed up ahead. The thought of having to explain Kat's absence weighed on her mind. She hesitated as her stomach churned and glared at Mitch. His pace never faltered and she ran to catch up. 'Did you plan that?' She asked.

A silence hung in the air before he answered. 'Do you want bloodshed?'

'You let them take Kat,' she said.

He stopped, 'No one takes a full grown marmoz. He chose to leave.'

His stare cut through her and she wondered if he would leave to. Once, she would have done anything to be on her own. Once, she had shed blood to be free. Perhaps later she would find a reason to return. The temple boundary walls clung to the earth. With faint remnants from a distant past. She wanted to be mad at the wizard, but Mitch had stayed by her side through more than she cared to admit. The morning sun warmed the stone floor as it gleamed in the strong light. Clara swept down the spiral stairs, 'Are you ready?'

Her eyes lit up with excitement, 'Took long enough.'

Saranon did not want to say she had lost the dragon. She hoped no one would notice. As she stuffed her belongings into the large sova bags, shrinking them down. She would have to sort out all the trinkets, but that could wait. The sloping valley hid the narrow treacherous path to the Pearl Castle. She took one last glimpse of the artefact. Before Clara wrapped the remnant of an elaborate hilt away from prying eyes. The bond-breaker had belonged to Zeralden Hadenvar, Queen of Darkania and the last Angeon. The sphere of heart stone at the centre had not a scratch. It still held a faint glow from the sorcery trapped within.

CHAPTER TWO

A risk worth taking

A matted dark hide rolled down toward Saranon at a steady pace. As the dragon took full advantage of the dry dirt, rubbing it well into his coat. She managed to leap over onto his giant belly as Katholomu halted in mid-motion. Turning his head to look her square in the eye. She stumbled while trying to stand. The great beast let out a warm snort of smelly sulphur. As she managed to cover her mouth in time.

'Kat!' Saranon shouted in disgust.

The dragon could be annoying at times. It was a relief to see the great beast that had snubbed her earlier, even if he was unhelpful. When she closed her eyes she could still see Kail glaring at her. Her friend Clara laughed in delight. As Kat gently moved her out of the way and kept on rolling down the hill. She had met Clara the on the first visit to

Odana Temple. It had been too long, it felt wonderful to relax in the moment. She watched as the dragon pretended to make chase. The deep red hair of the sorceress, Clara, trailed past tickling Kat's nose. He sneezed and slumped to the ground. Saranon could feel her face grow hot as he managed to flatten several trees in the process. The dragon merrily used his tail to squash down a patch of shrubs before curling up to rest. It felt good to have Mitch around, the wizard towered over her in comparison. As she stood on her toes and frowned. He smiled and said nothing which made her even more suspicious. As the sun set the cool breeze of autumn followed with a distant reminder of the days to come. Saranon made herself at home by the open fire as a scurry sent a spray of dirt overhead

She looked up and the dragon loomed over her. Katholomu's eyes shone with a purpose as he sniffed the open air. Before she could blink. The great beast leapt over their small campsite and into the shadows of dusk. Filling the sky with the last of the sun's golden rays. If anything she was glad he was gone, the dragon had been fidgeting all day. Clara filled the void with talk of the next step of their journey toward the army barracks. As the sounds of the distant wildlife echoed in the background. Saranon fell into a peaceful sleep. Finally the troubles of Darkonia were beginning to fade from her mind. They were all too real, but for now she could pretend they did not exist. Once again away from her homeland. A place that she longed for and loathed at the same time.

A tiny brush near the edge of her sleeping bag brought

her awake as the dawn crept in. The dull black outer shell of the giant millipede. Crawling unhindered as she watched in amazement. Its body seemed to be never ending. She crouched forward taking care as she picked it up. The creature appeared unafraid as she held it out of curiosity. She took it over to Clara. As the creature caught her friend's attention and screamed. It was then that Saranon realised it was not the greatest idea to pick up the creature and let it go.

Mitch stared at her in disbelief, 'That's a malicor.'

She tried to apologise to Clara who begrudgingly let the matter go. As they set out on their journey toward the Pearl Castle. The day shone bright as they made their way up the rugged hillside. This was as far as she had seen on the last visit. Odana Temple had magnificent sweeping views of the land. Travelling was exciting and rewarding at the same time. Her friend was intent on their mission. Saranon sighed and followed. Somehow she had been conned into helping. Yet the truth was she did not need much convincing.

Facing the wrath of the Darkonian Army again was less appealing than making the journey to the Mercidian Council. She wanted to say something, but all she caught sight of was a mass of fiery red hair. Clara shook her head, 'You had to pick it up.'

She apologised again and this time her friend relaxed. Saranon breathed a sigh of relief. She was so used to Clara talking that the silence was unbearable.

Before long her friend's voice filled the air with the

history of the great tomb of the old King. She stared ahead to where her friend was pointing. All she could see was the same dry brown grass and rocky ground. Still she did not want to dampen her friend's enthusiasm. Making a sound that resembled excitement. Mitch chuckled, then held back to join them. The wizard took great delight in joining the conversation.

She glared at him hoping he would change the subject, but the wizard was having none of it. Mitch extended out his wizardry as she watched in amazement. The images outside of the tomb glowed faintly through the ground. She glared at him in annoyance as the wizard showed off. The group walked on and Saranon stayed behind to watch the image fade. There was so much of the world she longed to know. She tried to imitate the wizard as her sorcery rose to the surface, yet it was too much. She grimaced as it scorched the edge of the grass.

Clara was moving way ahead and Mitch kept glancing over his shoulder. She let out a heavy sigh and she ran to catch up. She was not about to be left behind. As they cleared the edge of the ridge the trail led down. A whooshing noise caught her attention overhead. She gazed up at the shadowy underbelly of a marmoz dragon. The great beast flew without a care for the travellers below. They were nearing the edge of the great dragon colony at the centre of Alveron. Still, it did not make her feel any easier as several more dragons flew in the distance. Yet again she was being left behind. She rushed ahead and tripped, using her energy to block the fall. She bent down and wiped her tunic. Then as she moved forward the ground gave way underneath. It was all she could do to hang on as the earth slipped beneath her. She reached out with her senses, yet she could not hang on. As she fell further away from the distant light above. She screamed. All that came back in the darkness was a scattering of meaningless noise. She tried to focus using her energy to soften the blow. As the rugged floor of an old tunnel revealed itself. She continued to hold onto her energy lighting a path in the dark.

As she peered up, all sign of the outside world was lost. A scurrying sound ran behind her along the wall. Yet she could see nothing as she made her way through the tunnel. The ceiling had broken in patches worn with age as she made her way along. A scurrying noise caught her ear and she turned. The light reflecting back off the tunnel showed nothing. Saranon moved further down the passage searching for a way out. If there was one she could not see it. It was as though Tordoren had closed up trapping her in. She reached for her talik, but the small circular device was useless as she opened it. She was too far away from a Keep for it to work and she let out a sigh.

The grime coated the walls so heavily that it was hard to tell what lay underneath. She wiped away a small patch and extended her senses along the tunnel. She jumped as a faint signal returned like a tiny hum in the distance. It was not what she had expected as she strode toward the source. She moved out into the room and a faint sensation sent shivers up her spine. As something brushed against her arm. She peered in the darkness and held the light above her. Only the shadows playing tricks on her spun to life as she glanced around. The hairs on the back of her neck stood on edge. As the air grew cold and her heart thudded in her ears.

She froze as a soft breath filtered down the back of her neck. She swallowed, taking a deep breath and turned around. The giant creature that loomed in the dark, caught her attention with its piercing yellow eyes. The ockren stood still as its face drew back into a snarl. Before the she had time to leap out of the way a hollow growl rumbled through its belly. The giant magical cat that stood higher than she, leaped forward. She let out a soundless scream before her voice caught up. She blocked the creature, but all it did was slow it down. As she ran, hurtling through the nearest tunnel.

Somehow the creature managed to squeeze through. As it pounded the ground behind her with a speed that made the panic rise in her chest. She ducked through another tunnel, losing track of where she was going. As the ockren rounded the corner kicking the dust up in the air. The ground shook and it growled as the sound echoed around her in the tight space. Saranon summoned her energy as she tried to hold. Yet her mind could not focus. The attempt appeared feeble as the ockren gained speed. She headed further down as the trail tapered off. Skidding to stop before the edge of a giant void.

She peered down into a great hole in the ground swallowed by the darkness and gulped. Behind her the creature ran and her heart thudded hard as she tried to think. She peered up to the worn edges of the old wall poking out. Without a second thought she grasped the rough edge and heaved herself up out of the way. She clung above the opening trying not to use her sorcery. As the only form of light went out. It was pitch dark, yet she could sense the creature below and clung on. Sweat poured down her brow and she hoped the magical creature could not sense her. The ockren sniffed as it waited below in the darkness. She tried not to make a sound.

Saranon clung on hoping the creature could not sense her. As she held on hoping to stay hidden. The panic welled up inside her as she managed to keep her mind clear. Below she could sense the creature turning away. Then a thought filled her mind. How was she going to get out? While trying to remain calm she moved her hand down grasping the rock as her leg slipped. It was enough to send to send a clump of loose rubble rattling down the wall. Saranon cringed and held on hoping it would not attract the ockren. Yet at the same time a rush of air ran across her back. She flinched as her energy lit up the space.

She was caught in the beast's great paw as it yanked her away from the wall. She scrambled to hold on using her energy, but it was no use. As the ockren flung her into the abyss. She screamed as the realisation hit and she was sent into the air. The panic rose up through her stomach as her mind raced. Before she could think, her sorcery surged within. She used the energy to slow her descent. Until she found herself floating in midair. Her heart thudded in her chest as she managed to right herself from an awkward angle. As she stared upward a faint hint of daylight glimmered taunting her from above.

A deep low growl rang out. It echoed around her and without any hesitation she hauled herself upward. She hoped that it would be enough. As she strengthened the flow of energy while steadily rising. The glow became larger as she headed upward and out of the old tomb. As she reached the narrowest part. The strength of her energy threw her out with such speed that it took her a moment to hold back. She spun into the air before slowing near the dry brown earth. As the sun's rays beckoned in the distance. For a moment she saw no one as she searched around. Then a voice called from behind the clearing. 'We're over here,' Mitch said.

Her shoulders slumped with the reassurance of the wizard's voice. She found them waiting near the edge of the lay-line. 'Where have been?' Clara scowled in frustration.

Saranon tried to catch her breath. Before she could talk her friend had already entered the lay-line. Mitch reached over patting her on the shoulder as he urged her on. A frown crossed his face as he stared at her, 'We'll talk later.'

She was not about to argue. Her mind was still racing and she could not wait to get as far away from the tomb as possible.

The faint glow of the lay-line lit up in a circular fashion as they entered. A wave of relief spread over her as they made up time toward the barracks. Mitch eyed her occasionally with a look that said he wanted to say something. She was in no mood to talk as the image of the ockren stayed fresh in her mind. The travel did well to clear her head as she settled into her usual grumpy self. Almost stubbing her toe more than once on hidden rocks in the long dry grass. After a while she realised it was easier to let Mitch go first and he chuckled. She gave out a long sigh.

Her journey moved quickly as she stopped for a moment. Gazing down at a scattering of old carvings hidden in the long grass. She held the broken stone in her hand before taking care as she placed it back. They were near the end of the lay-line. She turned to find the others had gone ahead. She could make out Mitch near the opening. His hands were held high above his head and Saranon realised he was in trouble. As the faint sound of voices trickled her way. She held out her energy to the side of the lay-lines. It sparked before forming a hole and ran though. Her legs misjudged the ground as they crumpled beneath her. Panic began to rise as she lost sight of the wizard, then her senses indicated where he was.

He was some way off in the distance. As she found herself behind the wiccan who had cornered her friends. Her mind raced as she hoped Clara would provide an indication. Saranon felt lost without her friend. Clara would know what to do, but then her friend was the one who needed help. She tried to think as she listened to the voices. A rustle sounded close. As her heart sank at the realisation, she had been discovered. The wiccan cornered her in semi-circle as she froze, not knowing what to do. For all Clara's conversations she had not mentioned wiccan. A young man's voice shouted above the crowd, 'This is the one.'

She gaped in surprise as Oswin held out his hand in a welcoming gesture. Without knowing what else to do, she exchanged the greeting. He smiled, 'Jedd said we might see you.'

Saranon had completely forgotten her first encounter with wiccan community in Normisia. That did not explain how someone in the heart of Alveron knew. Her bewilderment was written all over her face as the strange misunderstanding melted away. Before she could ask, Clara whispered in her ear, 'Just go with it.'

She was not about to argue as their new friends led them to their town through the clearing. The place was sheltered and well protected with wards, yet the wiccan appeared nervous. As she remembered how unusual was for a sorceress to visit Bellington Castle. For a moment she forgot all about being a sorceress. As the small town reminded her of the castle in Normisia. Juren was less grand, but it was well-kept and full of life. She smiled breathing in the smell of fresh bread. Her stomach rumbled, a reminder it was lunchtime. As they sat down to eat the sorceress was too content to worry over the initial hostility.

She scoffed several mouthfuls before noticing Clara's calm gaze. She looked at Oswin, 'How do you know Jedd?'

It was a question she should have asked sooner, yet the thought had not crossed her mind. Oswin explained about the trade route between Alveron and Normisia. She listened while finishing the meal. The wiccan gazed intently.

As though there was something he wanted to say, 'You have been in the tomb.'

Clara gasped in astonishment as Saranon wondered what the fuss was about. She was still unsure as to how she had fallen in.

She began going red with embarrassment and spoke of the ockren chasing her. Clara's expression only made her feel worse. Oswin politely interrupted, 'The ward's have been giving unusual readings.'

He did not say any more, but then he did not need to. It was the first time Saranon had been chased by an ockren. She had the distinct feeling the creature had been grumpy. Well before she had fallen into its home. As the afternoon sun lowered over the hillside. She followed Oswin as he showed them around. Pointing out the wards on the outskirts. It had been over a year since she had taken a close look at the type of wards that circled the township. She place her hand on the stone and it tingled. She had spent half her life getting to know the wards from the camps. This one was similar as it shone with a faint glow.

The air above moved with a mild hum. She watched with a steady silence, as though waiting for something to happen. Clara had grown bored of the exercise as she began to talk away. Suggesting they move on when a fine wisp of magic broke in the air just above the ward. Her friend stopped mid-sentence as they gazed on. Yet whatever it was had fallen silent. She moved her hand just above the stone. It was as though nothing unusual had happened, even though they had all seen it. Mitch waited for the group to ponder in amazement before he added, 'It's sorcery.'

'Don't be silly,' Clara said, unsure of herself.

'I've seen it before,' Mitch replied.

Saranon looked at the expression on his face. She could not read his thoughts, but the seriousness of his tone made her cautious. As she stepped away from the ward. She was not sure if she wanted to know what was causing it. The hour was growing late as they welcomed the invitation to stay at the tavern. That looked almost exactly like the one she had stayed at in Normisia. She unpacked her belongings and Mitch sat down next to her, 'We have a problem.'

'What do you mean?' She asked.

'The ward,' the wizard spoke.

She sighed with resignation. That she was not going to get much sleep tonight, 'I'll take a look.'

There was no point arguing with the wizard. Since Jedd was friends with Oswin she felt obligated to at least do one check. The wizard offered to wake her later so she could get some sleep. Even though her mind was racing, she drifted off.

A hand waved in front startling her as the faint glow of light shimmered in the distance. Mitch looked on expectantly as he waited. She had not planned for the wizard to join her, yet she was not about to argue. As they crept downstairs trying not to make a sound she closed the door behind her. The place was even more beautiful at night. As the faint glow of lights sparkled throughout the buildings. Mitch stood behind her ready for action.

She could sense his irritation as they made their way out beyond the wards. They cleared the boundary as she peered back and froze. A faint green vapour emanated from the ground on the outskirts of the wards.

'Wow,' she spoke in complete surprise. As a horrible tingling sensation shivered down her spine. 'What is it?'

'I was going to ask you,' Mitch said as he stood beside her.

The two stayed there not knowing what to do as they watched and waited in the dark. She had not seen anything like it and wondered if had anything to do with the ockren.

CHAPTER THREE

The ancient sword

The lay-line led to the barracks. The last part of their journey before Saranon could ride a dragon again. The land was Katholomu's home. The dragon had hardly paid her attention since they arrived. A great roar loomed overhead as they peered up to the sky. A group of marmoz dragons flew in formation. She could sense no riders. As they made their way across without any fear of being seen in the light.

She stayed close to the wizard this time and he grinned. Mitch was amused by her acceptance of him. Clara had been unnerved to learn that Saranon had bonded a wizard as her companion. Her friend maintained a respectful distance. As the scenery changed from dry brown to patches of green. Along the edge of the forest the sounds of the creatures that lived there reached her ears. Before she knew it, the first sight of the barracks was revealed up ahead. She stopped in awe as the great building loomed out of the hillside.

The clearing led to a well-worn path and without thinking she walked towards it. A booming voice towered over her as a wizard stood close and jumped out of the way in surprise. She remembered to breathe as Gannon stood in her way. The wizard was accompanied by a small group.

Mitch spoke up behind her, 'She's with me.'

Gannon nodded and stepped aside to let them pass. A hub of life emerged as they drew near the barracks. Adeyorn revealed itself to be a full fledged wizard keep and she laughed. It did not matter where she travelled she always managed to end up at a wizard keep.

Saranon had not ridden a dragon for days, but it felt like ages as her eyes lit up with excitement. She was looking forward to the ride. Mitch placed a hand on her shoulder, 'The Shalough live near the colony.'

Her excitement caught in her throat as the words sank in. The Shalough could have helped her train and chose not to. Her mood dampened, yet she was determined to ride. She longed for the open sky and the wind in her hair. It would be nice to ride again after travelling from Odana Temple on foot.

She could smell the dragons before she saw them even though they were clean. Their hides glistened in the afternoon light. She reached out her senses to the one closest. As the great beast lowered its head and rubbed a cheek along her side in recognition. A great roar thundered from behind as she turned her head. In time to witness

Katholomu puffing out his chest in a grand stance. 'Are you jealous?' Saranon asked with an amused smile.

The dragon lowered his head until he was face to face. Then snorted blowing his fowl breath all over her. She coughed as she waved her hand in annoyance, 'You need a bath.'

She cringed at the thought knowing full well she would be the one having to clean him. Kat's coat was covered in dirt and the smell was not much better. The dragon ran ahead of her into the dragon pens. Hurling himself forward with huge leap into the shallow pool. The affect was instant as water sprayed everywhere except on the dragon. Saranon sighed, this was not the grand entrance she had hoped for. As great beast ruined any chance of making an impression. Perhaps next time would be different. Yet she doubted it as she managed to find a brush and started scrubbing. At least Katholomu would be clean.

As the air grew dark around her the glow from the lights in the keep illuminated her path. She watched the sun slowly set over the rugged rambling landscape. That marked the edge of civilisation. The heart of Alveron was a place that could turn. Even the most adventurous gave it a second thought. 'Are you sure you want to do this?' Mitch asked as he stood ready to go.

Saranon gave him a puzzled look, she had not expected him to be so keen.

They strode out toward the dragons. As the last of the sun's golden raise shone out from above the hill. The autumn breeze swept through her hair. Yet there was still warmth in the day as the memory of summer remained.

As she clambered aboard her dragon. Gannon climbed up beside her, 'What are you doing?'

The wizard said, 'You won't make it on your own.'

She could feel her anger rise and was tempted to say something. Katholomu was too excited to pay the new rider any interest. As he worked up to a mighty run before leaping into the shadowy sky. The cool breeze whipped along her cheeks. As she glanced downward over the approaching dragon colony.

The heart was home to much more than dragons. As her eyes caught sight of some unfamiliar creatures. The wizard directed Kat with an experienced ease. As he used his wizardry to search the ground. At first she could not understand what Gannon was looking for. Yet as he continued she could see the occasional flare striking back. 'Does that really work?' She asked in amazement.

'Most of the time,' Gannon answered.

As she gazed on watching the wizard work a surge of energy prickled along her senses. 'We need to return,' Gannon spoke.

The walls were full of laughter echoing up from the large rooms. Where the occupants of the keep gathered. A warm fire crackled away near the middle of the room. As she approached to take the chill from her hands. Mitch leaned down as he picked up a small parcel and presented it to her, 'Happy Birthday.'

She looked up rather embarrassed and accepted the gift. She had forgotten about her birthday. She felt much older than seventeen. Even though Mitch took great joy in reminding her how young she was. The parcel held a small book. It was not much to look at as she turned it over before opening the dark leather cover. Inside she saw a map of Alveron with details about the creatures that lived there in. She smiled and hugged the wizard.

As Saranon curled up in bed after a long evening she held the book illuminated by a tiny ball of light. She flicked through the pages and found the malicor. Mitch entered the room. He snuffed out her light with his wizardry and the room fell into darkness. 'Hey,' she exclaimed, but the wizard had already gone to bed.

She snuggled down. The Keep hummed away merrily underneath as she drifted off to sleep. Her dreams were filled of the strange land. As images of the creatures crept through. Then her thoughts turned. As the image changed and she could see the wizards from the barracks. They were running away from something. Every time she looked her eyes would not focus. All she could see was the cold grey sky looming behind, as they fled toward her.

A clap of thunder loomed outside and woke Saranon from her slumber. It was still dark as she rushed downstairs. The Keep sang with every step. It was speaking in amongst the hum, but not to her. She reached out her senses, yet all she could find was emptiness. The noise reached her ears as she opened the door. light filtered through from the dragon pens.

Before anyone could stop her. She was out in the courtyard with the grey sky looming overhead. The rain stopped short of the courtyard. She looked on as the wizards darted toward the Keep. A voice rang out behind them. The voice of a sorcerer and before anyone could stop her she answered. As the rain poured down, she answered with the strength of the Keep. The energy lit up the ground blocking the sorcerer out. This time she could sense the sorcerers. Saranon stood strong using the Keep to seal off any access.

She remained so focused that she had not seen the rain stop as the sky cleared. She remained locked in a trance waiting to be challenged, yet none came. It was then that she looked up at the building and saw the damage for the first time. The Keep had already begun repairing itself as the walls held strong.

Before she had time to ask what happened. Flynn rushed toward her, 'We need to get the artefact to the Pearl Castle.'

He did not elaborate anymore as he stayed. For a sorcerer, Clara's father had spent much time among the Athgar wizards. He held a rough and weary look with a well-worn coat that made him blend in. They had split up for the journey. To draw less attention from prying eyes and avoid the ire of sorcerer clans. She could do that on her own, yet had been asked to take the artefact. Her tummy rumbled, a reminder that she had not eaten. The fresh bread smelled delicious as the butter melted down the side. She scoffed down a mouthful as Mitch found her. The wizard looked like he had just woken up. Her head began to ring with the early thumping of a mighty headache.

Mitch smiled and spoke, 'That's what you get for showing off.'

'That's harsh,' Gannon interrupted,'Besides the keep did most of the work.'

Saranon lowered her head as she rubbed her forehead and the pain sank in. Gannon gently grasped her head in his hands. She could sense his wizardry and the pain numbed. She stared straight at Mitch with irritation, 'Why didn't you do that?'

Her companion was not showing any sympathy as he evaded the question. She gazed in annoyance at Mitch who would have let her suffer all day. An awkward silence fell over the room as the last of the early morning events were swept away. She stood not far from the opening to the dragon pens as Katholomu stuck his head out and gazed at her. The dragon had an unusual look on his face as he strained his head sideways and lowered his body. He managed to squeeze out the opening. Kat relaxed his muscles and scratched himself as though nothing had happened. She patted his hind leg and he jumped, gazing down.

The dragon was being difficult. As she searched for a way to climb on his back, Kat side stepped. Ever since they had entered Alveron the beast had been out of sorts.

A scorching sensation hit her shoulder before she had time to think. The pain creased through her body igniting the Angeon within. The sorcery of old soaked through her thoughts. As she blocked the blast from behind. Her mind raced, the attacker was heading straight for Clara. A shiver ran down her spine as she ran ahead. The corridor appeared empty even though she could sense someone.

Turmoil ruptured through the walls as she went, following a faint trace. It ricocheted off the stallic energy travelling upward. She ran further away from Clara and any sign of life. The only thing audible was the distant hum of the Keep. Saranon rounded a corner. Stopping short of an open chasm falling into the hidden depths. A flash crossed the great divide and she honed in, striking across the distance. A sound echoed from within the Keep pulsing as it went, getting louder with every step. She lost sight of the figure as the stallic energy swept up through the floor. From the edge of her vision a strange tinge crept into view. The hum of the Keep began to strain. Something else was there making its way through.

She leapt into the darkness. As the energy flowing up from the central core webbed around, hauling her down. There in the darkness the green tinge began to show. Her hand gripped the hilt. She held it, but the blade was gone. A shock ran through Saranon as she gripped the artefact. The ancient hilt felt warm in her grasp. The embedded heart stone gave a brilliant glow piercing into the void. As she floated downward the light wrapped around protecting her. It extended, evaporating the green tinge as it went. A deafening boom thundered along the outer edges as the light shielded her. Then it closed in melding into the hilt, forming the blade anew. Nothing could have prepared her as she held the bond-breaker. Once belonging to the last Angean, Zeralden Hadenvar. She gazed in awe as the Keep led her down toward the central core. For a moment she stayed transfixed watching the blade as it shone.

Her decent slowed as she reached the outer shell of the central core. A rim almost impenetrable. The words of the Keep Adeyorn were clear. Filtering through the immense void, use the blade. Saranon trembled as her knuckles went pale. She had only used her bond-breakers and this was Zeralden's. It was unfamiliar and cold, showing no sign of recognition. She willed it to work, but her nerves sank in. Stopping any attempt to use the blade. Adeyorn called out, waiting as she faltered. She cleared her mind, thinking of the central core and the pressure around it. Focusing on the heart stone as her sorcery surged. Still the blade remained cold, blocking her out. The frustration grew, she had to protect the Keep.

A tremor shimmered down the side of a giant conduit attached to the central core. It brought a sorcery that she had not sensed in a long time. The memory took her back to the detention camps and her friend Tasha whom she had lost. The central core shuddered. She had to act fast, but the thought of Tasha clung on as she opened her eyes. Her friend was standing there. Tasha reached out, holding the bond-breaker. As they both grasped it the heart stone flared. The blade came to life and her sorcery flowed through. This time it was the energy of the Angeon that filled the void. Sealing the fractures that had enabled the attack.

No trace was left as the blade did its work. Tasha's image faded and then vanished, leaving her feeling hollow inside. The burden crashed down on the emptiness as she stowed the blade away. The Keep lifted her upward once more. She was not ready to face the world and longed for the moment to continue. A sweeping silence greeted her. Before the activities of the habitable area echoed from above. She was so close. A numbness settled on her thoughts. It had been so long since she had truly seen her old friend. A sadness welled up and she tried not to show it, as she made her way through the corridors. The artefact held snug in her belt. She wondered if anyone would notice the short blade.

A smile crept across her face. It was reassuring to know that she was meant to be the Angeon. So many people shunned her and few had accepted. She hesitated as a hint of wizardry caught her senses. She held her hand to the wall of the Keep and extended her energy. The wall gave way to make an opening and it was then that the smell hit. She almost vomited. She entered alone as the sorcery bled through and melded into the barrier. Saranon hesitated as her mind mulled over the detail. Her heart thudded as the panic rose from within, she had to find Gannon.

Her sorcery strengthened and she turned toward the source. Yet still it would not focus. The frustration showed on her face. Her senses prickled as she made her way out toward a large open room and almost slipped. As she gazed down the trail of blood glistened in the light. Saranon's heart sank, she had to find Gannon. A sound rang out in the corridor and she ran toward it. Time slowed, yet at the same time it sped up. She could see Gannon lying on the ground. He was using the last of his energy so that she could see the intruders.

'No,' Saranon cried out.

As the Angeon rose without warning and she realised the wizard could not hold on. The energy rose around the Angeon, whirling as it gained momentum. The intruders placed all their efforts toward her as they forgot about Gannon. Her energy expanded through the melded wall, blocking the energy of the central core. It creaked with a massive deep sound that reverberated through the Keep. Saranon's anger welled inside her. The Keep answered as the wall disintegrated behind her. The Keep thrust the energy from the central core. Through the building with such harshness that she hesitated. The air around her froze with a stillness she could not contemplate.

She held out her hand in a void of calm as she stood in the eye of the storm. She remembered Gannon and ran toward him. The void of calm followed her as she crouched down. The wizard was so weak as he held on. He tried to speak and the words would not come out. She reached over. As the last of the Angeon withdrew deep beneath the surface, she healed the wizard.

CHAPTER FOUR

A dragon's greeting

Saranon stayed with the wizard as the energy thundered throughout the Keep. She closed her eyes as Adeyorn took over, until only she and Gannon remained. She shielded him from the stallic energy flowing out from the Keep. As it smoothed over the damaged walls. As the dust settled, sound returned in an inharmonious wave. It took her a while to make out someone approaching them. For a moment she thought it was Flynn, but as he came closer she could sense Mitch. There was a sense of urgency in his voice as they ran. The wizards of the Keep were heading down toward them.

Mitch found a small escape and they climbed through. Before she could utter a word. He used his wizardry to clean off the last remnants of dust from the attack. 'Now you help me,' Saranon grumbled as she used her energy to close the exit.

'This is not the time for talk.' Mitch whispered.

'Really.' She spoke with a hint of sarcasm.

He glanced around to make sure no one was following, 'The sorcerers were Shalough. If they find out it was the Angeon they will come after you.'

Saranon was not impressed, 'They ignored me.'

Mitch looked as though he was going to burst with frustration, 'You were not a threat.'

'Oh,' she exclaimed.

It did not make sense, but she did not like to say so. She could not understand how anyone would perceive her as non-threatening. When she last visited Alveron. She had always been the Angeon and nothing had changed.

The wizard could tell he was not getting through. He spun a fine ball of wizardry that floated in front of Saranon. The wizardry wrapped around itself as the energy ran around the sphere. She watched mesmerised. Mitch explained while the first ball of wizardry spun in on itself and dissipated. Then he made a new one and as the energy grew it shone brighter than before. 'Wow,' she gasped in amazement, 'I didn't know you could do that.'

The wizard gazed at her in disbelief. 'All right, I get it,' she frowned.

It was not the first time Mitch had taken great delight in explaining something to her. Clara's voice rang out behind them. Saranon was still dazed and found an excuse to leave. She sighed as she turned the corner.

The shock of the event clung on as she made her way

to bed. She closed her eyes, yet her mind did not want to rest. The door creaked open she stared at Mitch. He was moving slowly while trying not to disturb her. 'Are you awake?' He asked.

'You know I am.' She retorted.

'Gannon made it.' He spoke.

She could see the worry on Mitch's face. The former soldier hardly ever showed fear. 'The Shalough know you are here.' He spoke.

'How?' She asked.

'They blocked the pass to the south.' Mitch explained before he bid her goodnight.

This was not what she had expected. Saranon had a terrible feeling. She had been dragged into something that everybody else knew more about than her. With that her mixed dreams carried her away into an uneven sleep.

The building shook with a thud as the dragon misjudged the wall. The sound of a loud grunt crept in through the window. Katholomu grew impatient as she yelled at him for waking her up. The great beast took a step back, then as she leaned closer he picked her up on the edge of his nose. She let out an impulsive scream, before she could tell where the ground was. Mitch came running from below and called out, 'Quick, jump on.'

She was about to say something. When she caught sight of a fleet of dragons heading their way in the morning sky.

She gaped in astonishment. There would be no time to waste. As Katholomu ran in pursuit of the dragon riders as they launched into the sky. Saranon held her breath as Kat manoeuvred so close. His wing almost clipped another dragon, then let out a heavy sigh. Her stomach grumbled. This was not a good start to the morning and the dragon was picking up speed. She grumbled into the wind as all hope of staying in the background faded.

The dragon drove hard through the early morning frost. That hung in the air as the wind swept past. She wanted to call Kat back, but it was too late. They were heading straight for the attacking riders. Sorcery surged inside her as it reacted to the blast heading their way. The dragon swooped, almost knocking her off as she tried desperately to cling on. She yelled, only to find her voice carried away in the wind. Kat was travelling too fast and all she could do was hang on. The great beast ceased turning. Saranon peered over the top of his bulky head only to see yet another blast of sorcery. Before she could answer Kat exhaled at a phenomenal rate. A great roar from deep within his belly ignited in front of them.

She froze with fright, the result was instant as the dragon riders scattered. They had not expected the dragon to breathe fire and neither had she. The dragon chuckled. No one had warned her about Katholomu and she was not sure whether to scold or praise him. Given the fact that she was still sitting on his shoulders she opted to reassure him. He snorted and swooped over one last time, then stumbled into a rough landing.

She made her way down and stepped out of his way. Kat lowered his head as he coughed up the last of his fiery breath on a poor unsuspecting tree. The dragon promptly sat on it and curled up to go to sleep in the morning sun. Saranon stood in astonishment. Staring at the beast when Captain Trevell crept up behind her. 'You need to declare fire breathing dragons,' he stated.

'Do I look like I knew?' She responded, 'What do I do?'

The Captain smiled, 'You could boast about it.'

She frowned in bewilderment. She had known the dragon almost two years and not once had he breathed fire.

The captain broke her thoughts, 'We will be sad to see you go. Flynn is ready to leave.'

She could feel the exhaustion set in even though Kat had done most of the work. She trudged back to the barracks as two dragons waited in the courtyard. She began climbing on the one with Mitch, as Katholomu bounded through the clearing. The dragon nudged her onto his shoulder.

She hoped he did not breathe fire again as she held on tight. Kat was the last to launch into the sky and this time he stayed behind travelling at a steady pace. She breathed a sigh of relief and the dragon chuckled. The sound did nothing to reassure her. The Pearl Castle rose over the hillside as it came into view. The pale stone shone in the midday light as the sun warmed her back. It had been rebuilt after the Dreshan Occupation. In much the same image and towered over the land.

As Katholomu flew into the lower side of the castle she stayed close. The dragon pens took up a majority of the lower ground level. It opened up into the courtyard. Where the main level began further up the hillside. Saranon was astounded by the sheer scale, Clara had not mentioned it. She peered up into the void that led to the main floor. It would be easy to become lost as she tried to stay out of the way. A loud snort behind her sent the air whooshing down her neck. Kat snorted again as the sorcerers on the main floor stopped. Before she knew it, they had become the centre of attention.

She tried to nudge the dragon back into the pens. He was having none of it and ignored her attempts. Edelyn peered down over the balcony. The lady was everything Saranon expected a sorceress to be. As she realised her travelling clothes were worn and grubby. 'Your dragon does not belong in here,' Edelyn spoke with a firm tone.

Saranon's face grew hot and she spoke to the dragon as she tried again to nudge him toward the door.

Instead the great beast sidestepped her and lifted himself up to the main floor. The colour drained from her face as she gaped in astonishment.

She used her sorcery and nothing happened. A shock crept up her spine as she began to panic and nervously swallowed. She tried again, this time with greater strength and without success. She could not work out what was blocking her. The sounds of chaos rang out from above. As Katholomu moved without a care for anyone that came too close. Edelyn stood mortified. Saranon summoned the Angeon hidden deep inside. The energy surged within like a violent flood with no way out. A voice shouted near her in an attempt to restore calm. As the dragon keepers ran toward Katholomu.

A thunderous roar heaved its way up through the Keep. As she realised it was not her who had answered. She became lost in the haze of the Angeon as it swept over her. The energy thundered through after the mighty roar from the Keep. A shimmer of tiny sparks of light flowed like rain from the ceiling. 'Wow,' Saranon gasped in amazement.

Then the hum of the Keep broke through the silence. She smiled, watching Kat make his way down and out to the open courtyard. He flopped down, lapping up the warmth of the afternoon resting his head on the ground. 'What was that?' Saranon asked and jumped when Clara answered behind her.

Her friend had her arms held out as the last spark of light floated down. 'I've never seen anyone do that,' Clara exclaimed.

Saranon was still trying to work out how the sparks came into the equation. That would have to wait until later. Edelyn made her way toward them. She wanted to hide even though there was no way she could. Her only reassurance came from the Keep. As the central core whirred in contentment below.

Before she could speak, Clara took her hand and they darted away. 'What did you do that for?' Saranon asked.

Clara beamed with excitement, 'I'm so glad you're in Alveron again.'

Her friend's response did not answer the question, but she let it be. The last time they had met was at Odana

Temple when the Keep was under attack by the Otturin. Where she had first encountered Kat. The dragon was fidgeting in the courtyard which looked rather awkward given his size. He belonged to the Otturin before she had claimed him. Or perhaps he had claimed her, she was never really sure.

Clara clambered up on the dragon before Saranon could say no. Kat leaned down and nudged her. She made her way up the thick skin that shielded the great beast from almost anything. By the time she had reached his shoulders she was covered in dirt. She grimaced at the thought of having to clean him again. Kat leaped with a jovial step that made her stomach lurch as he flew into the sky. Autumn was beginning to show as the cool breeze swept past under the afternoon sun. Saranon had no idea where she was going as Kat circled down around Fendugal. The outer barracks marked the beginning of east Alveron.

The warm grey stone walls shone in the sunlight. As Katholomu ran across the open ground along the perimeter. The dragon had a habit of landing at the nearest wizard Keep. Today was no different as her enthusiasm waned. The Keep marked the beginning of the well-built roads leading to the nearest town. Yet she stayed on the western side where the great wilderness faded to a halt at the Keep's door. A familiar face came out to greet them. As Mitch approached she gave him a bewildered glare, 'What are you doing here?'

The wizard only smiled. Saranon shook her head before letting it be. He had braved the journey north all the way to Serenphel. Mitch knew more about Alveron than she did. Which made her feel like the odd one out as they went inside the Keep. The building stood with a simple splendour that continued inside. As they made their way to the large open hall. They sat down to enjoy that the sun streaming through the tall windows. As Clara made enquiries to view further into the Keep. Mitch spoke in a low whisper, 'There's trouble south, we need to stay away.'

He emphasised the word "we" as he stared at her. The wizard could be annoying.

A silent click reverberated in the hum of the central core. Creating a void between sound. Saranon turned her head away. Mitch answered for her, as though reading her immediate thoughts, 'Run!'

She strode toward the windows facing the edge of the wilderness. As the blast bulged through, warping the wall as it went. The great rush of air thundered around her. As she stood still in a silent void where the essence of time lingered. She raised her hands in a hazy trance as her energy rose to the surface. It ripped through the blast with an intense heat, as the air tore apart in a fiery rage. The ground trembled as Saranon stammered back with the shock. The wall stood strong and the shattered glass lay in piles swept back against the edge.

A chorus of rage echoed overhead as the dragon riders leapt into the harsh sky. She had not seen so many dragons take to the sky and looked on in astonishment. Mitch pulled her away from the windows and they ran into the depths of the Keep. She fumed as she realised they were being shut in. Mitch spoke, 'Stay here.'

They had been crammed in, it took a while for the sudden fear to vanish. She could feel the staring grow in abundance. Until a wizard a few years older made his way through the crowd. Clara gave a small bow, before thanking the Regent for his hospitality. Saranon stared in amazement. being crammed in a room full of wizards was not her idea of hospitality. The Regent, Robert of Ashden thanked her. For once she was speechless and could not think of anything to say as the Regent moved on. This was not how she expected to spend the evening.

Loud banging and a rustle came from the other side of the door. Much to her relief the wizards began to leave. Mitch stopped her, 'Do not get involved.'

'I already have,' she exclaimed.

He gave her a stern glare which only added to her frustration. They watched the wizards gather into action, reclaiming the sky. Saranon glanced around trying to make sense of what had happened. A rogue wizard group managed to get past the outer shield. She was not convinced, as she made her way out into the damp evening air. The energy of the Keep lit up the dragon pens and foreground as she made her way into the dark. She could not sense any remnants from sorcery except her own. Still it did not make her feel at ease, as she spotted Katholomu guarding the pens.

The great beast was resting. She was about to pat him when a stench wafted toward her. She coughed as the wizards let her through to the shallow pool. Kat stopped short of the water. She placed her hands on hips as she spoke, 'You need a wash.'

The dragon snorted in disgust as he began to arch his shoulders. A few short shouts rang out behind her. She took no notice as she tried to move the dragon. Instead she succeeded in being stared at with two massive grumpy dark eyes.

The thudding rang out when two dragons ran up behind Kat, racing toward the pool. She just had time to grab onto his leg, as he was shoved into the pool with her clinging on. Water sprayed everywhere and soaked through her clothes. Clara screamed in the background. Saranon managed to raise her hand and wave. She was safe for the moment as the dragons splashed around her. Kat's belly moved in a low growl that made its way to a chuckle. She was not impressed.

She requested a brush. Mitch threw it up as he tried not to laugh. 'See, this is what you get for dragging me in,' she told the dragon as she scrubbed his ears.

Finally she managed to make her way down, as he leaned his head forward. He splashed her one last time as he heaved his body out of the pool. Saranon used her energy to dry her clothes. At least the dragon was clean.

'You're not supposed to get in the pool,' Clara exclaimed.

She sighed. They made their way up to the hall where a wonderful aroma of the evening meal met her. The smell of food made her tummy rumble. She picked up a cup of soup and sat near the fireplace as it warmed her hands.

'You did well today,' Robert of Ashden spoke.

Saranon peered up and glanced around. Mitch and Clara were nowhere to be seen and she was unsure what to do. The Regent smiled. 'When you are at the Pearl Castle I would like you to meet the Oracle. Tell me what you make of him.'

She was rather puzzled by the request and nodded her head, 'Yes... your highness.'

Robert of Ashden was called away before she could think of anything else. Clara spoke behind her. She jumped using her sorcery to stop the soup from going everywhere. Clara giggled. 'I just meant to tell you we are leaving.'

Saranon made her way outside, where Mitch greeted her in darkness of the courtyard. 'I hear you made an impression.'

That was not the word she was looking for, as she told him about Robert's request. Mitch went quiet. 'You need to meet the oracle.'

'Why?' She asked out of suspicion.

'Let me know what you think,' he added.

Saranon had the distinct feeling she would be walking into trouble. She gave the wizard a disapproving glare before clambering aboard the sweet smelling dragon. If only Katholomu could stay clean, but that would be too much to ask. She held on tight as Mitch waved goodbye. Clara sat in front as she directed Kat toward the Pearl Castle. By the time they arrived only the night watch greeted them. The dragon needed no encouragement as he spotted a warm cosy bed. He did not let them down until he had curled his tail around and closed his eyes to rest. She could hear the hum of the Keep in the background, as it guided her up toward her room. Sleep was far from her mind, but it had been a busy day and exhaustion set in.

The room was large enough to look spacious without being extravagant. It made her wonder if the Mercidian picked the most average room in the whole Keep. She took out the sova bag and waited for it to expand before rummaging through her belongs. A knock at the door held her attention. Saranon opened the door a fraction. As she glanced up into the dark eyes of a sorcerer almost the same age. The familiar smell of dragon told her more about him than she needed to ask.

'What has Katholomu done this time?' She asked, dreading the reply.

Madoc spoke, 'We had to move him because he can breathe fire.'

Saranon's face went pale as the sorcerer tried to explain that nothing happened. She was not convinced and Madoc kept glancing over her shoulder. 'Would you like to come in?' She asked as he eyed the bond-breakers lying on the table.

She should have known someone would be interested, as she let him in. He held the blade before transforming it from a dagger into a sleek sword that would fit well in his hand.

She had made the bond-breaker Corsavere at Odana Temple. The old heart of Zyanthia in the north-west corner of Alveron. The heart stone shone with a warm glow of recognition at the sorcerer's strength. 'Will you make one here?' He asked with a hint of excitement.

'Is that a request?' Saranon asked.

'Maybe,' Madoc spoke, as he placed the bond-breaker back in its sheath.

After the sorcerer had left she settled down for the night. The central core of the Keep hummed away beneath. Her thoughts turned to the Oracle she had not met. The Pearl Castle was giving nothing away which made her wonder even more.

CHAPTER FIVE

The wizard lord

Creaking sounds made their way through a dreamless sleep. As Saranon stirred with the fresh morning light. The Pearl Castle had a different rhythm. A little slower, like it was dragging its heels. Yet the hum was strong. She held Corsavere to the light before attaching the bond-breaker to her belt. The corridor was quiet as she ducked away. A few people hesitated, glancing her way. Clara was further up the tower. She gave a knock as her friend opened the door and the two giggled, as they ran down the stairs. She had a task and Clara knew where to find the Oracle. They raced toward the courtyard.

Clara stopped in the middle of the gathering, 'That's odd.'

'What is?' Saranon asked.

'He isn't here,' Clara dismissed the thought, dragging

her through the Keep.

They darted to the courtyard on the upper level, as a crowd gathered. They hesitated, but the crowd parted letting them through to a manicured garden. Still they could see no sign of the elusive Oracle and Clara became worried.

'This is not supposed to happen,' Clara spoke aloud.

She was beginning to think the Oracle did not want to be found. The idea made her nervous as she glanced around. 'I know,' Clara said without explanation.

They made their way into a small foyer. Clara vanished around the doorway and Saranon hesitated before peering in. Her friend held out a Mercidian robe and urged her to try it on. Saranon sighed, she did not think it was going to make any difference. Clara gave her a look of approval before they made their way toward the great chambers. She followed through the stream of people, keeping sight of Clara. Then her friend shoved her back into the crowd.

Saranon gasped as she lost her balance and fell backward. Standing right behind her was the one person that had been avoiding her. The Oracle was a tall man, his eyes soft and sombre. Her voice had escaped her as she bowed and backed away into the crowd. Her cheeks grew hot as she leaned on the wall away from Oracle. 'Well?' Clara asked, startling her friend.

'Don't do that,' she exclaimed.

They managed to make their way out through the door. Clara was not going to let her be.

'What do you think?' Clara was itching to know as

they returned the robe.

'I don't think you want to know,' Saranon exclaimed.

The look on Clara's face turned into one of utter disappointment. As her shoulders slumped. Her friend looked like she was about to cry, then reassured herself, 'It's okay.'

Clara did not sound convincing, but there was not much Saranon could do. The man she had seen was not the Oracle. There was no spark of life that she had witnessed with the Prophet at Indarin. If anything there was an unexpected emptiness she could not explain.

The sensation stayed with her long after the image was gone, as she made her way toward the dragon pens. The place was almost empty as the afternoon sun shone through the high windows. The large arches led out to the courtyard where she could make out Kat's tail. As he waved it across the ground in irritation. The great beast turned his head to meet her. Yet he appeared reluctant to leave his cosy spot in the sun. She patted his smooth cheek and the dragon nudged her over his head and onto his shoulders. Saranon steadied herself as she turned around. The great beast leapt too close to the side of the building. She cringed as the angry shouts rang out behind them.

Fendugal came into view as the a cool breeze swept across the open plain. The Keep showed no sign of the attack and she breathed a sigh of relief. Lord Nemard Halleron stood in the doorway of the dragon pens. He was a tall brute of wizard with a face to match. 'What would a sorceress be doing here?' he enquired with a hint of interest.

Saranon had not expected to be greeted by the Lord and found herself lost for words. As she mumbled, 'I was... wondering if I could see the Regent?'

'Really,' he eyed her with an amused smile that was more menacing than friendly. 'Now why would you need to see the Regent?'

'He gave me a task,' her voice became meek.

Lord Halleron rubbed his chin, 'Well then, I will take you to see the Regent.'

She was not sure if she wanted to follow the overbearing wizard. That looked more at home in a tavern than the Keep. He glanced over to make sure she was following. As he led her up to the large drawing room with great windows. That looked in the direction of the capital Terrare. Voices travelled in a low murmur and stopped as she entered. The Regent, Robert of Ashden, was just as she remembered. His face showed the last traces of youth, yet his eyes were far older. The wizards around him parted to let her through. The Regent looked up with patient expectation.

Saranon tried to find her voice, yet it escaped her as she fumbled to find the words. She gave up and shook her head. 'He isn't the one,' she spoke softly.

'Are you sure?' The Regent asked.

'Ulrich is not the Oracle, not even close.' She may as well have been shouting.

Her words had the same effect. She could offer no hope to the Regent. It was not what she had expected, as she became disheartened. Lord Halleron gave a chuckle as he grinned. 'I am amazed Ulrich has lasted this long.'

With a hint of amusement the atmosphere in the room changed before she realised. It felt as though she had been left out of a silent conversation. Saranon politely bowed, her head spun and she longed for fresh air. She rushed out into the open courtyard where Kat waited. With his arms stretched out showing his shiny belly for all to see. The dragon moved sideways. While opening one eye then lied back with an air of contentment.

Mitch met her with relaxed smile. 'Stirring up trouble again?'

'Me,' Saranon gasped in annoyance, as she glared at the wizard.

He towered over her. 'I have accepted Lord Halleron's offer to stay at Kallawere... for the both of us.'

The wizard gave her an unwavering stare as she fumed. 'What!' She shouted and a few people turned around from the dragon pens. 'You did what?' She whispered.

'It's the least we can do…' The wizard spoke without finishing the sentence.

Saranon stood close which meant she had to crane her neck and stand on her toes, 'What do you mean?'

Mitch smiled and spoke in such a soft tone, 'You upset the Mercidian.'

She found the wizard rather puzzling and cryptic messages were not her strong point. She glared at him. While trying to figure out what staying with a bunch of wizards had to do with sorcerers.

'I don't think they were expecting you,' Mitch added.

Saranon was not about to argue as the wizard went

inside, because it did not make sense. She shrugged her shoulders and followed. The Keep remained silent underneath the touch of her fingers. A faint wave of energy caught her by surprise. As Fendugal reacted to her and she smiled before catching up to the wizard. Despite all her attempts to quiz him further, Mitch remained silent. She had trouble reading him. The wizard could hide his emotions well. Try as she might his calm mood did nothing to ease her thoughts.

She decided to explore the Keep by herself. She expected a reaction, but the wizard gave little away. The habitable areas were filled with activity. Yet the place had an open vastness that made it feel too large for its tenants. She ran her hand along the wall without thinking and it moved. Saranon froze, then turned and peered into a doorway with a staircase leading down. She had been thinking about going below the habitable area. This seemed like an invitation. She glanced around before darting down the dust covered stairs. The corridor was narrow and crept around as it lead further down.

She hesitated, then made her way into a small room. As she stood in the centre voices travelled from nearby. A wizard waved his hand through the doorway. She glanced around expecting to see someone behind her, even though she was alone. The doorway opened up into the entrance to a substation. A small crew were in good spirits as the exhaustion showed. Saranon wondered why she had not sensed anything. Yet the Keep had guided her here so perhaps that was her answer. Captain Lydia Grace waved in her direction. Words were not needed as the wizardess pointed toward the open conduit. She peered down into the depths. The empty conduit looked more like a long dark cave, which gradually made its way up to the surface.

As she leaned her head down into the conduit a great ball of black fluff growled. She jumped, fumbled and somehow managed to lose her grip all at the same time. She rolled down the side of the circular conduit. Placing her hand in the grimy layer covering the bottom. Captain Grace called out from above and chuckled after realising Saranon was okay. She turned to face the large ball of black fluff and asked, 'What is it?'

'This is Mina. If you are lucky enough you can meet her parents,' Captain Grace answered.

She smiled at the zennigh kitten. She had to admit it was one of the cutest things she had ever seen. The kitten took a tentative step back as Saranon approached. The giant black kitten had claws and teeth as sharp as its parents, so she did not walk any closer. 'There does not appear to be anything wrong with the conduit,' she spoke.

As she climbed back out. 'There isn't,' Captain Grace replied. 'This is supposed to be a routine maintenance check. We found this.'

Saranon wanted to ask what it was as she held out her hand to touch the rough surface of the broken seal. The carving imprinted on the fragments implied that someone had tried to break in. Her frustration grew. It had not been near the central core, it was far too small. 'It was caused by wizardry,' Captain Lydia Grace added.

'What?' Saranon's astonishment showed plain on her face.

'You aren't the only one who can do serious damage,' the Captain replied.

She attempted to hide her astonishment. As the Captain chuckled, 'Keep an eye open, I don't want to look after you too.'

Saranon grumbled, she thought she was able to look after herself. The old tomb in Alveron had frightened her, there was still so much to learn.

She made her way up to the habitable area via the main stairway. That opened into an elegant foyer hidden in the depths of the Keep. The lights along the walls were well lit as the last of the sun faded through the high windows. She peered up at the ceiling. Where the hexagonal frame of the columns flowed upward into the high arches. 'Beautiful isn't it?' The Regent had crept up behind her and she jumped.

He smiled. 'Come, I want to show you something.'

Saranon hesitated, then sprinted to catch up. The Regent waited for no one. She was fumbling for the right words, yet nothing came to mind as they entered a cosy library. A pile of books grew on a table near the centre of the room, as Lord Halleron flicked through them. The wizard was muttering to himself in annoyance. He took a moment longer to search. 'Ah, Robert just the man I want to see. Which one of these would help find the Oracle?'

The Regent, Robert of Ashden, leaned down to pick out a book. As he did so a sharp searing pain ran up

Saranon's leg and she screamed. The blast pounded through, as she created a shield for the Regent. Lord Halleron burst into action, hurtling a blast over Saranon's head. The air crackled as her ears rang and she filled with rage. As she turned all she could see was Lord Halleron taking a flying leap out the door. A series of agonising screams rang out, then a muffled cry and nothing. The silence that followed left an eerie tone. As the gasps to catch her breath filled the void. She brushed her hand along her leg, it felt fine. She looked down in astonishment. After all the pain there were no marks or sign of what had taken place.

A gruff Lord Halleron entered with the look of someone she did not want to anger. His voice came across with a firm certainty, 'It's nothing. I handed them over to the sergeant.'

'Who were they?' Saranon enquired.

'Hmm...' Lord Halleron had an amused look on his face. 'Whoever they were, they will not be doing much.'

She was not sure what he meant, but did not like to ask. The Regent stood up completely unhurt and calm. Which made her wonder if this was the first time he had faced such danger. Before she had a chance to ask. Lord Halleron picked up the book the Regent had given him and studied it in mild thought. He glanced at Saranon, turned back to the book then glanced at her again, 'How old are you?'

'Seventeen,' she replied.

'Hmm... You are rather young for the Angeon,' Lord Halleron remarked.

She frowned, placing her hands on her hips, 'What does that have to do with the Oracle?'

'No reason,' Lord Halleron replied, as he handed the book to the Regent.

She was not going to get any straight answers. As the two wizards idly changed the subject. Knowing full well that she was irritated. She found an excuse to leave and Lord Halleron gave her an amused smile as he bid her goodnight.

Saranon was not sure what to make of the Athgar wizards. Her thoughts were interrupted with the sharp smell of soot. As she entered the corridor, she gasped as her eyes followed a long charred trail up along the wall. It was not the marks that caught her attention. Rather the smudged outlines where the walls remained untouched. The ghostly reminder made her skin crawl, yet she would have done the same. She tried to block the image out of her mind, but the pungent smell clung to her clothes. The autumn cold brought a chill down the outer wall and she rubbed her arms.

The night had well and truly set in. Yet as she peered out into the courtyard a figure caught her attention. She hesitated before opening the outer door, there was something familiar about the figure. As she watched, Katholomu came out to greet the person. Saranon opened the door and reluctantly put on the coat. It reeked of smoke, but it was warm enough. She passed the outer rim of the courtyard. Before realising the sorcerer was Otturin and froze. He was almost the same age and hesitated as they stared at each other. Kat broke the silence as he gently nudged Kail forward. Saranon grimaced at recognising who the Otturin sorcerer was.

She had thrown him off the dragon and flown Katholomu north to Normisia. The dragon was hers by right, Mark Staragen had paid for the beast as a thank you for saving his life. Now she stood face to face with the Otturin, and for the first time he was not attacking her. In fact he seemed rather shy. 'What are you doing here?' She whispered.

'I came to see Katholomu,' Kail spoke, as he patted the great beast.

The dragon purred in return, much to Saranon's annoyance. 'Are you going to attack again?'

As soon as she had asked the question it sounded silly, 'That wasn't quite what I meant.'

Kail answered. 'It's been a long time since there has been an angeon.'

She gaped in astonishment. Another Otturin sorcerer appeared from the distance and called, 'Kail.'

The word was spoken which such a firm voice. That neither questioned the finality of the tone. 'I should go,' he gave a curt nod before retreating into the darkness.

Another voice cut through the air, as Mitch called out in alarm, 'Saranon.'

'It would appear I have to go to,' she spoke to herself, as she cringed.

Mitch held her arm as he led her inside and gave a strange look as he took a whiff of her jacket. 'I'm fine,' she said, not wanting to elaborate.

'Three sorcerer clans in Alveron and you manage to annoy all them,' he exclaimed.

As he peered down the corridor and caught the remnants of the smoke before it settled. 'That wasn't me,' Saranon retorted, before he could accuse her of anything.

She was beginning to wonder if it was too late to go back to the Pearl Castle. When a welcoming voice trailed out from the great hall. The warmth of the open fire greeted them as Lord Halleron shut the door. It made a small clicking noise that held her attention before she saw who stood in front of them.

There in the centre of the room standing not much taller than she was an Otturin sorceress. The Athgar wizards seemed completely oblivious, to the fact their guest was out of place. Mitch for once gave a bewildered glance. As Lord Halleron announced with an air of amusement, 'This is Adeen.'

Before Saranon could think of what to say Lord Halleron left. Making himself comfortable in a grand chair near the fireplace. The light from the Keep flickered as it washed down the walls. She had not expected to meet an Otturin. Welcomed by the wizards after the damage at Odana Temple. Her lips moved, but no sound came out as she tried think of something and stumbled. Adeen smiled. 'Odana recognises you, yet you do not seem like the Angeon of old.'

Saranon remained silent. She was beginning to get used to people not expecting to meet her.

'I have a task for you,' Adeen added as she eyed the Angeon up and down with a fleeting glance. 'Bring me the Oracle.'

Saranon gaped, 'Why would I do that?'

She was beginning to get annoyed with the Otturin. Yet as she stared around the room the wizards appeared calm. She felt as though she had been unwittingly led into a trap. Adeen turned to Lord Halleron and waited. The wizard did not miss his cue, 'The Mercidian and Shalough both want the Oracle.'

It was not an answer to her question. As the memory of pain still lingered from the attack at Odana Temple. Saranon spoke as she stared at Adeen, 'You are not worthy of the Oracle.'

'Neither are you,' Adeen replied with a calm confidence.

'I will not be drawn into this,' Saranon spoke as she closed her eyes.

Odana still held her thoughts. As she remembered the great central core from the deep.

'You already are,' Adeen responded.

She felt the sorcery of the Angeon swirl within her as she opened her eyes. Adeen clambered back as she turned away. In a moment the Angeon was gone, as it receded back inside.

With that a slow swell of darkness engulfed Adeen and she vanished. In disbelief Saranon waved her hand where the Otturin had been. 'That went well,' Lord Halleron said with a hint of sarcasm, as he rose from the chair. He grasped her shoulder and faced the sorceress. 'What do think will happen when we find the Oracle?'

She glared in disgust and Lord Halleron took no notice as he waited. 'Says the man who has not met one,' Saranon spat the words out.

As she stormed outside into the cold night air. Inside she was fuming, the wizards were so focused on the Oracle and she did not see why. Perhaps that was just as well. She was still agitated when a rustle came from the forest near the edge of the Keep. Adeen strode towards her from the darkness, 'Will you consider our offer?'

'It is not that simple,' she spoke and let out an uneasy sigh. 'Have you ever been near an Oracle?'

'We will not harm her,' Adeen answered.

'When I was in Serenphel, I became friends with the Prophet. It is not what you seek,' Saranon spoke in an anguished tone. There was no way she could make Adeen understand. 'I will search for the Oracle. Perhaps then you will understand,' she turned to leave.

There was no use trying to explain. The fake oracle had reinforced a false hope and she was being asked to unravel what was done.

As she entered inside the grand Keep. It felt as though she was the only one who could see the confusion. It would explain why the Oracle had not been found. If everyone was looking for a distorted truth. Chasing shadows of an image that did not exist, except in the pages of fables. The burden weighed heavy on her shoulders, as she slumped down on the bed for the night. The laughter and voices from the great hall echoed underneath the door. In the darkness she cried silent tears. What would become of the Oracle? The person would not live up to expectations, but then neither did she.

CHAPTER SIX

The betrayal

A steady rain ran down the window, the faint light crept through the curtain as she drew it back. Saranon glanced out and a movement caught her eye. There were too many people in the courtyard. She ran out into the foyer and Mitch greeted her warm smile. It was a pleasant change from the night before as she tried to forget the task she had been given. It grated on her mind like a dull headache not wanting to let go. Mitch had met the Prophet in Serenphel ever so briefly. Yet the wizard appeared oblivious to her concerns. She felt a wave of relief when Flynn made his way toward them.

'I thought you would like to ride with us,' Flynn said, as he led her toward the waiting dragons. 'We can meet up with Mitch at Felkrayer.'

'Are you sure?' Saranon asked with a hint of excited

hesitation.

She patted Flynn's dragon, as Katholomu nudged her with his cheek. About the only time Kat would fawn over her was when she paid attention to another dragon. She smiled then made her way up on her dragon, 'I'll follow you.'

'Of course,' Flynn replied, as he wasted no time taking to the sky.

As they made their way through the sky, she noticed Madoc off and waved. She saw no sign of Clara and frowned. It was not like her friend to miss an opportunity for adventure. Still, their journey had ended. When the artefact had been returned to the Pearl Castle. Now she had been lumped with the task of finding the Oracle. She let out a heavy sigh filled with frustration, she had no idea how to find an oracle. Alveron was beautiful with a vibrant greenery even in the middle of autumn. The chill air ran along her cheeks reminding her of the harsh winter to come.

Katholomu darted in and out. Revelling in showing off his homeland as he soaked up the brisk fresh air. The clouds faded to let through a soft sunlight. Filtering down over the trees and cottages spotting the landscape. They made good progress, as Flynn led the small group down under the glow of the midday sun. Saranon felt her stomach rumble. As Kat thudded along the ground in an uneven pattern. He used the slope of the hill to land. She scrambled onto his side, as he rolled over without a second thought for his rider. Of all the places to land, the dragon had managed to find a dry dirt patch. He merrily flicked his tail in the air, as he rubbed his back in the dirt.

She wanted to tell the dragon off, as Madoc's voice caught her attention. 'Where are you going?' He asked, as he hesitated.

She was not sure what to make of the sorcerer whose eyes showed he wanted to ask much more. Saranon glanced toward the waiting group and Madoc's carefree expression changed, 'Take care.'

She smiled at the thought, before climbing on top of the grubby dragon. Kat needed a bath, but that would have to wait.

The cool breeze turned into a sharp wind as it sent chills along her cheeks. She steadied herself close to the dragon's thick coat. Autumn had taken a strong hold over the land as they flew in formation above. The low hills and vibrant woodland reminded her of a homeland she had hardly seen. Katholomu beamed with excitement, he was only too keen to show off. As Flynn signalled for them to stay close. She hesitated then patted the dragon with a wilful encouragement. As he glided close to the ground in a steep dive. She felt alive and loved every moment as she breathed in the crisp air. Mitch was missing out on so much and then she remembered where she was.

She whispered near the dragon's ear and the great beast swooped around. Heading towards the group which had already landed. Katholomu had too much speed and she clung on and gritted her teeth. The dragon swerved into a clearing and as he lowered his wing she saw movement. Without thinking she dug her heel deep. The dragon flung himself upward with an ear piercing screech. A heavy weight fell on Saranon's back and she lost her grip. Falling the short distance to ground. The soft grass and fallen leaves cushioned her blow. As she stared toward a darkening sky, the shadows lingered as her muscles ached. When she moved, her whole body felt awkward and heavy.

As the shadows grew the darkness swept in, she looked up. There was no sign of Flynn and the dragons were long gone. She had lost track of time as the world moved around her and she went with it. A deep rumbling filled her ears, as the sound reverberated through the ground. She held on as the earth slipped. As she gazed skyward for one last time. Her eyes fell upon the stern faces of the Shalough looking down upon her. Saranon tried to say something, but her voice failed. As Tordoren opened up to swallow her. She clung on, yet all the strength she could summon was not enough. She felt tired and the weakness had ebbed its way through her body.

She tried to shout and the words were lost in the rumbling haze. Then the sky darkened, as she lost her grip. Anger seeped in, rising to the surface. It welled inside her as she fell, deep into the timeless tunnel. That sealed in on itself with a thunderous rush. She breathed, fearing what she might find. As her hands found the solid surface beneath. Then it moved and Saranon's heartbeat jumped into her throat with a rising panic. She opened her eyes and peered down holding her breath for a brief moment. There was a faint warmth emanating from the surface. She placed her ear next to it and a great rumble echoed upward, as she jumped bolt upright.

Time passed without the faintest measure, as she sat pondering her predicament. The small glow of light from her sorcery only added to her gloom. As it shone through the unending cave. She peered upward hoping for the answer to come, but this time she had run out of luck. She sat down on floor of the cave, a flat surface with a murky edge. The cave ran deep. As a thought entered her head to find a way out the surface moved with a jolt. Saranon tumbled backward until she managed to steady herself. She was swept down into the cave as the surface moved. As it did so she realised what it was. She was lying on the top of sheal, almost solid but it was still sheal.

The dark murky substance moved gathering speed. As it went hurtling her down deep underneath. Then the blood ran to her feet as the sheal rose with a fathomless might. The earth rumbled above as the tremors cascaded far below. The sudden rush kept her body flat to the surface as she clung on. Fearing what she would see as she peeked out through dusty haze. Then the sheal stopped with such a jolt that she flew up into the air. Saranon used her energy as a shield to soften the fall as her legs found the solid ground. She could smell the fresh damp grass pressing against her face. She breathed a trembling sigh of relief. As the sound in her ears diminished and for first time she noticed the stars above.

She rolled onto her back from exhaustion. She did not understand what had happened in the depths of Tordoren.

Yet her heart filled with an overwhelming gratitude. A silent tear escaped down the side of her cheek. Before she could stop the back of her head was soaked with an overwhelming sense of relief. Perhaps she could disappear and no one would know. Then she remembered Mitch, the wizard would find her anywhere. It was all a mess, the thought clung on as the chill wind numbed the ends of her fingers. A rustling noise caught her attention. As she turned and the dark silhouette of a figure emerged from the shadows.

She could tell straight away the young man was wiccan. She sighed as she called out and let the world in. As she made a small light she stared down at her grubby hands and clothes. Her hair was covered as well. The young man, Liam, smiled. 'We thought you might turn up.'

'Why is that?' Saranon asked, as bewilderment filled her voice.

'The Shalough are saying they trapped the Angeon and well... Here you are,' Liam spoke with a sense of awe and amusement.

She was too tired to ask how that was meant to make sense, she brushed the mud off her arm. 'I could do with bath,' she exclaimed to herself, as the dry mud made her skin itch.

Kylah smiled, the wiccan had stayed in Liam's shadowed. Her eyes shone bright. As she welcomed the opportunity to show the sorceress to their small town. Set in a well protected clearing. Saranon was not about to argue, as she was offered a warm meal and sat in a cosy chair near the fire place. The tavern was bigger than Mrs. Harper's in Normisia. Yet it had the same welcoming vibe that filled the air as she ate. The tavern was rather full for such late hour. As the sound of vibrant music floated out into the night sky. She had forgotten how much she missed the company of her friend's Celia and Jedd. It seemed ages since she had seen them.

It amazed her, how talk of her had travelled to Alveron. Her eyes were growing tired, as she placed the empty bowl down. As she rose to find a room upstairs Liam approached her. 'I need to talk with you, but it can wait until the morning,' he said.

She looked behind him to the open window. As the first rays of sunlight broke over the hillside. 'Perhaps noon,' she suggested.

Liam looked over his shoulder and smiled before nodding in agreement. As she found the door began to open it, it stopped halfway. She hesitated, yet she could not sense anything.

Mitch peering around the door, 'You're late.'

Saranon jumped with fright then pounded his chest with a tired fist. 'Where were you,' she cried in frustration. She pounded him again, before Mitch hugged her tight, 'We're in danger.'

Saranon stopped and glared up at his dark brown eyes, 'You noticed.'

'You were traded,' Mitch explained, 'Only the Shalough did not hand over the Oracle.'

She felt her blood run cold, as she slumped to the

floor. She wanted to scream and held her head in her hands. Her body shook with anger, yet she knew it would do her no good.

The strong sunlight worked its way into her thoughts, as her mind told her it was time to get up. Then the warm smell of hot bread and butter floated by and she sat up. Mitch was finishing off the last of his meal, as he offered her a plate. He said nothing though he did not need to, every sorcerer in Alveron was after the Oracle. She did not understand how she had been caught up in the chase. She sighed in deep thought, as she eyed the wizard. She had forgotten to ask Mitch how he had made it here. The wizard smiled in response, if only she could read minds. Mitch made it look easy and this annoyed her even more.

'Liam may know where the Oracle is,' Mitch spoke.

'I doubt it,' Saranon responded.

She had befriended the Prophet in Serenphel. Theron was almost the same age, it was not the only thing they had in common. She had a feeling the Oracle did not want to be found.

Her anxious gaze made the wizard uncomfortable. Yet Mitch said nothing as they made their way downstairs. 'I was wondering when you would appear,' Kylah ran to greet them. With an enthusiasm that bewildered the sorceress.

Saranon smiled even though the worry showed in her eyes. The tavern was as warm and welcoming as it had been the night before. Karraden was a humble piece of paradise locked away, far from the coast. She strode outside into the cool breeze bringing the autumn with it. Liam made his way toward her, 'I don't think I could ever leave this place.'

Saranon waited, she did not want to ask as she avoided making eye contact. 'I thought you wanted to know about the Oracle,' Liam spoke.

'I think I am only one who doesn't,' she sighed.

Liam smiled. 'Then we understand each other.'

She frowned at the comment, as Liam continued, 'Follow me.'

She did so as the wiccan spoke in a soft kindness barely audible above the breeze. His words withered away in the wind as soon as he had said them.

She was so intent on listening. She almost stumbled into the tiny stream that made its way across their path. Liam pointed toward the heartland. Her heart sank, she did not want to meet the Shalough again, in any form. Yet she followed his gaze and absorbed the meaning of his words. There in the distance, hidden from view. Were a clan of sorcerers that had unnatural luck at seeking the wiccan out. Liam did not speak the words as he gazed at her. She knew where the conversation was leading and a chill tingled down her spine. She nodded with the grim thought of facing the Shalough yet again. Any time would be far too soon.

Her head was still reeling from the dim darkness held far beneath the ground. Somehow she would have to find a way to deal it. The thought stuck in her throat, it was too soon. Yet if she waited it would be too late. She let out a small sigh and Liam gave her a comforting pat on the shoulder. He understood the meaning of such an enormous task. As she made her way back to the tavern Mitch was waiting with an enviable patience. The wizard was not at all keen to go with her. She breathed a sigh of relief, it would hard enough with just her. The sky consumed the warm afternoon light as she watched it fade taking her hopes with it.

The town of Karraden seemed far smaller than its actual size. It was a bustling lively place on the edge of the heartland. A beautiful bubble of serenity with an underlying air of anticipation, that yanked at her inner thoughts of turmoil. The Shalough were the last people in the whole of Tordoren that she wanted to meet. Even the Otturin seemed more appealing, then she let the thought go. Katholomu would be at home among the Otturin, but it would not be her home. She mused over her own silent thoughts, before noticing Kylah, who leaned against the stone wall beside her.

Kylah peered into the distance at the great rolling hills. That marked the home of the Shalough. The peaceful breeze brushed past in stark contrast to her mood. 'The Shalough will not expect you.' Kylah spoke in a soft voice.

She wanted to believe Kylah but then the Shalough knew more about the Angean than she did. She smiled then let out a long sigh, 'Look after Mitch.' She spoke into the breeze as she left.

'I don't think he needs looking after,' Kylah beamed.

Saranon never ceased to be amazed at how Mitch could blend in. Except for the time they were in Balquene. The thought scared her more than anything. She travelled away at a slow pace. All she wanted to do was stay. As she gazed upward she lost her footing and tripped. The soft fur of the misquew moved so that she landed on the hard ground. The large riding cat curled up, resting in the faint warmth of the sun. As she touched the ground she could sense the Keep running. It whirred with a magnificence that took her breath away. Then before she could blink she heard it. The sound was so slight she thought she had missed it. Then it reverberated again, the Keep knew she was here.

Saranon stood in disbelief, the Keep Sturanin had no fear of her. There was no awe or surprise. A great rumble seeped through the ground as the blood drained from her face and she ran. She wished she could leave, but the Keep had warned the Shalough. Without any hesitation she slipped in through the wall. As though it were not there. She could feel the vibrations shuddering along the walls as she ran. She slowed and glanced around, no one was following. In fact not one person was anywhere near her, yet the Keep was brimming with life. The Keep was under attack, but this time it was not her.

She let out a groan filled with frustration, the Keep knew she was there. Yet the occupants, the Shalough, were distracted. She was trying to imagine what could possibly distract the Shalough, then she froze. The Oracle had to be here. A tremor reverberated through the walls and she ran down the stairs toward it. The Keep gave a mild resistance. Letting her know she was not welcome, before allowing her to pass through the barrier. The air filled with the heat of sorcery. Building up with an energy that crawled along her skin. A great flame of sorcery hurled along without aim. She let it pass, as the energy around vanished in the haze.

She could sense the Shalough nearby. Yet none of it made sense, as she stayed in the shadows out of the way. The force of the energy thundered as it pummelled down the narrow passages. Rumbling in frequent succession as the lower Keep remained sealed. Veridan yelled with an almighty bellow that made her jump. The sorcerer was too close for comfort. The haze began to clear as the fighting ceased. To Saranon's disbelief she was standing right in the midst of the Shalough. 'You!' Veridan's voice boomed across the chamber.

She stood frozen to the spot. Then realised, it was she who should be angry with Veridan and glared at him in defiance. 'You will tear Tordoren apart before you are done,' Veridan said.

He struck out with his sorcery and watched as it dissipated into nothing. This enraged him even more, 'You were meant to remain imprisoned.'

'You were meant to handover the Oracle,' Saranon spoke in a flat tone.

Before Veridan had a chance to raise his voice the Keep shook. His gaze shifted back to the sealed entrance. Then to Saranon's astonishment the Shalough began pounding the seal. As though she did not exist.

As she watched, a force of energy struck her from behind and tried to fling her out of the way. It only succeeded in moving her to the side. Her annoyance clearly showed. As she raised her arm the whole group turned on her. A cataclysm of sparks cascaded around her bouncing off the walls. As she let the energy glide around rather. The sorcery flew in every direction. She raised her arm and the sparks ceased to exist. Veridan stepped back and his brow creased. He was not used to be challenged. As Saranon moved forward she stood outside the sealed entrance. Without taking her gaze away she held out her hand and the seal fell away.

A voice spoke from the open doorway and Saranon fumed, 'You!'

Flynn stood in front of her without any sign of remorse. 'I am going to leave you to kill each other.' She spoke with a hint of sarcasm.

Wandering off in the stunned silence that followed. Sturanin rumbled beneath as she made her way out into the darkness of night. The cool air swept by, yet it did not quell her anger. She sat on the damp grass as a fine rain fell from the sky. She stood in the land of the Shalough as her heart pounded in defiance. Sturanin remained silent giving nothing away.

Soft footsteps made their way across the muddy ground. As she waited for the Shalough to appear. She gasped at the sight of Madoc. Yet she had sensed a Shalough and peered behind him, expecting someone else. 'It's me,' Madoc replied, answering her unasked question.

'What are you doing here?' She glared at him in annoyance at being deceived.

'This is my home,' he spoke in a matter-of-fact tone as

he stood beside her.

'I thought the Pearl Castle was your home,' Saranon remarked.

'It was,' Madoc replied in a moment of regret.

They stood in a mutual peace gazing out at the night sky. As the rain eased and clouds let in the light from the stars. She could feel the excess energy she had absorbed burning underneath her skin. 'You wanted a bond-breaker,' she stated as they stood in the cool night air.

'That doesn't matter,' Madoc spoke as though all his dreams had been dashed.

She strode a few paces toward Sturanin then reached out her hands. The Keep hesitated before relenting. In the wind and the rain, with the earth of Tordoren and the fire of sorcery raging inside her. The sorceress wielded the blade made of heart stone as it formed in her grip. Sturanin gave one last rumble as it surged in the darkness. The blade was complete and cold to the touch.

She held out the blade as it shone in the light, then covered it in the sheath. 'This is a reminder of all the misunderstandings. That have happened this night, guard it well.'

Madoc made a humble bow as he received the gift. Staring in utter disbelief at the object he had longed for, 'I will guard it well.'

The sorcerer spoke with a sincere gratitude. Saranon sighed, if only finding the Oracle was that easy. As though answering her curiosity the Keep rumbled once more. In the distance the shadows grew as figures moved towards them. 'You need to leave,' Madoc whispered.

She could sense the Shalough approaching and hesitated. She was still no closer to the Oracle. Yet for all the attention, she was beginning to wonder if she would find the Oracle at all. She gazed over the growing crowd and stayed. She had no reason to run even as the numbers grew around her. Madoc stared at her as though urging her to run and she whispered, 'No.'

Veridan emerged. As he eyed Madoc he caught sight of the bond-breaker, 'What have you done?'

Saranon did not answer his question, 'You owe me an explanation.'

Veridan stared long and hard before standing so close she could feel his breath. 'The Angeon will break the world,' he said.

'Which one?' Saranon asked, 'Do you mean me or Merrick?'

The colour drained from Veridan's face as the horror of Saranon's words sank in. He had not realised there were two Angeon. 'Next time, I expect an explanation,' she spoke.

As the resounding beat of Katholomu's wings rose behind her. The dragon had impeccable timing. She could feel the great snort of warm air rush down her back. To her surprise the Shalough allowed her to leave. Kat wasted no time as he beat his wings hard. Bounding into the sky with such speed. That Sturanin became a mere memory fading into the night.

CHAPTER SEVEN

The Oracle

The safety of Karraden felt small as she mused over what had happened. She was still no closer to the Oracle. Mitch had packed the last of his belongings. While Kat was busy shredding the remains of tree. The dragon had taken a particular interest in sharpening his claws. She could not blame him. Ever since she had left Sturanin she had felt as though they were being watched. After all the attention they had to leave. The wiccan were a peaceful people. No match for the full might of their sorcerer neighbours hidden away in the hills. Kat would be easy to see in the sky and they waited for the brilliant rays of dusk to subside.

She preferred flying at night underneath the stars. The first two broke through and she breathed a sigh of relief as more gleamed overhead. Kat raised his head breathing in the cold wind as it swept past and she leaped on. The dragon's muscles became taut as he took to the sky with an astonishing ease. The great beast had been on edge all day and she did not blame him. She itched to be away, as far away as she could from both the Mercidian and the Shalough. The betrayal still stung, as her thoughts ran wild in her head, not wanting to commit.

Mitch clung on tight behind her, the wizard seemed so certain as she clung on to an all mighty mess. The dragon dipped and her thoughts strayed as she gazed through the night sky. It shone with elegant light as the stars made out their way in the darkness. The great beast flew higher into the thin cold air. As it clung to the sides of her cheeks, chilling her breath as they went. It gave her a thrill to be away from the Shalough and all the confusion. They would soon be after her. It was all a muddle that ran through her mind. As a great bolt of thunder flew diagonally from the ground.

Kat reacted before she did with an awful precision that made her heart skip a beat. The wizard remained silent behind her, but she could feel him tense. From out of the ground came another roar of flame. Only this time, it leaped through the sky behind her. Before she knew it Katholomu was surrounded in a tight formation. Symmetrical and elegant like a black diamond in the night sky. It took her a moment to realise they following Kat's lead. A dull black fleet of marmoz sucking in the light from the stars as they swept across the sky. Saranon felt the thrill surge through as her senses awakened. The dragon was honing in.

Several balls of flames answered from the ground. Lit

up as they headed toward them in the air. Kat accelerated and so did the fleet of dragons with a silent menace. They did not break formation. Then her stomach lurched as he dived. She could feel the pull of the sorcery below as it illuminated. Criss-crossing the ground and she gulped. For a moment she doubted herself as the energy welled inside. Saranon catapulted the blast with such straight aim. She almost singed the top of Katholomu's head. The dragon answered with a low rumble and she hesitated. The blast was not enough to extinguish the shield of sorcery. They headed closer at a steady pace.

The ground whirled into view and she took a deep breath. As the belly of the dragon gave a great roar beneath her. She closed her eyes and listened to the low rumble. Holding on tight as she summoned all she could. In the last few seconds before the shield gleamed below. This time the dragon dipped his head, as she let out one last blast. It shot across the web of sorcery with a grim finality. The sparks lit up the sky, showing the great fleet of dragons. It was only then that Saranon glimpsed the other riders on the dragons. She had no idea who they were. Yet as soon as the shield was down they took over. Moving ahead with a crushing blow and wizardry ignited the air around them.

The display of fiery colours would be brilliant. If it was not for the howling screams that followed. She wished she could block them out. Kat held his head high with pride. Then with a stretch and a flick of his tail. He gently knocked the two riders off and covered them under his wings. She tried to move the wing as it hung down with a heavy weight, but it would not budge. She wanted to hit the dragon, but she was exhausted. The panic still raced through her mind. Saranon knelt down on the grubby dirt covered by damp grass and caught her breath. The damp was soaking though to her knees, yet she did not move. There was so much happening outside, as the confusion set in.

Katholomu weakened his grip and relented. There was no end in sight as she ran through the mess with a blind haste. Not recognising anyone as the wizards fought on, ignoring her in their wake. A few steady eyes fell on her, hesitating then looked past as though she were not there. Then the ground cracked open with a low tremor. Whispering a challenge she did not want to accept. Yet no one came and she wondered if she had misunderstood. A cry caught her off guard. It was weak and she should not have heard it at all. Yet somehow amid all the fighting it pierced through the air and found her.

Another tremor embarked along the ground, as though taunting from the deep. Whoever it was did not want to be found. At the edge of her senses the Angeon waited within. Taunting from inside her thoughts. The energy seeped through her skin transforming her. As it blended in the shadows of the night. For the Angeon recognised the dull tremors more than she. It came as though summoned. It took Saranon a while to hear the whispers that had turned into a flood and filled her ears. She knew what it was. The Angeon came to life from within. With a calling that echoed through her thoughts. A faint sound, yet it screamed out in fear and she ran for all she was worth.

She blocked out the sounds of the battle around her as she raced. Time slowed and she felt her heart beat against her chest. Counting the distance with a mocking tone. Yet it guided her onward with a swiftness that ignited her senses. The cave ahead wrapped around her as she ran through the wall. There was no resistance as she swept through. The darkness wrapped around with a familiarity she did not share. As she moved down into the dim depths. A blast rang out, it curled around the walls and the ceiling in circular arc. The Angeon answered in a cold rage and the sorcery shattered. With shards raining around her before they vanished.

The sound rattled out with an unnatural call. That brought a blast aimed so close she could feel the heat across her neck. Before the protection of the Angeon set in. She ran forward with a rush and charged, there was no time. She could sense the voice calling. It was desperate, as the Angeon drew from the energy within. There was no time for empathy. As she fought ahead. Carving the path hard against the tumult of sorcery that followed. She seared through, not wanting to hesitate as the voice called. Pleading with her and weeping into her thoughts. Saranon wished she could shut it out, but could not. She knew who it was, as the oracle cried out in her mind.

The sweeping grimy corners led her down to a pungent smell. That filled the air and stuck to her clothes as she ran. Moisture trickled in tiny pools on the floor making it hopeless to be silent. Another blast rang out up ahead.

Only this time the wall ahead gave way, heading towards her. She took a deep breath and held her energy around to shield the blow. As she ducked and sped through. Then a mighty crack fled up the outer wall of the chamber and another. The sharp splitting sound made the Angeon freeze on the spot as she glanced around. She had to leave and soon. A cry rang out, only this time it was not in her mind. The wall splintered and she pounded on the web of lines creasing across the wall and floor.

Her energy hit its mark as she managed to break through. She stretched herself upward and held her hand out. As the Oracle clung on with all her might. The Oracle let out a scream, as a chunk of rock and dirt fell on the Angeon's shield. Then the girl, all of twelve, jumped over Saranon's shoulder and ran. Christine needed no convincing. The girl fled with such blind luck that the Angeon struggled to keep up. A great jarring sound rang out behind her and she held her breath. She had alwost reached the exit with the light of the full moon shining the way.

Yet as the sound had finished its dooms day call, the whole tunnel around her collapsed. She bolted through with she a dive and slid at the same time. The might of the cascading dirt sealed the cave behind her. Dust sprayed in a horizontal gush showering her with a dim reminder of how close she had come. Yet the Oracle was no where in sight. Her heart sank. She brushed off the dirt as she clambered upward. The ground rumbled and this time it was not from the sunken cave. The Angeon felt the surge of sorcery. Before she saw it gather strength along the ground. She ran toward it and saw the Oracle with her hands held high in a protective stance. They were being surrounded faster than the Angeon could count.

Anger swelled up inside her as she made the last distance and reached the Oracle. Her hand grabbed the hilt belonging to Corsavere. Her bond-breaker formed from the depths of Odana Temple. It swung high as she grimaced, yet she was not aiming for the group of sorcerers closing in. Christine shrieked. Her look filled with terror as she realised the Angeon was after her. Saranon's steely gaze locked on the Oracle. As she brought the blade down hard with both hands. The bond-breaker struck so close. It sheered through the Oracle's sleeve as the girl froze from fear. The blade landed hard into the stony ground. As the Oracle regained her strength and stood, pale as the moon above.

The Angeon plummeted her energy down seeping far into the ground and Tordoren answered. The Oracle screamed. As she caught glimpses of what was happening and shouted for the Angeon to stop. Yet the deed was already done, as the energy of the Angeon bled her energy to the surface. Creating a wide ring of sorcerer's stone as it expanded around them. The Angeon and the Oracle stood at the centre. With the sorcerer's growing agitated along the outer rim that kept them away. A pattern broke along the surface of the stone. At the last moment the Angeon twisted the blade of the bond-breaker. The pattern changed.

The Oracle barely had time to tell her off for making

a wizard's circle. As a rustle sprang undergrowth from behind them. Mitch leaped forward in open defiance and ignited the energy within the stone. The shield sprang into being. Lord Halleron's voice rang out above the crowd. More wizards ignited the wizard's circle as the shield grew stronger still. The Oracle watched in open disbelief. Then Mitch turned his attention to the left and right as if knowing. The ambient light from another wizard's circle ignited, then another and another. Lord Halleron's troops needed no convincing. To ignite the row of circles set hard in the earth.

As the pulse of the shield strengthened the sorcerer's disappeared into the darkness. Mitch eyed Saranon wearily as the Angeon seeped back within. 'If no one knew you were here, they do now.' he said.

Then gazed at the young Oracle and wrapped a cloak around her defiant shoulders. 'You, on the other hand, need to keep a low profile.'

Christine stomped on the wizard's foot, as she marched past without uttering a word. Mitch turned to Saranon, 'You can deal with that.'

'Me?' She said under her breath.

The wizard replied, 'I am only dealing with one sorceress.'

Saranon glared at him, she was not ready for a babysitting job. In fact, that was the last thing she was concerned about. She made her way to the great beast Katholomu. As she clambered up the Oracle was already there waiting. With an unimpressed look since the dragon would not budge. Saranon clambered on as Mitch shared another ride. He had made it clear the Oracle was one too may. She gave out a reluctant sigh, as she motioned for the dragon to fly. He obediently headed toward Auden, the great Keep of Lord Halleron, in Felkrayer.

As they flew the Oracle moved sideways, as though searching the ground beneath. She was about to say something and then motion in the dark caught her eye. It was not clear, but whatever it was it worried the Oracle. Katholomu swung at a hard angle. As he glided sideways spiralling down around the curve of the Keep. With a flick of his tail he lowered his wings and came to a screeching halt. Skidding across the courtyard toward the dragon pens. Before she had time to steady herself the Oracle had jumped off and was nowhere to be seen. She grumbled as she made her way down. The dragon let out a low rumble as he chuckled with amusement. 'Don't you start,' she spoke as she let the beast be.

Auden was huge and unfamiliar, it did not resemble any Keep she had come across. Like the Lord, the Keep remained silent. Several times she found herself going around in circles. Only to be greet by a friendly chuckle. 'You have passed this foyer three times,' the wizardess said.

Captain Lydia Grace smiled and showed the sorceress up to the great hall. The warmth hit her in a welcome burst as the door opened. Sounds of merriment and too much drink followed. As she attempted to enter unnoticed and the room fell as silent as the Keep. Mitch had positioned himself in a comfortable chair. Well away from the door and out of reach.

She frowned in dismay, the wizard could be rather unhelpful. He was seven years her senior and taller than most men with a frame to match. In comparison she was still an awkward seventeen. Saranon still had her hair out in much the same way a child would. Lord Halleron paused, before he rose to his feet and lifted her off the ground in a warm embrace. He patted her shoulder and moved her toward the head table with a grin. That showed an uneven row of teeth. If she were anyone else, it would be an intimidating sight. This was not the first wizard lord she had encountered.

The food smelled so good as she sat down. That she began piling her plate before the lord had time to sit. He said in a low voice, 'I think the Shalough have it right.'

He stopped to hear her pause with a worried glance. The Lord continued, 'It is you I should fear.'

Lord Halleron turned his gaze to the young Oracle who shouted in disgust. While no one was paying attention. There were a few warm smiles that made the Oracle erupt in another outburst. As she stomped her feet and sight of Saranon. She had time to hide, even though she knew hiding would serve no purpose. Christine, who had changed into a beautiful pale dress. Grabbed hold of Saranon's arm demanding that she go with the Oracle.

When the girl realised her attempt was futile. Christine sat down in a loud humph right next to her, 'Do you know how much trouble is coming? You are wasting time.'

Saranon smiled. 'I am no good to anyone with an

empty stomach and no sleep.'

The Lord chuckled with a big belly laugh as he ate. His large grin was in stark contrast to the Oracle's frown. The night continued on with a range of drunken song. Somehow every wizard managed to avoid Saranon. An act that she found quite impressive given there was more than one brawl. That had begun with an awkward stumble. As she rose to go to bed the Oracle went with her, the girl showed no intention of leaving her side. She let a sigh, then held out her hand as they made their way to bed. Perhaps in the morning the Oracle would find someone else to annoy. For for now she was all the girl had. The company was welcome given she was in a wizard Keep. There were almost no other sorcerers in sight.

Her dreams were filled with the rage of battle as the voices rang out around her. The last sound that came was the thunderous roar of the cave as it collapsed around. A mighty thud woke her as she stared up at Christine who had jumped on her bed. The girl had already begun ordering her out of bed. Saranon attempted to tell the Oracle there was no need to rush as the girl pushed her out of the way. She grumbled as she gathered her things in haste. It was not the start to the morning she had been hoping for, as the late autumn sun broke across the sky. She eyed Mitch in the corridor who showed no intention of intervening. Even under a stern gaze.

The wizard appeared to enjoy leaving her to occupy the Oracle. As everyone stepped out of their way. She held up her hand to block the rays of the morning light. As they ran out onto the courtyard adjacent the dragon pens. Katholomu opened one eye to peer at them, as he remained curled up in a sleepy fashion. Then to her surprise held out his front paw and gave a gentle flick with his claw. Moving the Oracle toward the door. A scream filled the air, then Christine shouted at the dragon in haste. Saranon took a deep breath, but the dragon did not move. She let out a sigh and in that moment Kat decided he had had enough. The dragon let out a fowl warm gust of air from his lungs. It was enough to give the Oracle a start and she ran out into the open field.

'Really?' She gazed at the dragon. 'Well, at least you didn't squash her.'

She chased after the girl, when she would much rather be curled up asleep. In the distance Lady Halleron had found the Oracle and she breathed a sigh of relief. Someone else could look after the girl, at least for the moment. Mitch stood at the end of the courtyard in a solemn stance at his full height as she peered upward. 'There is someone waiting for you,' he remarked.

'Pardon?' Saranon asked.

The wizard held out his hand and gestured without a reply. There in the largest sitting room she had ever laid eyes upon. Stood a tall and nimble sorcerer. His eyebrows raised in a monotone form as she entered. 'The ockren requests your presence,' Halwende spoke as though it was a mere formality.

'What ockren?' She asked with a puzzled expression.

'The one that sits on the last wizard circle. You so

promptly made,' Halwende replied.

Staring in a matter-of-fact tone as he cleared his voice with a cough. As Saranon stood in a baffled silence. Christine's voice rang out across the room, 'I'm coming with you.'

The Oracle announced in a proud stance with her hands on her hips. Halwende bowed his head in a smooth motion, 'And this young lady, would be the Oracle. The one whom we are to teach in the art of sorcery.'

Christine gave him an uneasy stare then announced in a stern voice, 'I am not going.'

Saranon looked at her agape as though she had missed something. 'I am not going,' the Oracle repeated.

Lord Halleron and Halwende gave a knowing smile. As though the arrangement had already been agreed.

Before thinking Saranon exclaimed, 'Do you know what you are getting involved in?'

Halwende gave her a warm smile, 'Why yes, the oracles of old were from this region.'

Lord Halleron arched his back in a fine gesture of grandeur. 'The Fellowyn's know more about the Oracle than anyone else,' he said.

The Lord looked as though he was about to say more. Instead stopped himself short as he left their company. He was a wizard of few words, but what he did say carried weight. She had the distinct feeling he knew far more than he would ever admit.

The day was cool, yet the sky was crystal clear. As they made their way at an easy pace to see an ockren without a

Keep. Saranon had never heard of such a thing, yet it did not surprise her. She grew anxious as they became closer and the great magical beast could be seen up ahead. She stood and took a deep breath near the edge of the wizard circle, as the ockren raised it's head. The faint marking on the beast appeared different and more notable in the light. She stepped with hesitation and made her way forward. Until she was almost level with the ockren's yellow eyes. The giant cat moved in a way that was not quite right. As it spoke in a hollow tone. That rumbled along the ground, 'Angeon, you have passed your second test.'

Saranon stood expecting something else to happen, but the ockren waited. As it's short rough coat moved in way that did not allow for the movement of muscles beneath. She hesitated, 'What do you mean by a second test?'

She had not recalled her first test and the ockren did not make sense. The ockren smiled, if that was at all possible. Then it let out a low rumble of a laugh that clung in the air and chilled her skin. Just as the sound ceased the ockren arched forward. Light criss-crossed along its skin as though breaking through from underneath. The outer layer melting away before she could take a breath. The energy that had been held within sparkled as it cascaded. A strong gust blew toward her. Before she could move the energy contained within the ockren blew through her. The sensation tingled as she blinked and opened her eyes in a different phase.

The world she had been in was swept away by the

sorcery trapped in the ockren. There before her on the wizard's circle, stood Tasha, the only person she could see. The spirit of her old friend glowed with a warm vibrancy. Silhouetted by her fawn coloured hair, waving free of her shoulders. It had been so long since she had seen her old friend, 'Why have you brought me here.'

Tasha smiled, 'Welcome to my world.'

CHAPTER EIGHT

The memory that remains

Tasha stood still as though waiting for the right moment. Then spoke, 'I could not tell you that you had passed the first test. You would not have survived the Shalough.'

The grim reality of what her friend was saying sank in. The Shalough really had tried to kill her. 'What was my first test?'

Tasha appeared amused by the question, 'You encountered the other Angeon.'

Saranon exclaimed, 'Merrick Calthazard.'

The different phase held few people, only those who could travel there. The uneven wind that swept around them made a hollow sound that made her anxious. Yet she knew she had to return. The ground blurred underneath. She was back where she began on the wizard's circle. Mitch gave her a knowing stare and held out his arm to comfort her. The wizard could read her mind at all the wrong times, just when she hoped for some quiet.

The memory of her friend held so much pain, it was hard to let go. They made their way back to the wizard Keep. She sat down, the anguish plain on her face. By all accounts she should be dead. She had been betrayed by one of the few friends she had. Mitch could not stand still. She could not read his mind, but his anxiety showed. She asked, 'What's going on?'

He hesitated before responding, 'Lord Halleron is gathering support. To meet on the edge of the heartland. I told him we would join them.'

Her face grew hot as she fumed. It was not like him to make a decision, but she could not think of an alternative. 'You want me away from the Oracle,' she quizzed.

'I think it's best,' he said.

It was a blunt reply. She did not want to stay near the Oracle, but the choice had already been made. The last night at Felkrayer moved slow as she wrestled in her sleep. Waking too often in the dark. She woke again as Mitch approached. They left before the light reached over the mountains. Katholomu greeted her and they clambered on. She waited as Mitch steadied himself near the thick folds of the dragon's shoulder.

The great beast jolted into the sky, his wings spread and they gathered speed. The chill of the late autumn wind numbed her face and she held on. Guiding Kat through the morning light. 'I passed two tests of the Angeon,' she spoke her thoughts aloud.

He was quiet for a while, 'You are meant to be older.'

She asked, 'How would you know?'

'The Angeons of old did not experience the tests until they were older,' he said. 'Have you read the books you kept?'

'I missed that,' she exclaimed.

It annoyed her when Mitch knew more about the Angeon that she did. 'So what if I'm a bit early,' she retorted.

'You will not be ready,' he responded.

The dragon remained quiet, as he glided above the hills and dense forest below. 'Mitch,' she said, 'I would prefer it if you didn't tell anyone.'

'I am your hilazen,' he answered.

She was not sure if that meant yes or no, but was not about to ask.

A golden sun shone over Hestrel Keep and Katholomu circled down. Gliding too close to the wall and his claw scrapped. She winced at the sound and the dragon took no notice. As he hit the ground, leaning over to warm his back. She slid off as Kat rolled, it was one of his softer landings. Captain Grace headed toward Mitch, 'You took your time.'

Before Saranon had time to ask she was alone in the stone courtyard.

The sun shone along the grey walls. Warming the courtyard that linked around the Keep. Opening up to the garden that buffered them from the thick woodland. She wandered around to the dragon pens, where supplies were being offloaded from the carts. She darted through a gap into the warmth of the pens. An open hearth gave a welcoming glow from the end of the room. She accepted a drink and found a seat as the wizards rested between work. A blanket moved near the hearth and she jumped. Elethea laughed and an infant marmoz dragon poked its head out. The creature was tiny compared to the full grown dragons.

It wandered over and sniffed her holding one paw up, then curled up in her lap. 'You won't be able to move now,' Elethea smiled. 'Kallie will stay as long as you let her.'

The hatchling felt so fragile as she patted it. The seat provided a good vantage point. As she watched the equipment and weapons being hauled into the Keep. She asked, 'What are you preparing for?'

Elethea grew silent and an officer answered. 'Guarding the trade link,' Bayard spoke.

She asked, 'Is that from the Shalough?'

'No,' he replied.

'It's always been a rough journey to travel inland,' Bayard relaxed.

While taking a break. Yet his eyes took in everything watching. As the last of the supplies vanished into the building. A growl shot across the courtyard. Katholomu squeezed his head sideways through the archway. Saranon glared at him, 'Are you jealous?'

He huffed a snort of warm stale air into the room and she placed the hatchling down. She patted his head while nudging him out of the doorway. The pens were a good size and Kat fit comfortably. He flopped on the floor letting her pat his head.

There was something odd about the supplies. The Keep did not appear lacking in anything. Yet she said nothing, as she began to groom the dragon. Her ordeal had taken its toll. Her friend Clara had betrayed her and Alveron was no longer the safe haven it may have been. Katholomu's offered a small respite from the storm inside her head. If two tests were done, how long did she have until the final one? She was lost in her thoughts when Mitch approached. 'The Athgar need our help,' he said.

'Don't include me in this,' she spoke before he had time to answer.

'Wiccan have disappeared,' he explained.

Ever since Mrs Harper's tavern in Normisia the wiccan had welcomed her. It was more than many had done. The night caved in as the clouds drew close, the days were getting shorter. She let the great dragon rest and entered into the Keep. The outer rim turned from a worn rustic appearance. Into sleek hard walls beautifully formed with wide corridors. She held her hand up against the cold stone and Hestrel Keep responded with a vibrant hum. Its strength shone in the lights illuminating the walls. Mitch led her to the control room. Where Captain Lydia Grace studied several maps spread across a broad table.

As Saranon approached she spied the markers highlighting the wicca towns. Close to the trade link to the south of the heartland. There was something else. She leaned forward picking gazing at a mark for the Athgar, yet it was not the same. The Captain read her immediate thoughts, 'The Athgar are divided.'

It was the only explanation Captain Lydia Grace was willing to give. She made her way to the cosy apartment that waited part way up the wizard Keep. The room was a welcome relief as she sat curled up near the fire. A quiet knock came from the door and Mitch let himself in. He sat on the chair next to her. The wizard had been her companion for over a year and she was yet to figure him out. 'Hold out your hands,' he asked.

She did, there was nothing there and he gave a look of dismay. 'If anything appears let me know,' he said.

She asked, 'If what appears?'

'Anything different,' he replied. 'To mark when the final test is near.'

The thought made her shudder and Lord Shakar's words stayed with her. If she chose the wrong path he would kill her. If she chose the right one he could use her to rule Zyanthia. Mitch hugged her before he left. It was little comfort and she hoped that sleep would bring relief. The wind whirred around the Keep, with a sound that penetrated through the walls as she drifted off.

A clamour woke her with the dawn as Mitch opened the door. She glanced out the window, and asked, 'Do you know what time it is?'

He ignored her protest and waited as she hurried. The smell of warm toast wafted from the great hall and she wandered in. Kat had flattened a corner of the garden including two trees. While warming his belly in the sun. His long tail swished in a dangerous carefree motion. Keeping a buffer between him and the trainers. 'Katholomu,' she shouted so loud the dragon stood up to greet her. She exclaimed, 'Can you be discreet?'

The great beast laughed and his body rumbled magnifying the sound into a low growl.

Kat had never been discreet. She thought she would ask before she climbed up on his shoulders. Mitch motioned for the dragon to fly before she had a chance to hang on and almost slid off. The cloud covered sky hid the dragon as the chill wind set in. Her rough coat had been borrowed from the Athgar. It kept her warm as they flew high staying amid the grey sky. Hestrel was well placed. Guarding a fork between the main road to the south and the road east to Felkrayer. Kat swooped low on the verge of the hillside as it met the forest sweeping along either side. The dense woodland parted to form a road held together with worn stone. She gazed along the road yet it vanished darting in and out of view.

A loud crack caught her attention. She turned to find a tree collapsing under the dragon's weight. Kat rested without a care and she exclaimed, 'Did we have to bring the dragon?'

'The road veers close to the heartland. We will draw attention if we don't,' Mitch explained.

Saranon was tempted to ask if they could bring a different dragon, but Kat may not take the hint. She trudged along, her every attempt to avoid the mud muted by the damp ground. Mitch showed her the first marker along the road and she went pale.

The stone marker was too familiar. Identical to the

ones that had trapped her inside the detention camp. He spoke, but the words did not sink in, '…Are you all right?'

She asked, 'Can we leave?'

He hesitated then took her back to the upside down dragon. Kat had managed to stick his tail and hind legs in the air. While rubbing his back against the muddy ground. The great beast turned and grumbled at the sight of her muddy boots. 'Don't you start,' she said.

They travelled in silence, as soon as the dragon landed she slid down. Mitch caught her halfway and she nose planted into the dragon's dirt ridden scales. He let go and Saranon slid down covered in the mud. Mitch began to laugh and she stormed off. It was not the reaction she had expected. Before she had a chance to sit down he found her, 'I can travel alone.'

The frustration showed on her face, 'No.'

He nodded and let her be. She knew the road had to be protected, but the markers still sent a chill down her spine.

The memory of the detention camp had seemed so far away. The glow of the marker dimmed and she moved. The glow returned, and she glanced around trying to figure out what had happened. She reached out her hand yet there was no change. She tried again and the dragon roared with laughter. He gave a firm nudge with his front leg and she fell toward the rock.

Again the glow dimmed and she peered down. All she could find was her bond-breaker. She placed it on the stone marker and the glow dimmed. 'Oh,' she exclaimed.

The dragon gave a loud snort and rumbled. 'I didn't know,' she said.

'Angeon,' he snorted.

'You know I am the Angeon,' she responded.

The forest parted around them as they were met by a group of wizards. Mitch shouted, 'What are you doing?'

'It was him,' she said pointing to the dragon.

'Don't blame this one on Kat. You tampered with the markers,' he accused her.

She glared at him, 'Yes.'

'They protect the road,' he motioned for her to follow.

The Athgar wizards moved with ease through the forest. The branches shook behind them as the great dragon plodded through. 'Now everyone knows we are here,' she exclaimed.

Mitch responded, 'Dragons are common...'

Before he could finish two juvenile dragons ran past. 'All right,' she retorted.

'If you must know, you are the odd one,' he added.

The Athgar wizards checked the stone markers while she stayed at the edge of the group. The glow held too many memories trapped away, she tried not to let it show. The two younger dragons ran close to Katholomu. He leaped out, sending one to the ground. 'No,' she shouted and Kat released his hold.

The juvenile dragon whimpered and scurried away. Kat stood in front of her stomping his front leg hard on the ground. 'I said "no",' she glared at him.

Mitch spoke, 'Saranon.'

Kathomolu jumped straight over her. Every muscle tense as Kat narrowed in on the adult dragon, ripping into the flesh. Kat's opponent backed down screeching in pain. 'Finish the fight,' she yelled at the dragon who glanced at her.

Mitch stared at her in horror. She yelled again, 'Finish the dragon.'

Katholomu heaved and lay down, breathing heavy. Saranon strode toward the dragon, 'You only get one chance to attack me.'

She let the Angeon flow through, the adult dragon hobbled further away.

Her energy flared into a narrow arc, hitting the dragon's heart. It stood for a moment before falling with a heavy thud. Only then did Kat wince in agony. Saranon searched the dead dragon and found a small trace, the mark of the Shalough. She took a closer glance holding back the dragon's thick coat. The second mark below showed the fires of chaos. It matched the mark on her arm, given to her in the detention camp.

'We should go,' Mitch said.

The sun was beginning to set as the breeze deepened its chill and she nodded.

Katholomu let her climb on and she glanced back. Watching as the dead dragon disintegrated. He flew strong and she clung on until they landed in the courtyard near the dragon pens. Kat lowered his head and winced. Bayard rushed to examine the dragon. The wound was little more than a graze, yet a crowd gathered to dote on the giant beast. Saranon eyed the dragon with suspicion when Mitch spoke, 'He defended you.'

Captain Grace added while patting the beast, 'He did a good job.'

She asked the captain, 'Do the Shalough use the symbol for the fires of chaos?'

'Before the Dreshan occupation, you won't see it much now,' the Captain answered.

She waited to make sure Katholomu was snug and warm inside the pens. He rested with a gentle purr that rumbled through his body. She leaned close and whispered in his ear, 'Did you know I was the Angeon?'

The dragon responded by nuzzling his head against her. She stayed long after the night fell and made her way to the great hall. The large room was almost empty and she spotted Mitch by the fire.

He spoke, 'You killed the dragon.'

'I had to,' she responded.

'That is not what I meant,' Mitch said. 'Anyone else would hesitate.'

'Or run away,' she added.

He asked, 'You doubt my ability?'

'No. Well...' She began.

Mitch gave her an annoyed glare. The wizard was seven years her senior and made it clear when he was not impressed.

Hestrel Keep stayed almost silent. As she slipped through the empty corridors to her room. The thick walls made the place feel smaller than it was, but the room was cosy enough. She took out the bond-breaker Corsavere holding it up to the light. The heart stone embedded in the hilt glowed. The device could nullify her oldest fear and she held it in her hand. The fear was long gone, or so she thought before seeing the stone markers. It had been a long time since she had thought of the detention camps in Darkonia. Tasha's death stayed a constant reminder. The loss of her friend and leader had been so great. It weighed on her mind even more.

She took off her coat staring down at the mark on her arm. The fires of chaos were still there, yet her palms were clear. A faint shadow appeared as she stared at her hands and she gasped. The second test was complete. She should have guessed her marks would begin to show. They were so faint if she pretended they were not there no one would know. Saranon let exhaustion take her as she fell asleep. The turmoil of the day crept into her dreams and well into the early morning.

CHAPTER NINE

The price of survival

An awkward atmosphere hung over the room as Saranon failed to find the right words. Mitch interrupted. It was a welcome relief as she followed him into the fading light covering the dragon pens. Hestrel Keep had been silent, there was only one way to find out what had happened. The thought chilled her more than the wind that took hold. She slipped by the wizards. Making her way down to the indolin chambers below the habitable area. The Keep was strong and sturdy, yet it had fallen to the Dreshan Army that had taken Zyanthia. The region had since been reborn into five countries. Armedicia, Taria and Normisia and in the south, Darkonia and Alveron. Hestrel Keep stood near the midway point joining the south to the north. She should have known it had seen war, yet the thought had not occurred to her.

She made her way further down to the imbenik chambers. The hum from the central core rose above the background noise. A solid sorrowful sound that filled the air. She called out in her mind and it spoke. The foundations reverberated she could sense the shudder from the dragon pens and ran. It came again ever so faint, yet it broke through the low hum of the Keep. At first the pens were empty then the great dragon rammed against the side of the building. She shouted mistaking the beast for Katholomu. The dragon glared at her. His features were similar with a scar running down the left side of his jaw.

Kail stood in the cold night air. The Otturin sorcerer gave the same glare as his dragon, 'Where is the Oracle?'

Captain Lydia Grace and the wizards blocked him from entering the Keep. She glanced around, 'Where is Katholomu?'

'Mitch took him with the riders,' Bayard replied.

She was not impressed. Kail stood close, 'You were supposed to return the Oracle.'

'You haven't had much experience with a real Oracle, have you?' She remarked.

He mused, '... And you have?'

'Yes,' she replied and asked, 'Can I ride with you?'

'You are not stealing another dragon,' he spoke, climbing atop Dramakor.

She gazed over the dragons that were left and let them be. A small group of misquew made their home on the edge of the garden. She called to one and it came. The riding cat was well built for speed, yet not for long distance. She made her way to the first stone markers. Highlighting the gateway to the road and let the misquew go. She stood next to the marker, hesitating before reaching out. The sickly glow wavered and she tried not to let go. Her hand slipped, she took a deep breath and tried again.

She let the flow of the Angeon guide her. Gripping onto a remnant of sorcery in the stone and stepped onto the road. The chill wind faded as she dropped out of phase and the world grew silent. The road passed beneath her with no rhythm as she walked. The distance melted as she picked up speed. A dragon broke through the sky shattering the peace. It threw her back into the real world and she hit the ground with a thud. She glanced up in time to watch Dramakor fall, a web of sorcery dragging him down. She ran to the dragon and Kail's scream cut through. The wizards were guarding the Oracle, but the attackers had caught Kail. Their sorcery rose and the small group became twelve Shalough.

The formation began to close and the energy of the Angeon rose. She ripped through the corner of the circle. Her energy scorched a long trail as it blasted the group apart. The last of the Shalough ran. She grabbed Kail. 'No. Leave me,' he cried out.

'He won't make it,' Mitch said.

She exclaimed, 'What?'

Kail held out his arm, his sorcery was bleeding out. No matter how much he tried to make it stop. 'Leave,' he cried.

Mitch opened a small sova bag, as it grew in size he

took out a hyrik. Saranon jumped back. The metal band made of wizardry had been placed around her neck once.

She shouted, 'What are you doing?'

'It will stop the flow,' Captain Grace explained, 'or he will bleed out.'

Her face grew pale, 'Do you have to?'

Kail screamed even more as the hyrik was placed around his neck. To her amazement the sorcery stopped flowing from his arm. 'You can take him back,' Mitch said.

She protested, 'Me? I don't think so.'

He asked, 'Would you rather stay?'

She wanted to stay, a few of the attackers had escaped. Mitch nodded as though reading her immediate thoughts.

She watched as the group left and Katholomu stood watching her. He did not blink as he stared. 'Let us hunt.' She said.

The dragon flexed his shoulders in eagerness and she climbed up. This time the dragon stayed low to the ground and his muscles moved in a fluid motion. Every step calculated, as he ran through the edge of the forest. The rustle of the wind called to her as she sensed the lay of the land. Waiting with the patient dragon. She drew her bond-breaker Corsavere to the length of a sword. This time there would be no survivors. Katholomu honed in through the darkness, it was all she needed.

Saranon slid down his shoulder while her focus stayed transfixed. She rushed forward taking the first sorcerer by surprise. The marks of dark sorcery revealed as the body slumped beside the brittle bark of the tree. Her heart thudded in her ears as the energy of the Angeon flooded through. She ran along the muddy ground with the last of the autumn leaves underfoot. Two sorcerers up ahead were so close. That the energy took them down in the same blast as it lit up the night. She had not meant to worn the others, as the embers glowed throwing shadows past the trees. A sorceress moved in the distance and she ran toward her. A blow of sorcery knocked her from behind, but it was not enough. As the energy of the Angeon shielded her.

She moved forward still catching her breath and hit the sorceress hard. The energy of the Angeon was so great it ripped the dark sorcery from the sorceress. A hideous scream pierced the night. Saranon hesitated taking a step back. The impact frightened her and she tried not to show it. 'We need to go,' Madoc shouted behind her.

The sight of the dragon trainer was enough to snap her out of the trance. Her attacker lied dead on the ground. Madoc's blade glowed from the impact. She asked, 'What are you doing?'

'Same as you. We have to leave,' he said.

They raced toward Katholomu, she climbed on last. The dragon jolted into the sky while she watched for any sign of attack. The great beast made good speed. They were well away as the first signs of sorcerers scattered across the ground. 'They took my brother,' Madoc explained. Saranon knew what that meant after witnessing the attack on Kail. 'Is that why you hid among the Mercidian?'

'Yes,' he replied.

Katholomu glided into the courtyard and flopped

sideways to let them down. Before curling up into a large ball inside the warmth of the dragon pens.

Mitch ran out to meet them. Eyeing Madoc with caution before speaking, 'Kail has sealed himself in the Keep.'

She shouted, 'What?'

'He is below the habitable area,' he answered.

She made her way down the stairs and Madoc ran after her. He asked, 'Can I join you?'

They made their way down, the corridors were silent. The Keep guided her toward Kail. She made her way through the catacomb of tunnels to a simple room. An altar had been carved out of the far wall. Kail still wore the hyrik, the sight of the band made her hesitate. She reached out with her mind, I cannot take your pain but I can share your burden. Kail opened his eyes, it was the look of exhaustion.

'The Oracle is safe,' she said.

'You should not have taken her,' Kail said.

'Madoc and I just saved your hide,' she spoke as she helped him stand.

Saranon waited until they were out of sight, 'The oracle stays at Felkrayer.'

'You steal my dragon and now you steal the Oracle,' Kail said.

'...And save your life,' Madoc added.

The two sorcerers stared at each other in silence before letting the matter lie.

Mitch stormed along the corridor, 'I want a word

with you.'

Madoc and Kail left her alone to face the wizard. The fact that he was her hilazen did not make it any better and she cringed. Mitch took her to the side, 'What are doing?'

'I... I had to go after the Razen sorcerers,' she explained.

'I meant the young men you were flirting with,' he glared at her.

'I was not flirting,' she shouted. 'I was not flirting,' she repeated in a softer voice.

He asked, 'How old are you?'

'Seventeen,' she rolled her eyes. 'I was not flirting.'

'You are going to be a full Angeon soon,' he said.

She could feel her cheeks grow hot. 'Be careful who you choose,' he added.

The change in Mitch's words surprised her as he left. At Balquene the thought of her having a boyfriend had shocked him. It was not the type of conversation she wanted to have.

The thought clouded her mind and she went beneath the habitable area. Hestrel Keep had survived the Dreshan Occupation and the temptation was too great. She made her way down until she stood at the lowest part of the indolin chambers. The last area before the central core. She waited calling out to Hestrel with her mind, yet the Keep was reluctant to let her in. She listened to the hum of the central core whirring underneath.

She was about to speak and the floor slipped away. The central core caught her off guard as it dragged her down into the deep. It barely spoke above the rhythm that reverberated around. The outer shell closed, trapping her inside a thick storm. The current of the winds picked her up as though she was floating through the air. An array of light glowed along the rod, yet the clouds were so thick, she could only just make it out. Then the light was upon her and she crashed with a thud. Clinging on as the clouds whirled around. She held on and moved around to an opening leading into the control room. Saranon fell on the floor as gravity returned. The makeshift room was in immaculate condition. She took a seat at the control panels, trying to remember how it operated.

A lever moved on the floor and the whirring increased. She turned it the other way and the storm began to slow. Hidden behind the whirring clouds was a central core in perfect condition. The outer shell held no signs of stress. The structural frame leading down was sturdy. She peered down at the rod and the surface was smooth. Somehow the central core had survived the Dreshan occupation. She smiled as she gazed. Watching the stallic energy rise at a steady pace charging the central core.

The core rumbled and she made her way out of the enclosed room. Letting go of gravity as she floated upward. The winds that swept around the core caught her. As the outer shell opened guiding her to the surface. Her feet made contact with solid ground and she reached out. Touching the sorcerers stone. The end node was partially covered by the undergrowth of the forest. A fair distance from the main building. Flynn emerged from the edge of the forest in the morning light. Her anger swelled within as more Mercidian sorcerers arrived.

The Mercidian attacked and the shield surrounding Hestrel Keep flared. Bringing the attention of the Athgar wizards. She was too angry. She tried to calm her thoughts as she watched from distance. Madoc ran toward the Mercidian sending a flare into the sky. She should have known he would bring the Shalough.

Saranon shouted to Flynn, 'You have no place here.'

She turned to Madoc, 'You had to make it worse.'

Madoc hung his head and did not answer. Flynn stared at her, 'You were never meant to live.'

Saranon stepped outside the shield protecting the Keep, 'You are too late Mercidian.'

The energy of the Angeon surged within and Flynn backed down. She waited as he left.

'I was trying to help,' Madoc explained.

She headed toward the Keep, 'At least you have a clan.'

The Keep had become silent as she fumed. Captain Grace was the last person she expected see. 'We have a problem,' the Captain said.

'Kail,' Captain Grace continued. The colour drained from her face.

The stairs leading down below the habitable area, opened into a foyer, lit from above. A pool of dark sheal lapped near the rim of the floor as she entered the underground room. The hyrik was removed and Kail remained slumped at the base of a column. His fingers swinging close to the sheal. His sorcery surged and he let it drain into the sheal. 'You cannot stay here,' she said.

He leaped up and shouted, the sorcery surging along his skin. 'You should have returned the Oracle. Get out!'

She stayed and Kail stumbled. She caught him, but he pulled away from her grasp. 'Leave,' he said. 'Leave.'

He stumbled again. 'You are going to fall in,' she said.

He glared at her as he sat on the floor in resignation. 'I need to be with my clan,' he spoke.

Saranon knelt down, 'Stay away from the Oracle.'

She clasped his head in her hands. The energy of the Angeon rose within. It crept through her and entered Kail sealing his sorcery in. He grabbed her hand and saw the faint mark, 'Well, well. You've been keeping that one secret.'

She pulled away, 'That's none of your business.'

He gave a knowing smile of satisfaction and she fought the urge to shove him into the sheal. 'You owe me,' she said.

'You stole my dragon, I call that even,' he replied.

She lunged at Kail before he was able to leave and they rolled close to the edge of the sheal. A heavy hand picked her up and Kail wrestled free. As soon as Mitch placed her back on the ground she turned on him. His expression was cold and firm. Saranon backed away teetering on the edge of the sheal and fell in. The cool liquid began draining the energy from her. She managed to heave herself up on the floor. Mitch's stance was unwavering. 'He...' the words trailed off as she glared at him. 'Do not annoy the Otturin,' Mitch said.

'He's not...' She began.

Nothing she could say would make the wizard understand. Saranon pulled away from his grasp. The impact of the sheal still plagued her senses. She sought refuge below in the depths of the Keep. The walls became silent as she descended far beneath the habitable area. A great chasm loomed at the edge of the floor, marking the decent to the central core. The magical entity that flowed through the Keep. Nothing above had survived the Dreshan Occupation. Yet the floor held the pattern of the Keep. Hestrel had been alone in the dark, cut off from the outside world. She let the low hum sink through and peered over the edge. A dull drone crept up with the warm air weaving its way up the vents.

She took one step reaching out into the void and held out her arms embracing the fall. The darkness wrapped around, hauling her down. The voice of the Keep hummed welcoming her back amid the drone, as she fell ever closer to the core. The descent gave way in a rush as the outer shell came into reach. Each time she hesitated unsure of what to find, yet knowing too much. Hestrel spoke urging her to enter. Only a few could and even fewer dared. She reached out expecting to find the shell solid. Yet it ebbed away beneath pulling her in. A mass of clouds swirled in the haze as the charge crackled through. There was no way up or down as Hestrel waited. The control room revealed again as the haze lifted and she clung on. Gravity took hold in the circular structure secured at the centre of the core.

A man sat at the controls and she froze. It was the embodiment of the Keep. She backed away. He held out his hand and beckoned her. 'Only you can drive the core,' he said.

'You want something,' she eyed him with suspicion.

She waited and the man became agitated. 'When you want to talk let me know,' she moved away.

'Rebuild the Keep,' Hestrel said.

A smile crept across her face as she slipped into the comfortable seat. Hestrel leaned over and she gently blocked him. He did not resist. The Angeon surged through as she waited for the energy of the core to reach them. It ignited along the rod embedded deep in Tordoren weaving its way toward them.

The Keep began to move upward with a slow pace at first. The great structure rising from the ground. The towers of old rose around the end nodes forming the outer rim. The Keep stopped as it moved into its final resting place. It felt like a life time as Hestrel lifted her back through the open void. Her ears still humming with the sound of the Keep.

Mitch whispered, 'You have been gone seven days.'

The exhaustion found a way to creep in as the sun shone through frost. She left while the wizards shouted with excitement. The room was warm inside the thick walls and she soon fell into a deep sleep.

Mitch's voice cut through the dark as she managed to open her eyes, 'We have to leave.'

Saranon asked, 'Why?'

'We will leave before dawn, be ready,' Lord Halleron said as he closed the door behind him.

'Tathen has been attacked,' Mitch said.

She sat bolt upright and rushed to get ready, it was not what she wanted to hear. The frost had thickened in the night. The Athgar wizards prepared the horses for travel. She asked, 'Why not take the dragons?'

Lord Halleron answered, 'Wizards prefer to stay together.'

She hesitated, then went outside to call to the misquew. One answered and she waited as the wizards formed a tight group. Lord Halleron stayed in the centre. The hilt of his bond-breaker gleamed in the dark. The misquew sat lower than the horses. They made their way to the road where stone markers lit the way ahead. Her stomach churned, yet she held on. Lord Halleron waited for the last wizard to enter the road then gave the signal. The road spun past as the wizards used the stone markers to move at a quick pace. A glimmer of faded light broke over the hill and through the trees. Smoke from the chimneys marked the cottages of Tathen. The smooth stone broke into an uneven trail underneath.

A white layer of frost circled Tathen. They exited the edge of the woods to find Captain Drevon waiting. The group continued through the town growing as the wizards gathered. Saranon glanced around. By the time they reached the end of the town the group verged on a small army. She stayed close to the Lord as they picked up speed. Shouts rang from up ahead as a blast rang out from the hillside. The wizards charged leaving her behind. She sensed the wizardry and hesitated, they were fighting their own. Mitch swung around and yelled out, he pointed ahead and her gaze followed. Still she lagged behind. The wizards took the fight into the heart of the group.

Mitch shouted in anguish, 'What are you doing?'

'I can't,' she answered.

He re-joined Lord Halleron as she watched on, trying not to tremble in disbelief. The Lord stormed into the opposition with his soldiers swarming around him. She wanted to run, but a rustle in the woods caught her attention. She turned to see a wicca girl beckoning her to follow. Saranon left the misquew behind and entered the woods losing sight of the girl. Stubbing her toe on a rock. It gave a green glow that faded until she reached out. As soon as she touched the rock it glowed faint green. She gripped it with both hands and turned it over. The mark of the fires of chaos was etched deep in the surface, but that was not what caught her breath.

She dug into the shallow pit grasping a small leather pouch and opened it. The stolen sorcery leaked into the ground. She glanced over at the wizards as the skirmish slowed and the woods fell silent. Mitch ran toward her and stopped, she was still holding the pouch. It took a moment for him to realise what she held. Cheers rang out around them and she spoke, 'We're in trouble.'

He took the empty pouch and they made their way into the town. A cart went by holding some of the wizards who had fought against Lord Halleron. A wizard glared straight through her and a chill ran down her spine. Time had slipped away as the day turned to afternoon. She managed to squeeze her way into a packed inn. Filled with wiccan and wizards who had fought on both sides.

She could not make sense of the rambling scene as beer and hot meals were brought out. The inn keeper Delores held more beer mugs than she imagined possible. Not spilling a drop. Lord Halleron greeted them, he sat at the head of the table. The wizard who had glared at her, sat near the Lord with his hands bound in front of him. 'Do not worry about Irvyn.' The Lord said.

Mitch threw the pouch on the table. 'Ah,' Lord Halleron picked up the pouch with his knife. 'This is what you've been up to.'

Irvyn's face went pale, 'No… my Lord.'

'Give it here,' Delores inspected the pouch. 'You've been running off with my people for this.'

Lord Halleron beamed showing his crooked teeth, 'Perhaps I should leave you two alone?'

Irvyn's eyes grew wide and he hunched his head. The Lord continued, 'What were you promised? Riches beyond your wildest dreams? The crown?'

Lord Halleron did not wait for an answer, 'We may be staying a while.'

Saranon began to speak and Mitch jabbed her with his elbow while thanking the Lord. He led her away to the courtyard. She glared at him, 'Why did you do that?'

'Shush,' he said. 'The Lord needs your help.'

She was not impressed. Delores came out the kitchen door with two large meals. Placing them down on a small bench, 'You will bring my Fergus back, won't you?'

She hesitated. 'He's a good man,' Delores said.

Saranon nodded, she had no idea what to say. Mitch filled the void, 'It's a small town.'

They sat in silence as the shouts and laughter continued from inside. In complete contrast to the fight that had taken place before. The shouting grew louder as a brawl began to flow out into the courtyard and they left. Mitch stayed close as they strode around the outskirts of the town. Saranon searched the ground for another sign of the glowing stone. He waited every time she hesitated, yet there was nothing.

He suggested, 'Maybe it was just the one?'

'I doubt it,' she replied.

The ice chill of the wind set in as the sky grew dark and they made their way to the inn. The door to the barn was open and a crowd gathered around the open fire in the courtyard. A few glanced their way, but let them be. She made her way up the narrow stairs to a warm room overlooking the gathering. Mitch made his bed and tended to a bruise on his arm while she peered out the window. She was exhausted, yet she had gone beyond the point of sleep. The bed made Mitch look like a giant, his feet hung over the edge. She stifled a laugh and continued to watch the wizards below.

As the night wore on she tried to rest, yet the shouts from outside kept her awake. She tip-toed past Mitch and shut the door. The inn filled with voices from downstairs. She darted out the back and slipped past the barn. A frost had settled in and she drew her cloak near. She made her way past the town's edge and into the forest. It had a restful peace. A patch of wet ground lay amid the frost and peered into the shallow cave. In the dark of night a slit opened to reveal the large eye of a dragon. 'Katholumu,' she said.

The great beast looked as stunned as her. Hesitating before stretching out to welcome the sorceress. She curled up underneath his wing and he rested his head beside her.

CHAPTER TEN

Enter the Fires of Chaos

Kat remained in a peaceful sleep as she woke to the sound of thundering hooves. A glimpse over the dragon's wing showed wizards riding toward Tathen. Saranon gazed at the numbers she did not have time to warn Lord Halleron. They were still some way from the town. A gap appeared and she unravelled herself from the sleeping dragon. The battle worn beast was silent, ignoring the world outside. She strode toward the edge of the cave and shouts rang out above. Her heart pounded as she froze, she thought there were no wizards left. If she extended her sorcery it could attract attention. She back-tracked staying close to the dragon. The voice was strong, but she could not place it.

As the last of the wizards disappeared from site. A Shalough sorcerer rode forward on the misquew. She glimpsed his fine dark cloak, on the side it held the emblem of the fires of chaos. It was the only time Katholomu had stayed away from conflict. The giant beast was silent. She could feel her breath in the cold air. The sorcerer stopped while surveying the path toward Tathen. The silence prolonged time and all she could hear was the rustle of the wind. As it whipped along the frost covered grass. His head turned as though sensing something, yet he did not look her way. His thick cloak draped in a fine edge with the emblem for all to see in a silver outline. The sorcerer, Caddell, showed the first wisps of grey through his shoulder length hair.

A glimpse from the bond-breaker on his belt caught in the first ray of light over the hill. He settled back on the misquew. Saranon crouched down careful to draw the bond-breaker. It shone and transformed into a sword. A faint shrill ring broke the silence. Caddell turned, staring straight into her eyes as she charged toward him. Caddell raised his arms sending a circular blast outward. The first impact knocked through her, yet she held her ground. The shield began to crumble inward around the sorcerer. She waited letting the energy of the Angeon rise. Forming an arc, pushing the energy against the shield. The frost melted as the sorcery burnt a sharp edge into the ground. A web of sparks spread across the shield covering the entire sphere. It shattered carrying the sound through the air.

In the void she glimpsed a few figures on the hillside. Her focus remained on the sorcerer. She let the energy of the Angeon rush toward him. Caddell hurled a blast in retaliation. It spiralled in a fiery arc roaring as it gathered speed. She held out her hands and the energy concentrated deflecting around her. The thunderous tone echoed past her ears as it diverged up the hill behind her. Caddell realised what he had done as his companions ran for cover. She struck out and he faltered, kneeling on the ground. She strode toward him and he stood with the bond-breaker at full length. She lunged and he deflected the blow stepping sideways. Her energy shielded her as she ran through, but he was prepared.

The bond-breakers hit the air as the two forces struck created a shield. Each time neither blade struck the other. The compounded air between echoed with each impact. He deflected the blows with a fluid ease. Saranon's frustration showed with every swing. He did not give her time to meet his blade and in shear anguish she slammed down the hilt. The smooth stone in the centre glowed bright and Caddell fell to his knees, his face pale. 'Yield,' he cried out, 'I yield.'

Saranon staggered back as the words filtered through, she glanced around. The entire legion of Athgar wizards from Hestrel Keep gathered. In a semicircle watching in silence. 'Took you long enough,' Lord Halleron's voice boomed.

Caddell stood and greeted the Lord while brushing off the dirt from his robes. 'Of course it was a close fight,' he said.

Katholomu chose that moment to stretch. His forearms reaghing out of the low entrance to the cave. He poked his head out twisting his body through the narrow gap. He flexed his wings after they cleared the opening.

Ruffled his mane towering over the sorcerer. The ground shook as he flopped into the early frost. 'I am sure it was,' the Lord spoke in an amused tone, 'Now, about my wiccan.'

Caddell bowed and invited the Lord to visit. She glared at the sorcerer as he left and asked, 'Why did you do that?'

Lord Halleron remarked, 'You haven't had much to do with bargaining have you?'

'No,' she replied.

'I want my people returned alive,' he said.

Saranon joined the band of wizards as they made their way to Tathen. The signs of battle lay embedded in the thin layer of frost. As the wizards cleared the ground. She was about to wander into the inn when Lord Halleron waved her into the barn.

The large well-built structure had been converted for the wizards. The fire kept the warmth within the thick walls. The Lord began to remove his armour and the wizards shed their weapons. A corner had been set up for the wounded and Irvyn sat on bench against the wall. They made eye contact as the Lord spoke, 'He will offer you a temptation or the wiccan.'

She asked, 'Me?'

The Lord responded, 'Did you think I was going?'

'Yes,' she answered unsure as she said it.

Lord Halleron laughed, 'The invitation was for you.'

He stood over her, 'You will return the wiccan.'

She began, 'But I thought…'

'Make sure you return the wiccan,' he said.

The Lord's voice carried with it a tone that ended the conversation. She wandered out into cold light air, Mitch stood at the edge of the courtyard. 'Show me your bond-breaker' he said.

She took it out and he examined the hilt. 'Caddell has a bond he did not want you to break,' he spoke as he handed it back.

'I thought it was meant to be used at the sharp end,' she exclaimed.

He laughed then the expression changed to a serious one, 'You will have to face your fear.'

She hung her head in thought, 'It's not…'

Mitch had already walked inside and she hurried after him leaving the thought unsaid. The inn was cosy and warm, yet there was a sadness that filled the air. She wondered how many were missing. A thud rattled through the building. She rushed outside as Katholomu used the barn to scratch his back. He gave her a quick glance and continued while the wizards shouted in disbelief. There was nothing subtle about the dragon. He leaned into the courtyard and nudged her onto his shoulders. Mitch climbed up beside her. Kat removed himself from the gathering before taking off into the sky.

Saranon stayed closed to the giant beast, he flew over the edge of the heartland. A tall hill rose above the land covered by the forest floor that wrapped around the slope. She sensed the outer boundary of the Keep. As the dragon glided through swooping to the side. A platform wedged in the slope came into view. Kat lowered his hind legs, slowing the descent. A lone figure greeted them. Caddell was tall and well-built yet Mitch still managed to tower over the sorcerer. The fine robes wore the mark of the fires of chaos and she hesitated. It was the mark on her right shoulder placed there from the detention camps. The reminder made her uncomfortable.

'Welcome,' he said, 'It has been a while since Ledueran has been host to an Angeon.'

The Keep hidden in the great hill made almost no sound. The only person to greet them was the lone sorcerer. If she had hoped for clues there were none, the rooms were simple and sparse. Their footsteps echoed along the narrow corridors. The Keep was stark and silent. The wind echoed from outside as it whirred around the building. It sent a shiver down her spine, the Keep was the last place she wanted to be. Caddell led them into an open drawing room that extended into a gallery. He took his time meandering along talking of everything, but the missing wiccan. The place was almost peaceful if it was not for her anxious thoughts filling the void. She waited for a cue to speak, but it did not come.

The Keep was surrounded by the forest making its way up the steep incline. She glimpsed back to where they came, 'Where is Katholomu?'

She spoke before the thought had time to settle in her mind.

'We thought you were staying,' the sorcerer answered in a smooth tone.

'No,' Saranon responded.

She could see Mitch's expression change, yet its meaning was lost. 'It must be so troubling always on the move, always on the run, always having to hide. How many near escapes have you had? It would be so nice to have somewhere to stay. We are in the company of many great sorcerers. You are not alone.' Caddell's voice was soothing.

If it was not for Mitch's expressionless face she would not hesitate. She asked again, 'Where is Katholomu?'

A bell chimed echoing along the corridor. 'We will be late for the meeting,' he hurried down out of the room. 'Come we will be late, and you don't want to be late do you?'

She bellowed down the corridor, 'Where is my dragon?'

Caddell said, 'You didn't think there would be a price did you?'

Saranon ignored his remark, 'You had three chances. It's time we found out what you were so afraid of.'

She held out her bond-breaker, but it would not glow. 'We do not permit such devices here,' his voice was calm, yet the threat was there.

Saranon seethed underneath the surface. The possibility of rescuing the wiccan faded. She was not prepared to leave the dragon. Caddell turned and had almost disappeared. Mitch whispered, 'You need to follow.'

She glared at him, the memory of the fire mark from the camp burned in her mind. She rubbed the permanent symbol on her right arm. It was a constant reminder, one she would rather forget. Mitch pushed her forward and she stood firm. 'We will lose the wiccan,' he said.

The energy of the Angeon rose from within. She sensed the stallic energy of the Keep trickling along the walls. It clung in a weblike fashion through the uneven pattern. Ledueran stayed silent. The flickering traces showed in the gaps spread across the walls. Her energy slipped through. She could sense Kathomolou and the wiccan. Her anger flared with the memory of Tasha searing to the forefront of her mind. She peered down at her hands, Tasha's blood was still there. Mitch's voice faded in and out, as the memory took her back to Antavagon. Tasha's lifeless body flashed before her eyes and the anger of the Keep. A faint voice called out from afar. At first she thought it was Tasha, but then the voice became clear.

Antavagon called to her from the depths of Tordoren, break the core. The image left, Saranon stood in a cold sweat. Mitch was staring at her, yet the words did not filter through. Caddell was about to close the door up ahead. The last link to Antavagon slipped away. As Ledueran blocked out the Darkonian Keep, yet the damage was done. Time lapsed into eternity as she raised her hands. The first Keep to embrace the Angeon had summoned her and she answered. The energy flooded through so hard the floor around her shattered upward. Ledueran howled, the rage from beneath thundered along the heavy walls. For a moment the void held her gripped in an unenviable calm. As the stallic energy rose from the deep.

Saranon held out her arms waiting for energy of the Keep to reach out. Mitch shouted through the turmoil,

'No.'

The stallic energy ruptured as the sound became deafening. Yet it could not grip her as she fell toward the central core. Ledueran's angry shouts rang through her mind. Yet the only words she could hear belonged to Antavagon. 'Break the core,' her voice was lost in a cataclysm of fire.

The Angeon held strong against the stallic energy. Yet the searing edges of the shield closed around her. It was a race to the central core and she could not lose. Her hold shrank and when she reached her farthest point she pushed onward.

Stallic energy pressed around her taking the shield ever closer. Yet it was the central core that caught her attention. The outer shell's rugged surface was just beyond reach. Ledueran laughed, it reverberated through the stallic energy. Her rage hit the surface before she had time to think. The blast slammed into the shell protecting the central core. All momentum was lost as the stallic energy flung her upward. A great thunderous roar bellowed from underneath. As the blast from the Angeon found its mark. She smiled with reassuring confidence until the momentum stopped, leaving her in mid-air. The great black marmoz dragon broke through the building. His magnificent wings stretching full length and taking him straight into the sky.

Saranon glanced beneath her to the gaping jaws and let out a scream. The dragon flew into her with a thud. She began tumbling over his thick skull, clinging onto his mane as her legs dangled in the wind. Kat flew so hard it was all she could do to hold on. As the great beast slowed to a comfortable speed. She brought her leg around to sit between his shoulders. The moment was short lived as gravity disappeared. Katholomu swooped straight at the Keep. His lungs sucked in the cold air and his belly grew warm. 'Wait,' she cried out.

It was too late. The flames licked the side of the building and she covered her face from the heat.

The air crackled overhead, she could hear the dragon's powerful wings swooping low. A whirlwind of sorcery spiralled upward. Mixed with the dust and broken shards from the building. Ledueran Keep stood, yet the creases lining the grounds showed. Cheering rose catching her off-guard. She could feel Kat tense his shoulders, as he turned toward the noise. The small group of wiccan swarmed around, their weary faces filled with excitement. Caddell's stone voice cut through the air from the balustrade. The Shalough sorcerer stood parallel to the dragon's gaze. She tried to speak, but the dust caught in her throat turning her voice to a whisper. 'Our offer is no more,' Caddell spoke, 'Take the wiccan and be gone.'

Katholomu took his time as he turned to stare straight into the sorcerer's glare. The great beast said one word, 'Coward.'

Caddell's face went pale as the rage washed over him. Saranon responded, 'Your offer was never there.'

She tilted and the dragon turned with her. Lord Halleron broke through woods bringing his troops with him. The wizards spread forming an arc around the wiccan in a protective stance. At the first sign of movement away from the Keep, Katholomu leaned down. He bounded off the broken stone courtyard spreading his wings high into the sky. The chill wind caught her hair and cooled the dragon.

They flew in a great arc veering to the heartland. Home of the largest dragon colony in Zyanthia. It stretched farther than the eye could see. The great beast made his way to a rocky side, swooping just below the ridge. The dragon stopped with a jolt and she slid down. He wheezed gasping for air and his body shuddered. A lump began to make its way up the dragon's neck. She just had time to jump out of the way as Kat coughed up a pile of charred remains. The smell made her gag and she ran upwind. Before she could look, she heard the crunch as Katholomu ate his own vomit and she winced. Perhaps Caddell would think twice before capturing the dragon again. She made her way down the rocky hill forming the ridge line. The sun began to set as dragons swooped low to perch.

Kat glanced down then rubbed the side of his head against her shoulder. She only just had time to hold her breath. The great dragon rumbled with deep affection as though sensing what she had done. Finally she gave in breathing the smell, with a violent cough, as he moved out of the way. Mitch's voice rose from the valley, 'There you are.'

'Don't come any closer,' she said waving her arms.

The wizard, Mitch, did not change his stride until the smell hit. He pointed to a shallow stream and she headed toward it. 'Not you, the dragon,' he said.

Her cheeks grew red with embarrassment and she called the dragon over. Kat hesitated wiggling from side to side then flopped into the ice cold water. A jet of steam rose around him and he let out a comforting sigh. She sat by the water's edge. Mitch created a small ambient light. She watched as it flickered across the dragon's thick skin. As Katholomu stood up he took half the pool of water with him. She held her arms up as he shook his body, the water dripped off her shield in mid-air. Mitch ran toward her with his hair soaked and she laughed. The dark night covered them as the dragon curled his great body. Making a warm shelter from the frost gathering on the ground.

Mitch sat with his back against the dragon. His pensive gaze gave away his thoughts, 'You did not accept the offer,'

It was a statement more than a question. Saranon removed her coat, the fire mark still showed on her right arm. 'There was only one chance to accept the Angeon.'

The mark remained a stark reminder of her days in the detention camps. Any trust for the sorcerers had vanished long ago. She rested near Katholomu's chest listening to the faint rumblings as he slept. 'You damaged the Keep,' Mitch said.

She glared at him, 'It was the least I could do.'

He did not look impressed. 'Antavagon helped me escape the camp and he asked me to,' she responded.

He said, 'Would you take on the clan if it asked you to?'

She did not answer and the silence became deafening.

Finally she gave in, 'Yes.'

She had never seen Mitch's jaw drop so fast. She asked, 'What did you think I was going to say?'

'Anyone else would have said no,' he replied.

The wind droned around the rocky hillside. As a clear night sky let the frost settle and she tried in vain to calm her mind.

Caddell's image loomed when she closed her eyes. Keeping her awake long after Mitch had fallen asleep. She climbed out of the warm cocoon underneath Kat's wing. Making her way along his shoulders. The dragon's eyes opened with a thin slither and he let out a gruff snort. She stroked his matted coat and he went back to sleep. The moon shone bright over the tops of the trees as the branches swayed in the bellowing wind. A glimmer of light broke through the shadows and she followed. A silhouette formed among the trees holding out a beckoning hand. The spirit of her friend Tasha stood in a flowing white dress. Her fawn coloured hair caught in the light. Tasha moved further away and Saranon ran, not wanting to lose sight.

She ran on through the chill night air leaving marks on the frost covered ground. She moved faster, yet Tasha remained out of reach. The silhouette faded and the woods grew dark around her. She wrapped her cloak around and made her way back. The branches whistled in the dark as the wind picked up speed and she ran to find Mitch waiting. He stood not far from the dragon. His tall muscular frame held a firm stare. 'Chasing shadows,' he remarked.

She nodded and climbed into the warm makeshift camp as Katholomu rested. Mitch watched as her eyes grew heavy.

A wisp of the cool breeze woke her. The dragon had long moved, yet his imprint remained in the shallow snow. She jumped up and breathed in the crisp chill air. Mitch laughed, 'Took you long enough.'

She stood beside him watching a tiny trail of smoke in the distant horizon. 'What's that?'

'Nothing,' he replied.

She was not so sure. 'I saw Tasha in the woods,' she said.

Mitch hesitated before walking in the direction she had seen her old friend. She asked, 'Did you see her?'

He nodded in reply.

The snow had stopped. The early chill of winter held it in place underneath the morning sun. Mitch strode with a purpose and she followed. He moved through the forest with ease. As she clambered through avoiding the low lying branches. The first warm rays broke over the hillside and the dragons began to stir taking to the sky. She glanced back to see Katholomu settled beneath the ridge line, lazing in the sun. 'Mitch,' Clara cried out.

The sound sent a chill through Saranon. She had not been expecting to find the Mercidian sorceress. Astonishment held her in disbelief. Clara was pale and ragged, nothing like the proud cheerful person she knew.

Mitch stiffened at the sight he voice held firm, 'What are you doing here?'

Clara's eyes were red, 'I didn't know, I swear. They've taken the Oracle.'

'No,' the words escaped Saranon's lips.

'I didn't know what to do,' Clara had tears running down her face. 'I didn't mean for any of this.'

'We have to return to the Keep,' she waited for Clara who whispered thank you.

Katholomu uncurled his tail and stretched as they approached. The dragon was slow to accommodate them. He flew toward Hestrel Keep in a silent gesture and the trail of smoke grew closer.

Kat veered sideways and a dragon broke into flight so close she could feel the air rush past. The woods came to life as a fleet of dragons followed with their riders. She glanced toward the Keep. There on the horizon. She could make out the faint line of dragons spreading their wings. They were caught. Clara screamed into the air, 'No!'

Saranon could sense Flynn and her anger rose to the surface. She flew Kat close to the ground and held the thought in her mind hoping that Mitch would read it. He tapped her shoulder then grabbed Clara and they rolled along the soft undergrowth. Katholomu heaved back into the sky rising above the oncoming dragons..

The first blasts of sorcery hurled from both sides aimed at each other. The blazing inferno barely missed the great dragon's tail as he swung upside down. The void of weightlessness held a moment of calm, then she reached out into nothing. Her arms flung wide as the sorcery gravitated around her. Turning into a swirling array as neither side hit. The blast engulfed her in mid-air and she reached out absorbing the energy. The air broke into a crystal blue sky and the Angeon rose from within, the Angeon of old. Shouts rang out as both fleets of dragons dived for the ground. To escape the energy pulsing from the Angeon. She could feel it intensifying as she held on waiting, her heart beat thudding in her ears.

A lone sorcerer broke the silence, just one. Flynn stood on the grounded dragon. He held the blade of the bond-breaker raising it toward her. The Angeon released her energy in a circular arc. It reached Flynn and he fell instantaneously. The blade fell away and he stood alone on the dragon. The Angeon neutralised the flow of sorcery and shouted, 'Leave.'

CHAPTER ELEVEN

Stand strong against the darkness

The Mercidian sorcerers wasted no time making their exit before she found Mitch. She asked, 'Where is Clara?'

'Gone,' he replied.

It hurt, but it did not surprise her. Clara had only found her to help Flynn. Katholomu purred with a giant rumble and rubbed his head against her. Mitch climbed on sitting at the front, he flew the dragon in a wide arc around the Keep. The pillars of smoke rose from the damage along the outer walls.

She could tell Mitch was not impressed and said nothing. The damage revealed itself as the dragon made a smooth descent lowering his head. For once, Katholomu did not fumble as he landed. There was no one to greet them and the panic began to rise. She ran into the building to find Bayard he sat near the fire. She glanced around at the tell-tale signs sprawled along the walls. 'We lost eighteen good wizards,' Bayard said.

Madoc greeted them, 'You should have been here.'

He shouted the last words in disgust. Saranon did not know what to say.

Madoc spoke, 'I'm leaving.'

'No,' she said.

It was a hollow threat, yet she treated the words with the weight by which they were spoken. 'I have to deal with this,' she told him.

'Make them pay,' he said.

She did not answer as she gazed around the dishevelled room and left. The Athgar wizards were still shaken by the event as they began to repair the building. She had not thought the Mercidian would attack. Yet Flynn had been willing to sacrifice her for the Oracle.

Kail gave her a cold glare and she chose to ignore it as she made her way through the corridor. The wizards had team work down to a fine art. The process of rebuilding and strengthening the outer walls was underway. Captain Lydia Grace called out, 'We will not last another attack. Not while the barrier is down.'

She asked, 'What?'

'We changed the connections to hold the shield. It won't last,' the Captain explained.

The shock showed as the colour drained from her face. 'I have to go down,' she said the thought aloud.

'Be careful it's a wreck,' the Captain said.

Saranon hoped Captain Grace was wrong. Smoke

wafted up from below as she avoided the wizards working away to fix the damage. A chunk had been taken out of the wall and a voice called out, 'Mind your step.'

She glanced down and part of the floor was gone. The cavity exposed a broken conduit. The sight in the dark depths far below was almost nauseating and she looked away. Bronwyn, the wizardess, made her way up the ladder. Her head level with the gaping hole in the floor.

'Ever wondered why the sorcerers want the Oracle so bad?' Bronwyn asked.

'Because they don't know what she is,' she answered in a flat tone.

'Christine can stop the Angeon,' Bronwyn said.

Saranon burst out laughing, then stopped when an awkward silence fell. 'Let's get this Keep back up?'

She clambered down to the lower levels. The building was sturdy and the attack had been aimed directly for the shield. Hestrel fared well, she just needed to bring the shield up. Debris littered her way. As she trailed her fingers along the walls listening for the rhythm of the Keep.

All her focus went to the hum emanating from below. She strode passed the wizards until the corridors became empty. The imbenik chambers sat above the pathways leading down to the central core. The hum from the core grew audible as she made her way to the altar. The stone was warm to the touch. She braced herself clearing the thoughts raging inside. As her head lowered the stone altar began to soften and the Keep reached out to greet her. It melded to her skin and her sorcery linked with the energy rising from the central core. She gave all her concentration to guiding the stallic energy in place. Along the damaged walls that had stood against the attack.

She reached out her hand and Mitch held it. Almost breaking the connection with the Keep. Her eyes opened in a haze and she sensed him. She could feel his warm breath on her ear. The connection broke and she stared at him. 'Were you expecting war?' Mitch asked.

'No,' the word escaped before she had time to think.

He led her up toward the light. The stone spread across the floor of the chamber. As the sun shone from the high arches overhead. The pattern embedded in the stone swirled in the same fashion as the temple in her dream. If Saranon closed her eyes she could reach out and see Tasha. The image was gone all too soon. She could almost hear the dark stream. There was just one thing missing as she gazed into the centre of the chamber. A tear fled down her cheek, it still hurt knowing her friend did not make it. 'I appear to have rebuilt the Keep,' she said.

'It's more than that,' Mitch replied.

He waited for her to follow through the high arch doors. She had been expecting to walk out into the courtyard. Stopping at the balustrade around on the balcony. The courtyard was at least three stories below. She eyed Mitch with an amused gaze, 'Maybe.'

'You have lost eight days,' Mitch watched her expression change.

She glanced around, the Keep was calmer than it had been since they arrived. She made her way toward the dragon pens. Katholomu lowered his head out through the open archway. He grumbled as he squeezed out and hit the arch as he went. The Athgar wizards ignored the thud as they worked, preparing the dragons for flight. She stayed on the stone courtyard beside the great beast as he nudged her. A small group stood around the long wooden table near the hearth. The room had access to the dragon pens and the wizard stronghold. The high windows kept out prying eyes and kept in the warmth. Captain Lydia Grace surveyed the map strewn over the table.

Saranon strode toward the group and the Captain lifted her gaze. 'The supplies are not getting through. We have had to resort to the dragons.'

The words were spoken in a matter of fact manner, as though the element of surprise had gone. She asked, 'Who?'

'Our own,' the Captain spoke as she rolled up the map.

Saranon wanted to ask but no more was said as the Captain left the room. Madoc stood by the door, 'I think there is something you should see.'

She was not sure whether to trust the Shalough sorcerer. The wizards paid him no attention.

She followed him down the corridor. Around the edge of the wizard stronghold to the warden's quarters. She hesitated at the threshold, the last time she had been near a prison it had not ended well. Madoc waited as she walked through. Banging resonated from the cells. She stayed in the foyer and backed into Hobson. The wizard towered over her, he carried a band of keys on a thick leather belt. 'You want to see the traitor,' he said.

Hobson walked on before she had time to say otherwise. Saranon glared at Madoc for dragging her to the last place she wanted to be. He smiled and followed behind.

The cells were clean and light shone through from overhead. A wizard sat in the last cell and she spoke his name, 'Bayard.'

The word escaped her lips and took away her breath in the moment of horror. She had never dreamed that there could be a spy from within. Madoc left and she turned hoping for an answer as he left her alone with the wizard. Saranon hated being in the place. The bars and silt covered floor brought back the memory of Antavagon. A memory she tried to forget. Bayard's expression changed as he mistook her sad gaze. 'You heard,' was all he said.

She did not want to admit she had no idea. As she responded, 'Yes.' The awkward silence grew between them until she asked, 'Why?'

He leaned in close wrapping his hands around the bars. 'You know what it's like, when you get the offer. What did he offer you?' He asked.

She flinched and took a step back as their eyes met. She felt the fire mark on her right arm and stepped further away. Her words were bittersweet, 'He offered me a place to belong.'

Mitch had urged her to accept and she almost had. The air was growing stuffy and she backed away avoiding the urge to run.

The corridor filled with light from the high windows across the rough walls. There was not a person in sight, yet voices carried along interrupting the silence. There had been so much damage caused by the sorcerer clans. Yet as she made her way around the Keep, all she could see were familiar faces. The fire from the hearth warmed the great hall together with the central core. Bronwyn waved her over to a plain wooden table where they ate, 'I like what you did with the Keep.'

She felt her face grow red. It had been Hestrel more than she who had restored the building. Making it strong enough to withstand an attack. The ease at which the wizards chatted made her relax as she sat to eat the evening meal. The sky grew dark through the high windows along the far wall, carved into the thick stone. The fire beckoned as she held out her hands to warm them near the hearth. A ripple of air move in a vertical wave and the chairs around the hearth became vacant. She blinked and the room filled with the chatter of voices once more. She scouted the grand hall gazing on the faces and turned to leave. Mitch followed and she spoke, 'I'm all right.'

He waited a moment, 'Perhaps.'

It was no use lying to the wizard. He could read her immediate thoughts, but she was trying to convince herself. Saranon made her way to the sorcerer quarters. The lights were low. Darkness hovered over the edges of the corridor leading to her room. She rolled her coat down her arms and folded the thick worn leather that had kept her warm. The woollen rug was a welcome relief from from the stark wooden floor. The furniture was plain, yet beautifully carved with a smooth finish. She rubbed her fingertips along the thick stone wall. The Keep hummed from beneath. The wind swept around the outer wall keeping her awake. The last of her thoughts drifted away into sleep.

A bell tolling in the distance broke through. Disturbing her as she woke to darkness. The Keep hummed away in the silence as she glanced around. She did not recall seeing a bell and wrapped her coat tight. making her way down the narrow circular stairs. A light shone in a long thin band up the corridor and she walked toward it. The carved wooden door creaked as it opened. A dim light flooded the great chamber from above. The sorcerer stone that covered the floor, showed the trails of a faint carving along the surface. Saranon made her way to the columns marking the large dome in the centre. A lone figure in a long white dress stood with her back turned. The flowing fawn coloured wavy hair could only belong to one person, Tasha.

Saranon moved further into the chamber until she stood beside her old friend. The bell tolled in the distance and Tasha spoke, 'There can only be one Oracle.'

She asked, 'What should I do?'

Mitch shouted from the doorway and Tasha's image faded in the light. She was exasperated, 'Did you have to?'

He took hold of her arm and urged her to follow. Voices entered the chamber as they ducked to the side. She was about to speak. Until she heard Captain Grace's voice trail past the outer columns. Mitch stayed close, she could feel his warm breath. The scraping of the chains etched its way along the floor. As Bayard was brought to the centre kneeling to the ground with his head hung. A whisper of light from the morning sun escaped down the length of the columns. Surrounding the circular dome. It shone along the bond-breaker as the Captain raised it. Saranon let out a gasp and Mitch held her tight as the blade fell. She whispered Tasha's words. As though they would be forgotten, 'There can only be one Oracle.'

She had to leave and Mitch ran after her. 'I did not have time to warn you,' he said.

It broke her out of the frame of mind, 'I was not thinking of Bayard.'

'You should be, he was Corathy,' he said it.

As though it had an important meaning and she gave him a blank stare. 'A wizard from the south,' he explained.

She did not want to be caught up with the Athgar wizards. Hestrel was strong enough to keep the Oracle safe, that was what mattered. She strode out to the courtyard to find Kat and hesitated. The dragons were being readied to enter the sky waiting for their riders. The closest dragon barely acknowledgement her as she wandered through.

Bronwyn glanced up from handing out supplies. Saranon asked, 'Where is Katholomu?'

'He left last evening. No one has seen him since,' Bronwyn answered while continuing her task.

'You can take Holdvar,' Mitch offered.

'No,' she snapped, 'I need to find Kat.'

After the encounter with the Fires of Chaos the

missing dragon made her uneasy. She made her way across the courtyard along the pebble path. Until she found a group of misquew. She patted one of the riding cats and it lifted its head. The grounds of Hestrel kept the harshness of winter at bay, with the energy rising from the central core. The grass was wet underneath. It did not share the covering of frost glistening on the outer edge. She pulled her cloak tight as the misquew made its way along the path. Almost invisible in the fallen snow. Mitch rode beside her. His misquew was a little taller making him appear larger still.

She glanced around, but the snow covered the hillside. In a white blanket hiding any trace of the great dragon. She motioned for the misquew to speed up. It ran into the clearing marking the entrance to the main road. The stone markers gave the frost a pale green glow yet the road remained clear. The well-trodden stone shone in the pale light. Mitch went to turn back. Facing the direction they had come, 'We won't find anything.'

It was not the answer she wanted to hear and rode on. He turned to follow, but his face was stern. He had made his point. As Saranon headed onto the road. The faint glow reminded her of the detention camp, Tasha had been alive then. If only her friend had made it out.

A grumble shook the frost from the trees surrounding the heartland. Kat rose above the branches. His eyes peered just high enough to stare at her as she called his name. She slumped down in the snow and ran through the trees avoiding the branches as she went. The cold wind whipped at her cheeks as she raced ahead. On the ground beneath the great beast, the white snow ran red. It seeped out from where he rested. He lifted his weight to show his thick scales revealing a dark mass below. She had to ask, 'Did you sit on someone?'

The dragon tilted his ears in disgust. The great beast had squashed the metal plate armour of the soldier beyond recognition. She grimaced.

Mitch took one look, 'We have to get out of here.'

He held her arm and she stood firm, 'Wait. If they were heading to Hestrel we would have seen them.'

Mitch was about to argue, his chest heaved. 'I will check where they went.'

She had a better idea, 'Kat, where did the soldiers go?'

The dragon pointed north to the Pearl Castle and Temare. Mitch gave her an exasperated glare and climbed onto the great beast.

She hesitated, 'You go, someone needs to warn the Regent.'

He nodded, 'Don't get caught."-

She laughed and Mitch gave her a stern glare, 'A lone sorceress will be an easy target.'

Saranon wondered if sometimes he forgot that she was the Angeon, 'I will be fine.'

She stood back as Katholomu jolted into the sky. His wings spread wide casting a shadow along the ground. The woods were covered in a layer of thin snow and a rocky path edged its way around. She stepped onto the path and it glimmered pale amid the snow. The lay-line was weak underneath. It would speed up the journey, but the wizards would know. There would be no surprise.

A chill settled through the calm blue sky. As the morning held over the frost covered ground. She trudged along the path. As the wet snow melted underneath from the magic in the lay-line. The trees with their bare branches clung in a tight ring around the edges. Blocking any hope of a view from the road and the hills that hid Hestrel Keep. The path led her deeper into the heartland. As the dragons came into view melting the snow as they rested. The frost tapered away and she glanced around, up ahead the lay-line ended. It touched the edge of a grassy field that appeared out of place amid the white covered hills.

The path ended in a low valley, where she walked there were signs across the rocks on the ground. She leaned down near one and touched the rough surface, her senses prickled. A great raging fireball gleamed overhead. The shield from her own energy protected her. Saranon glanced into the fiery blaze. The heat hurtling overhead with barely a fraction protecting her. At the farther end, deep in the heartland, three figures stood. Behind them, the marks around the building shaped the edge of the Keep. Hidden deep in the hillside.

As she strode closer a Shalough sorceress, not much older, hesitated. A sorcerer stood off to the side. For a moment she thought they were going to turn and run. The sorceress held out her arms and Saranon braced herself. She could sense that buildup of energy and was still far away. she chose not to run and instead waited, watching to see what would happen.

The energy flared into a heavy storm crackling with lightning through the sky. It arched in a random pattern. Saranon watched it all, but the pattern broke. Shattering around her before it approached. The fog lifted as she walked closer at a steady pace. The two sorcerers were aghast as she approached in silence. 'I'm Bridget,' said the sorceress. Not knowing what to say. 'And this is Troy,' she added.

'This is not the right place for that type of sorcery,' Saranon said. 'Is there somewhere else?'

'There's the stadium,' Troy pointed toward the building.

Bridget glared at him and he shrugged his shoulders. Saranon followed the two sorcerers inside, past the field leading to a stone entrance. It was small and humble, but large enough to welcome them inside. The rooms were plain and simple with grey whitewashed walls. As they moved in deeper she noticed the colours change and become more vibrant. At the end of the corridor, around the architrave was a carving of leaves and dragons. Marking the entrance to a grand room.

Deep inside the building the light from the Keep shone. The floor sloped down at a gradual pace toward the centre of the lower stands. The great columns held another row of stands above, arcing around the central stadium. At the end was a heavy wall, sturdy enough to absorb great sorcery. She had travelled far, all the way to Indarin in Serenphel. To be able to learn the art of sorcery so that she could control what she had. Saranon felt sorry for Bridget whose sorcery was not under control. At her age it should have been.

Saranon made an offer to teach as she stood on the floor of the stadium. The two sorcerers looked at her hesitantly. Troy said, 'How can you teach another?'

'I finish my training at Indarin,' she replied.

With such certainty that he backed down. She stood at an even pace. Allowing for a buffer between her and the immense wall that could absorb sorcery. She beckoned for Bridget to begin and the sorceress was hesitant.

'Focus,' she said.

The air blurred in front as the sorcery swelled. She could see it emanating from Bridget as the air heated. The great blast shattered around the stadium.

The energy took up the space with a glow that threw shadows from the columns. It headed toward her uneven swirl, she held her hands and stood steady for the embrace. It swirled overhead and to the sides. She disappeared in the maze and swirl of sorcery. Yet behind remained a gap visible between. Where she stood near the wall there was no rebound from the Keep. No reverberation and instead it dissipated. A ranger shouted from above commanding them to stop. His voice boomed around the last crackles of sorcery. The three sorcerers stood pale and she was about to speak, but the ranger stopped her.

He made his way down from the stand, each footstep echoed in the grand stadium. His presence was felt as he stood tall over the three. He stared at her and said, 'What are you doing here?'

She was about to speak, but Troy said something odd and she stayed silent. She did not understand what completing her training would do. Yet the explanation made the ranger's shoulders relax and he welcomed her. It was an awkward moment. He was not sure how to respond and neither was she.

CHAPTER TWELVE

The path of a guardian

Sounds echoed from the entrance to the stadium saving any need for a reply. The ranger, Korben, followed as they entered the dining area. The room captured the light from the narrow windows spanning from floor to ceiling. The tables were spread around the walls with chairs wrapping around an open hearth. The large opening where a fire would have been, let warm air from the central core flow into the room. Saranon held out her hands, yet the Keep remained silent. A bellowing wind thrust against the windows, 'You are welcome to stay the night.'

'No. I really...' Her words trailed off.

As the soldiers of the Shalough rode across the distant fields. Their steeds kept in a close formation. Only the golden emblem glinting from the uniforms gave them away as sorcerers. 'Perhaps,' she said.

Bridget gave a knowing smile, 'Commander Meghan is enough to scare anyone.'

Saranon caught a glimpse shimmering near Bridget's shoulder. The different phase drew her in with a rush that took the breath from her lips. She stood out of time with the world. Three sorcerers stood around her all bearing the same eyes. Those of the Keep Serensa. Why are you here? The Keep spoke through a sorceress, yet she could hear the words in her mind. Saranon hesitated, she was unsure.

'You know Bridget better than I. How long does she have?' She waited for the answer.

We do not interfere, a sorcerer mouthed the words of the Keep. 'Then why do you ask?' She responded.

Are you only here for the girl? The Keep asked. 'I was on my way to the Pearl Castle. I was going to leave...'

You are welcome on one condition, show yourself. The sorceress who spoke for the Keep held out her hand. Saranon knew what it meant. She had kept her sorcery hidden for so long, creating boundaries to fit in.

If she broke down the boundaries it would warn the Shalough before she attacked. Then it would reveal more than that. 'Only here,' she said waiting for the Keep to answer.

We accept, the words of the Keep clung in her mind. She reached out and the image faded around her. She fell out of phase hitting the floor. Voices floated around as her hearing returned. Someone reached out. 'Don't,' she shouted.

She stood up and Troy stepped back hitting the bench.

The dizziness slipped away leaving a numb resonance. She glanced at the small lights above glowing with the Keep's energy, as did the Ranger. A difference in the faint glow gave away everything in one small detail.

Footsteps echoed along the corridors. Commander Meghan rushed in and the Ranger held up his hand. The Commander stopped, her cloak giving away the impulse of her action. As it fluttered through the doorway. Korben shook his head and the Commander bowed. Her shouts could be heard down the passage. A queasy sensation gripped her. 'What are you?' Korben spoke then hesitated. Her voice was lost as she coughed. She tried again to speak, 'Not the myth you were expecting.'

Her thoughts cleared as the cloudy haze from the conversation with the Keep lifted. The energy of the Angeon pulsed under her skin. It was barely visible, but she could feel its rhythm.

As the Keep settled for the night a storm swept across the grounds. She had wanted to leave earlier. Serensa's request had made a world of difference. The Shalough sorcerers stayed at a distance allowing her to pass through. Yet they watched, conscious of the recognition the Keep had given her. The snow faded as the cold set in carried by the wind lashing at the trees through the forest. Stars shone bright overhead. Dimmed only by the low lights around the walls of the building. The glimmer gave a faint glow through the soft haze as she peered upward. The Keep was nestled tight in the hillside, rising in a manner that belonged. Perhaps she was wrong about the Shalough.

Shouts emerged as she made her way through the foyer. It remained open, but kept the cold outside shielded by the energy from the Keep. Troy grabbed her hand and they darted away as he spoke, 'We have to find Bridget.'

'Why?' She asked.

'That's why they're angry,' he pointed back where the shouting came from.

The response did not answer her question, but he had already run ahead. If she did not catch up he would soon be out of sight. The stairs lead higher and she gripped the rail. Glancing out the narrow window before continuing on.

Shadows fell along the floor. From the beams framing the space tacked away between the walls. Bridget sat gazing out into the darkness covering the frozen land. She stayed a moment longer before acknowledging them. 'I won't go back,' Bridget said.

Troy urged her and she refused. Saranon felt out of place and asked, 'Why not?'

'I'm not supposed to hit the wall,' Bridget said.

Saranon burst out laughing and they both gave her an uneasy look. 'You are supposed to hit the wall,' she said.

'But what if it breaks?' Bridget said.

'That could happen,' Saranon replied, 'Let me show you.'

'You're going to break the wall?' Troy asked in astonishment.

'Maybe,' Saranon said.

She dashed down the open stairs leading into the

stadium. The solid wall at the end stood as a continuous plain form as high as it was wide. Reaching the edges of the main floor that curved around in an arch. The Shalough sorcerers were scattered around the area in front of her. She thought of asking them to move, but it was not necessary for what she intended to do. Saranon felt the energy close to the surface. It came willingly, building up as she held it in place. A loud crack boomed as it flew through the open gaps hitting the wall. The reverberation echoed carrying the thunderous tones around with clear precision.

For a moment silence fell and she raised her arms again for the second blast that hit the wall. As the sorcerers fled to the sidelines. It crackled again and again, each time the reverberation echoed. She continued almost relentlessly until it was clear the wall would not fail. Then she stood to one side and beckoned Bridget to follow her lead onto the stadium floor. Bridget hesitated, her face pale, 'I cannot do that.'

'That is what it's for,' Saranon said.

Korben began to interrupt, but he was cut off mid-sentence by the blast as it hit the wall. Bridget tried again with a renewed sense of certainty. Concentrating all her efforts on the wall.

By the time Bridget was done she had honed the blast and her stance. Silence clung in the air as their audience inspected the wall. The hour was growing late, yet Saranon stayed. Long enough for the Shalough to be assured that the wall would not crumble. 'How did you know?' Korben asked standing by her side.

'There are many like it at Indarin,' she replied.

Her answer appeared to satisfy him. They made their way back to the outer rim of the building, that formed the Ranger's quarters. The wind howled around the stone surface of the walls. It was enough to keep her awake, but she needed to sleep and closed her eyes.

The shudder of the morning bell broke through her dreams and she woke. It had been filled with vague images none of which made sense. She peered out the small window to the icy blanket below. The wind was still, at least for time being. The wooden door creaked loud enough to the let the Rangers know she was there. As she strode into the dining room. An aroma filled the air with the smell of warm bread. Without hesitation she joined them for breakfast. Bridget gazed at her and the silence began to make her uneasy. 'I was told the wall would break,' Bridget finally said.

'Only if your intention was untoward,' Saranon answered. 'There is a difference between lack of control and attacking the Keep.'

She hesitated before adding, 'You should have been told that.'

Her words were harsh and they were meant to be. Bridget had learned fast and the sorceress should have been farther ahead than she. Korben rose to make a start with the days' work. 'One day we will be Rangers looking after the heartland,' Bridget spoke.

Saranon almost choked. Korben and the entire room filled with sorcerers glared at her. 'You are no Ranger,'

Saranon said as Bridget tensed.

'I meant that is not your specialisation,' she added.

'My path has already been chosen,' Bridget said growing confused.

'Not well enough,' Saranon said. 'If you really want to know where your path lies I can show you.'

She was hoping the answer would be no. Especially with the stunned look on Bridget's face. 'I think you should,' Korben replied.

She waited for Bridget to accompany her and pulled her cloak around. 'Where are we headed?' Bridget asked.

'Serensa, though he may be outside by the time we get there,' she answered.

Troy tagged along as the Keep let them pass. The small lights glimmered revealing the way. The stairs opened up leading higher and the cold air hit as they strode near the outer wall. Saranon could not see him, yet the Keep was sure he was there. The walkway trailed into a large open platform. The sorcerers stone underneath lay almost hidden. In the faint clumps of snow drifting down. Commander Meghan turned to greet them. It was then that Saranon pointed ahead to a solitary figure overlooking the great building. He glanced then returned to his silent vigil. Bridget drew in a sharp breath, 'That's Dargon.'

She went no closer and began to leave. 'Are you sure?' Troy asked and she nodded in reply. A deep firm voice shouted across the open space as Dargon locked eyes with her. 'Angeon. Why are you here?'

He closed the distance fast in a motionless effort. His

face carried the scars of an unknown battle and his brow deepened as he towered over her. 'Perhaps we had better go,' Troy tugged her arm. 'It is not for the Guardian of Gate, but for your successor,' she answered.

The Commander stared at Troy. 'Not me,' he explained pointing at Bridget who appeared frozen to the spot.

'A girl,' Dargon spoke the words too soon.

Bridget ran from site, Troy followed after her. 'A Guardian of the Gate is no job for a girl,' Dargon said.

'You cannot choose,' Saranon said.

She ran down into the Keep as the wind set in overhead. Footsteps followed behind her on the staircase, the Guardian's shadow swept over floor. 'A Ranger does not have the makings of a Guardian and you are not a full Angeon,' he said.

She was about to find Bridget and hesitated, 'How did you know?'

'Bridget's path has been chosen,' Dargon said.

It was the answer she was looking for, but she did not want to delay finding Bridget. Serensa led her toward officer quarters. At first she thought the Keep may have misled her. As she made her way through the corridor it opened up to a stadium hidden inside the building. The benches were wrapped around one side, with a second tier in the balcony above. The walkway had a gentle slope down to a floor half the size of the one she had seen near the entrance. The great wall that protected the Keep from sorcery appeared twice. One at either end. The columns surrounding the floor were thick and sturdy made with heavy stone. The small group of Shalough sorcerers training finished their session. They gave her an uneasy glance.

She walked straight past Bridget sitting on the bench and waited. As the sorcerers left the main floor. The space was ideal for sparring and she invited Bridget onto the empty stadium. 'Do you want to spar?' She asked.

There was a moment of hesitation and Saranon removed her cloak. Flinging it on the bench. She reached down and removed her bond-breaker from the belt. 'I thought we already had?' Bridget said.

'No,' she replied.

Before there was time to answer she opened her arms the energy crept along, but it was enough. Bridget deflected the blow and responded. Saranon gave her a chance to warm up and held the energy strong. As the Keep absorbed the remainder around them. The air stayed clear from the sparks of energy. She watched as Bridget skirted around the space, becoming more confident with every move. She kept her pace steady giving time between each attack. Showing the actions before using her sorcery. She stayed close to the centre and Bridget was beginning to show frustration. As they fought the sorcerers began to group around the benches and the balcony.

The strain showed plain on Bridget's face and she came in for the attack. Saranon held strong and answered the blow knocking her opponent down. The fight was over and the Shalough sorcerers clapped their hands in unison. Making beats of noise echoing in the space. 'I failed,' Bridget stood up and they shook hands.

'When you fail you know who you are,' she replied.

Saranon stepped back as the crowd clapped in a rhythm, 'They cheer for you.'

'I didn't do anything,' Bridget said.

'You sparred with an Angeon,' she answered.

Dargon peered down from the balcony and she gathered her belongings. She had lost much time and her mind returned to the task her old friend Tasha had given. She made her way up the walkway and Dargon met her. His heavy cloak still settled around his shoulders. 'Congratulations. You found a Guardian,' He said.

She was about to head toward the Ranger's quarters. 'It is quicker if you go that way,' he pointed north to the main entrance.

It would reduce her time. Yet it would also take her deeper into the territory of the Shalough. She followed his lead through the corridors. As the sorcerers stepped away to let them pass. The grounds were laden in white snow. Not enough to hide the wide paths leading away from the Keep. It was the furthest she had been among the clan, where the Shalough had permitted her to be. Dargon strode as far as the outer gate. The ruin of a heavy stone wall protruded from the earth. As a remnant from a battle long forgotten. Its walls had been lowered, but the sections that lasted still conveyed the perimeter. The two columns stood with a stone bowl filled with a fire. An ornament marking the emblem of the clan. 'Zeralden Hadenvar was one of us,' Dargon spoke as the wind caught the edge of his cloak.

'What?' Saranon exclaimed.

'You are Vandragamond. The blood of the Angeon has abandoned our clan. There are many who would go to great lengths to see it return,' Dargon said.

'I thought it was random,' she said.

'Nothing with sorcery is random,' he said.

With that Dargon turned. All sight of the Shalough sorcerers vanished in the light. As though the Keep had been abandoned. She watched as the wind blew along the ground, yet all that appeared was the building. She let the energy of the Angeon go, falling deep within. The agreement had only been with Serensa. She would rather avoid meeting anymore Shalough.

The path grew narrow as it veered out along the hills. The rocky slope provided an alcove for her to rest. A sacra seal shielded her from the wind. She warmed the air as the trees rustled with a hollow sound. The small seal the same size as a coin sat secure atop the rock's surface. Saranon opened a sova bag, when it had grown large she pulled out a thick cloak. To keep away the last of the cold that crept through the shield. A patter of feet scampered past and the cloak moved. The infant dragon ran underneath. Its eyes poked out and she patted the tiny creature. 'I am not sharing my bed,' she said in a stern voice.

The hatchling did not move.

She took the cloak and the infant began to shiver. 'You are not cold,' she said.

She reached out a hand to make sure and the infant dragon dived in the cloak. It stared out into the white forest and back up at her. 'It's not the cold that makes you shiver,' Saranon spoke her thoughts aloud.

A great thud landed from the sky skidding down the hill. The huge dragon turned to stop and stuck his head next to the alcove. 'Kat,' she said and the dragon snorted.

He flopped down covering the alcove leaving a small gap. The hatchling curled up in the cloak to rest and she did the same.

Katholomu shook off the melted snow as the shield from the sacra seal kept her dry. The spray of water ran down and she stayed wrapped in the warm cloak. The great black dragon edged his claw near the sacra seal. 'Don't you dare,' she said.

He flicked the sacra seal toward the hill and the chill air came in with a rush. She ran out into the thin layer of snow and the dragon laughed as she shouted at him. She gathered her cloak leaving a patch of cloth for the infant dragon who refused to let it go. The hatchling was the same size as a cat. Albeit a rather pudgy one with wings and a tough underbelly. Its tiny sharp teeth glistened with content at claiming the cloth as a prize.

'You returned early,' she spoke as she approached the great dragon.

Katholomu snorted in disgust and stepped back. 'Fine, I'll take the lay-line if you don't want a rider,' she exclaimed.

A line of wizards appeared along the ridge of the low hill. The southern emblem of the Corathy flew from their flags and shone on their cloaks. A ball of flame similar to the emblem worn by the Shalough. The line grew thick as the troops gathered, flanking the front lines. The hooves of the horses at the rear could be heard through the silence. The great beast beside her lied down and purred as his tail swung from side to side.

'A warning would have been nice,' she glared at the dragon.

Kat glanced at her. If the great beast could appear amused he certainly did. 'We have your wizard,' shouted the Captain.

His thick cloak and heavy helmet gave him a broad stance. 'Are you sure?' she asked.

The wizards shoved Mitch to the front row for a brief glimpse then hid him among their ranks. '...And I am expected to do what?' Saranon asked.

'You will surrender,' Captain Harkin said.

'The trouble is I'm not feeling so inclined,' she answered.

Kat stopped his gracious purr and stared at her. '... And I don't think it would be much of a fight,' she said.

The great dragon pricked his ear back. The Captain lifted his hand and the wizards responded. Kat flew away as the wizardry flared striking straight for her. She stood, letting the wizardry pass through the energy of the Angeon. It hurled through into the heartland, home of the Shalough. The sorcerers responded rushing with their troops to meet the wizards. Panic took hold and Captain Harkin's troops began to run. As they broke scattering into the forest she caught sight of Mitch. He used his wizardry, desperately trying to break the chains that held him.

A wizard turned, took one look at her and ran. Mitch broke through before she reached him. Screams carried along the wind as the sorcerers clashed with the wizards, then silence. The Shalough stood around the edge waiting. The wizards stepped forward as a large group. Using their wizardry in unison and the Shalough retreated. 'You think you can take on that?' Mitch asked.

She was about to leave their hiding place and he placed a hand on her shoulder. He shook his head to warn her and she glared at him. The sound from the horses veered close and she could sense the rider. He was Shalough. She went to move and Mitch held her in silence.

Rustling branches filled the void. As the wind swept through creeping into the edges of her clothes. A great thud hit the ground and Kathomolu gave a low growl. She scurried up the embankment as the air around heated. A blaze of sorcery swept overhead. Singeing the wisps of her hair before managing to shield herself. The sorcerer held his gaze then fled a moment before the dragon stampeded. Kat ran so hard he went straight over Saranon's head. She lost sight of the sorcerer before he vanished from view. The woods moved as the wizards of the south revealed themselves. Captain Harkin strode forward, his cape bellowing in the icy chill.

The wizards circled in forming a tight arc as Saranon held her ground. Around her she could see the Captain's troops had taken damage. Yet they stood strong. She steadied herself and a great vacuum of air pulled her cloak back. As Kat ran to greet Captain Harkin. The dragon rolled over showing his belly and rubbed his head against the wizard. 'How do you know my dragon?' She asked.

The Captain nudged the great beast. Kat would not move and instead began a deep purr that rumbled through the ground. Captain Harkin let out a laugh, 'When he listens to you, you can say he's yours.'

She glared at the wizard who was beginning to be as annoying as Mitch. 'Kat!' She shouted.

For once the dragon raised his head and somehow managed to stay lying on his back. Before shaking melted snow on everyone. His ears pricked up in the direction of Sturanin Keep. An uneasy silence fell on the wizards of the south. 'Who was the sorcerer?' She asked.

'It does not concern you,' the Captain said.

'His name is Devaughn,' Meredith spoke up.

The Captain gave her a sideways glance. The wizardess, Meredith, stepped back in line.

The great dragon had dozed off between them giving out a loud snore that rumbled on the wind. The day had been wasted as the night fell early behind the clouds. 'I have a more pressing matter than you,' Saranon held his gaze.

'How quaint?' The captain spat the words out.

Meredith spoke, 'Forgive him, he doesn't know when to quit.'

The two wizards shared a discussion without words, it was over almost as soon as it had begun. The troops relaxed in a visible wave of relief. They gave her a cautious welcome into their midst. 'Your wizard is welcome if he can restrain himself,' Meredith said.

Gazing in the direction just below the ridge. Saranon ignored the cold edge to the comment, 'I have to make it to the Pearl Castle.'

The Captain managed to contain a laugh, 'Only a fool travels in this weather.'

As he spoke a storm settled above. The shield from the wizards kept the icy flakes from breaking through. Mitch joined her, staying close to her side. 'The bear makes an appearance,' Meredith said as she eyed him. The wizards worked around her, ignoring her existence. She stared up at the hills to the north as the last light faded. 'You really want to take on the Pearl Castle?' Meredith asked.

'There is much more at stake,' she left the last unsaid.

The troops would descend on Temare and she had no way to warn the Regent. The Pearl Castle was closer, yet it would still take some time to reach. There were many questions she wanted to ask Mitch, but it would have to wait. The storm set in over the wizards' shield wiping away all hope of travel. She strode over to the sacra seals keeping the troops warm. When a heavy wind broke through the shield dumping an icy blast of snow on her shoulders. 'I'm going to regret this,' she muttered aloud.

Using her energy to strengthen the shield. 'It is a pity you are not going the same way,' Meredith said.

'Do you really want an Angeon meddling with wizards?' She snapped.

'The Shalough do not share your sentiment,' the

Captain said.

CHAPTER THIRTEEN

A worthy foe

Saranon felt the dragon's breath on her back keeping them warm. Mitch glared at her, but his words were calm as he suggested they sleep for the night. She watched the storm skim over the wizard shield, rest was the last thing she could think of. He made his bed as close to Katholomu as he could manage. 'You have a volatile hilazen,' Meredith remarked of the bonded wizard.

It was a word she was used to hearing, but not for Mitch. 'What makes you say that?' She asked.

'He is too ready to fight,' Meredith spoke.

'People say that of me,' she replied.

'You are a sorceress,' Meredith gave her response as though it explained everything.

She changed the subject, 'How do you know Katholomu?'

'He grazes on our herds,' the Captain said. 'And eats the kultier that stray too close.'

'I thought he belonged to the Otturin,' she said.

Meredith laughed, 'No one can keep that dragon. What do you want with the Pearl Castle?'

She remained silent as the wizards watched on, 'The false Oracle.'

A hush fell over the group. 'So it's true,' Meredith said.

'Yes,' she answered and left for bed.

Kat nudged in close as he slept, as did Mitch giving little room to rest. Caught between the dragon and the wizard she fell into a broken sleep. Filled with dreams carrying the great rumble of the snoring beast.

She woke during the night dipping in and out of sleep. Listening to the wizards' voices blend into the wind. That whirled above the still air inside the shield. Once she woke to see Meredith staring straight into her eyes. Over the head of the dragon as he slept. 'Do you sleep?' She asked and the wizardess only smiled.

The morning took hold through the shattered sky. As the shield fell with the fading storm. The last remnants of energy dwindled low into the ground. Until there remained no trace. She breathed in the fresh air. Then the dank sulphur smell of the dragon's coat caught in her lungs. Katholomu glared at her as though daring her to give him a bath. 'You stink,' she said.

'There's a hot spring toward Sturanin,' Meredith explained, 'It's a short walk.'

The troops took their time. Still settled in the slope

and gathering equipment as they went. It was a good excuse to stray from the camp and she could not stand the smell for much longer.

Mitch led the way with an eager step and she hurried to catch up. 'Are you all right?' She asked, but he did not answer.

The spring was long enough for Katholomu to lie in while she did her best to scrub his thick skin. She used her energy to dry him before the chill took the last of the waters' warmth away. A rustle came low from the edge of the woods and she turned, yet there was nothing. Mitch could sense her unease, but the dragon paid no heed. The crunch of snow from heavy boots crept along the breeze and Madoc appeared. 'What are doing here?' Saranon asked, she thought he had stayed at Hestrel Keep.

He held the deep red blade of the bond-breaker free. 'You are in Shalough territory,' he said with a firm grip on the hilt.

She touched her bond-breaker tucked away in the form of a dagger. 'No. I meant...' Madoc explained, 'Sturanin...'

Tiny flecks rose from the ground and Madoc's words were swept in a great catalyst. As the air whipped violently toward Keep Sturanin. Her arms felt the heavy weight dragging. As she moved through the pain to raise one blade, Corsavere. The deep sea green of the heart stone shone with the energy of the Angeon as it swung through the air.

She transformed letting the façade fall to the unnatural wind. The sky began to fill with the swarm of dragon riders. A heavy thud reverberated through the ground. Madoc lost his calm and stumbled back. Katholomu waited for the riders to come closer. As he stood strong, spreading his wings in anticipation. The rumble of the outer edge of sorcery kicked up the fresh snow and shallow earth in its wake. A low cloud hung in the air racing toward them with a crackling sound, that followed as it tore up a path reducing the distance at speed. She strode out facing the edge of the oncoming rush of sorcery. As the sound thickened through the air. Madoc found his strength and stood beside her. 'Brace yourself,' he said as it came ever closer.

Saranon held up her sword arm and called to the bond-breaker she had so readily given up. It pierced the heart of the raging storm. Creating a wedge that cut a gaping hole in the flowing sorcery. As it burst into the air the remnants of sorcery vanished. Madoc let out a harsh rush of air from the breath he had been holding. The Shalough appeared and she could make out Devaughn in the distance. 'I'll handle it,' Madoc said and he went to meet them.

'Do you trust him?' Mitch whispered.

She was about to answer and changed her thought, 'Are you jealous?'

'No,' he said.

The response was not convincing and she smiled. Madoc made his way toward the group of sorcerers and Devaughn let his cape flow in the wind. She could almost hear them. The way the group stood their ground told her all that was required. 'I should have sent you,' she exclaimed.

Mitch strode toward the small group and a shadow crossed the hill behind them. As it extended forward the group made their leave. The horses galloped through the narrow path. The clear markings of the riders shone in the light. Their armour hidden underneath their cloaks, shown by the helmets they wore. Mitch went out to meet the Commander and she waited.

She took her time to meet them taking in the entire band, their sword hilts gleaming. They were calm, but ready and watched her at every step. The Commander gazed down with a casual stance. Yet the alertness in his eyes remained. Saranon stayed where she was until the sorcerer invited them to follow. At each step she could feel the Commander judging her, almost waiting. Every time she turned, his eyes locked onto hers with an even gaze. His cropped grey hair escaped from the edges of his helmet. His skin was worn, yet his poise was strong. The wrought iron gates opened to the grounds surrounding the fort. The entrance was for display with the wall trailing low. The Shalough sorcerers were enough to keep people away.

The inside of the building was plainer than she had anticipated. Commander Regner saw her disappointment, 'We're you expecting something else?'

'Perhaps,' she said.

'It has been a while since our fort has seen an Angeon, more than 200 years. When Queen Zeralden graced her ancestral home,' the Commander said.

Saranon glanced around at the stone walls. With the

thick timber frame breaking the monotony. 'Was the last Angeon a Shalough?' She asked.

'All the Angeon were,' he said with a calm interest. 'I have a question for you. Why would Tordoren choose a Vandragamond?'

The room fell silent and Mitch backed away. Madoc spoke first breaking the Commander's gaze, 'Perhaps it is the Tethaweir?'

She was about to speak when the Commander snapped, 'What would you know?'

He turned to Saranon, 'Stay here until the Athgar have had their unrest.'

'I'm not...' She was interrupted while Madoc shook his head.

Commander Regner raised his voice, 'I will not have anyone interfere with the wizards. If the Armythral had taught you properly you would not be so eager to break the Uvalen Code.'

They were left in an awkward silence. As the Shalough tried to accommodate them after the Commander had gone. 'What is the Tethaweir?'

Cassidy spoke up before Madoc could answer. 'It is when Tordoren disadvantages a sorcerer clan to create balance.'

'That might be, but I have to be somewhere,' Saranon said.

'If you want to take on the Commander go right ahead,' Cassidy replied.

Madoc finally got a word in, 'The Shalough Council

will not cross him.'

'Are you serious?' Saranon asked in exasperation.

'Do not argue with the Commander,' Mitch said.

'Lord Shakar lost to him,' Cassidy added. 'Not that the Lord would admit it.'

Saranon could feel her mission slipping away as she was stifled yet again. An idea occurred to her, 'I thought the Vandragamond stayed at Validain.'

'You are here,' said Cassidy, 'but then the weak can travel freely.'

'I am not weak,' she snapped.

'If you want to prove it. There are many here who would be willing to spar with you,' Cassidy replied.

The sorceress, Cassidy, showed them along the path. That the led through the open grounds. The officers that stood around the perimeter glanced their way. The courtyard was protected by a faint shield that kept the harsh chill of winter at bay. Saranon peered through the tall windows as the sorcerers inside stirred. Madoc grinned, 'I don't think they were expecting us.'

'Perhaps,' she replied as an uneasy feeling rose.

Mitch stayed close, his silence and short glances spoke for him. The air filled with the spray of snow and ice. As Katholomu thudded against the boundary wall. The dragon held his wings wide blocking out the last rays of sun. Enveloping the courtyard in shadow.

He flicked the melted ice with a rapid shake and bounded into the courtyard. For a moment Saranon thought the great beast would stop. Instead he reach over them and scratched his claws down the side of the stone wall.

'I'll show you around,' Madoc said.

She hid her surprise at realising he had been at Melacront. The barracks seemed simple enough and worn with age.

When she stepped across the threshold of the main building. The image fell away revealing a Keep with thick sturdy walls. 'Wow!' She exclaimed showing her astonishment.

'Cool, huh?' Madoc said.

She had not expected to find the Keep wrapped in secrecy. It felt like her chance of a short stay was starting to vanish. They followed him through the building that wrapped around the hill side. He led them up a narrow stairway to the tower overlooking where they had been. The chill broke through as they made their way above the shield and she held her cloak tight. Mitch pointed to a glimpse of the Pearl Castle from a distance.

She waited until Madoc left and asked, 'Did we just gain him entry?'

Mitch nodded in reply. 'I thought so,' she said.

They made their way down as the guards changed. The Commander brushed the last of the chill from his coat. The thin wisps of hair remained straight after the helmet was removed. 'It is not fitting for an Angeon to have a wizard,' the Commander said.

As he glanced toward Mitch. 'The wizard stays,' she replied.

It was not the first time she had heard the remark and she stood close to Mitch to prove her point. The Commander brushed it off as he made his way inside. The place was cosy for a sorcerer Keep and the corridors were small. It was almost impossible to move through without walking into someone. The wizard with his broad shoulders managed to glide along unnoticed. Yet she had to dart around. For a moment she stood in a completely unfamiliar place. Hello, Chronasett's voice trailed through her mind. She jumped back slamming against the wall. Saranon followed Mitch into a decorated lounge. With thick woollen carpet and finely carved chairs. The low table was laden with food and drink.

The Commander sat behind a desk with a heavy stain and leather bound folder to one side. He took a moment to breathe in the warm air. 'I will discuss the terms with the clan. In the meantime do not stray far,' he said.

'What terms?' She asked.

'Your surrender,' The Commander said.

Saranon could feel her anger rise. Mitch reached out and gave a curt reply while leading her toward the door. When they were in the corridor she whispered, 'Why did you do that?'

Mitch waited until they were far enough away, 'Not now.'

She glared at him, the wizard could be infuriating. They were stuck within the grounds of a building barely large enough to be a Keep. It was impossible to find a quiet moment with Shalough watching her. She strode through the courtyard and gazed up at the tiny flecks of snow falling. The flakes melted on the surface of the shield, yet the wind found a way to sneak through. Whipping at the edge of her cloak. She stared at the hills blocking her view. Over the ridge and far off in the distance stood the Pearl Castle. Home to the one whom she had been asked to deal with. For all the desire to find Christine. There was an absence of concern for Ulrich, the false Oracle.

A festive cheer rose up through the corridors as she made her way in for the evening meal. The open friendliness took her by surprise. She had to remind herself that she was a prisoner. As darkness fell the lights of the Keep lit up the space with a warm glow. The sound of the wind sweeping past echoed with a steady drone. Above the faint voices that reached her from outside. The decoration in the large room made up for its lack of size. She struggled to find a spare moment as the sorcerers strode by.

The iron lever holding the thick wooden door creaked as the wind caught it and she went out. Mitch ducked through before it had a chance to close. The night sky shone clear as the clouds hastened their journey. The chill worked its way to the edge of her fingers and across her cheeks. The courtyard opened with an archway above. A night watchman called out and Saranon heard the swooping of giant wings. She gazed up to the underbellies of the dragons. Flying low over the turrets, marking the roof top of the Keep. She ran to the outer yard in time to watch the dragon riders circle and land. The first rider came in too fast. A flurry of fresh snow sprayed across the guards that stood close.

Commander Meghan greeted her with a wry smile, 'I didn't think you would get far.'

Saranon's face went red, though it went unnoticed in the chill night air. 'Follow me,' Mitch whispered behind her. He ran ahead creating a distraction as he let out a blast toward the guard tower, 'Run.'

She watched as the guards went for Mitch and could not let the wizard fight alone.

She let her energy rise outward and it met against a heavy shield from the Keep. Saranon narrowed the source and aimed for the guards. The surprise of an attack stunned them more than the impact. She ran passed grabbing hold of Mitch. Guards swarmed around the way out. They darted to the side through a small courtyard. The shield still held at the outer barrier and she ran through. No one followed and she turned. Mitch was stuck inside the shield with no way out. The Shalough were closing in. 'Leave,' he said.

'No,' she cried out.

She stepped back gathering the energy of the Angeon. As it welled up inside the Keep gave ground, at the last moment it let the wizard through.

Sorcery prickled within and she managed to aim the blast upward. To avoid hitting the Keep head on. The energy crackled engulfing the shield. The sound followed echoing, so loud, that all stood stunned. The shield shivered in an array of bright colours, then finally it fell. Mitch took hold of her and they ran. She glanced back as the first flakes of snow wilted down onto the rooftops. They trudged off the wayward paths. Their boots squelched through the layer of snow. She lost sight of Mitch, but he reappeared. Beckoning her through the darkness of the hillside. It was a tiny slither of an opening just wide enough to pass into an archway. He braced the worn flat wall of the rocky hill and it gave a soft glow.

Shouts rang out in the ice cold wind and she could sense the Shalough. She placed enough energy in the old gateway for them to meld through. Mitch went first. As she glanced back a faint glow of energy streaked through the night sky. Her foot lost the ground while stepping back and Mitch caught her. They clung to the wall and she peeked over the edge. It was a long drop down into the destroyed foundations of an old Keep, piled on the cavern floor. The ledge was narrow and she glanced ahead, 'There's a path.'

Mitch jumped from the ledge. His lower half disappeared and he reached over to help her down. The steps were worn and crumbled, but sturdy enough. She ran, gaining speed and he shouted after her. The stone slipped away and she landed with a thump as the dust scattered. Mitch ran toward her and she held on. He bent over and went pale as the pain showed on his face. 'You didn't tell me,' she gasped.

'There wasn't time,' he said.

He collapsed against the wall. A corridor remained intact opening up to a small set of rooms. Yet all she could hear was a faint droning of the wind above. She opened a sova bag and pulled out some bedding as it expanded. It was an excuse to get a closer look at Mitch's leg, but he kept her away. 'I need to look at it,' she said.

There was blood trickling from the wound. He flinched and pulled away, the shock of blood on her hands made her pale. She rinsed them then ripped the cloth before he had a chance to protest.

Underneath, the wound was small and beginning to heal. Saranon glared at him and put her hand above the deep gash. Her energy coursed through the wound. It closed leaving only the dried blood on the surface. 'I appreciate what you did,' she said.

'That's all right,' he responded.

She made sure he was warm for the night. They were below ground, but the air carried with it a chill.

The odd sounds that creaked from every direction broke her sleep. Mitch had rolled over, his face pale with sweat. He coughed and his eyes held pain. She placed a hand on his chest and reached out her senses. 'Why didn't tell me?' She asked.

'You were supposed to leave me,' he whispered.

'I'm not going to leave you,' she said in an angry tone, trying to concentrate.

She managed to block the wizard's pain so he could sleep. She reached out with her energy finding the damage left behind by the Shalough. As the wound healed he gently removed her hand. Her back ached and she stayed close while he rested. The sounds of the distant wind filled the darkness. She wondered why Mitch would conceal his injuries. Then it occurred to her, he did not expect to live.

She reached over and glared at his sleepy face as he woke. 'Don't you ever do that,' she said.

'Do what?' He asked half asleep.

'I didn't ask you to die,' she said.

'I'll try not to,' he said and rolled over.

'I'm serious,' she said.

'So am I,' he answered.

'Mitch,' she said, 'If anything happens to you Captain Mirshendy will never forgive me.'

He put an arm around her and drifted off to sleep without saying a word. As she closed her eyes she slipped into a strange dream with the Captain chasing after her. Through winding corridors that wrapped around with no end. A tiny strand of light broke through from above. She reached over to find an empty spot where Mitch had been. She glanced around becoming frantic and called out.

He appeared with a makeshift breakfast of dried food they had been carrying. 'We need to keep moving,' he said as they ate.

She eyed him carefully watching every strain to see if the wizard was struggling. He hid his injuries well and she did not like being duped. 'It can wait,' she said.

He was about to argue and she glared at him. 'You aren't going anywhere after I healed you,' she continued.

Knowing full well the effort could be undone. A silence clung in the air and Mitch shrugged his shoulders. They spent the morning wandering through the ruins at a casual pace.

A few paths had led to dead ends, but they made their

forward deeper into the hillside. All signs of natural light faded. She cupped her hands until a faint glow lifted above them. Offering a soft light in the mountain of darkness. 'I should've told you,' he said.

The words were yet another reminder that the wizard could read her immediate thoughts. It was a gift that somehow missed the sorcerer clans, much to her annoyance. 'Come on, I suppose we need to find a way out,' she spoke.

With reluctance not wanting to follow his advice. He grinned and ran ahead leaving her to catch up, before disappearing from sight.

CHAPTER FOURTEEN

Race through the ruins

A thin light beamed onto the rubble of the fallen Keep. Saranon steadied herself on the cold hard surface where the frost marked the outside. They were high up with a view that stretched along the valley. Mitch stayed close as the wind picked up carrying the chill through a clear blue sky. To the east in the distance shone a small glimpse of the Pearl Castle. She strode out into the open and the chill ran across her face. They continued, staying close to the hillside. To the far north loomed the Menna Range, home to the Otturin. The hills remained quiet giving the impression that no one lived there. Yet hidden away were several towns, that traded with the sorcerer clans across the region.

The empty branches of the trees allowed the wind to pass through. The valley between the three sorcerer clans remained barren. A land that few crossed as it kept the old ruins of Zyanthia. The resting place of Galdamore, a once great city where the sorcerer clans met. The stone remnants broke free of the path. Offering a glimpse of the vast buildings that had once stood. A faint green tinge spread in the morning light across the pale white snow. She hesitated, yet as the sun's rays strengthened it began to fade. Mitch caught her gaze and pointed toward the Pearl Castle. Where the haze lingered before it disappeared. 'Do you think...?' She asked, lost in thought.

A horn blew sharp in the distance behind them. Carrying its sound through the clear sky and they turned. Back across the ridge the Shalough on horseback made their way ever closer. 'Run,' Mitch said.

This time he stayed with her. Saranon caught the glimmer of a lay-line up ahead. 'There,' she said.

The Shalough were in the valley. She could make out Devaughn near the lead. They rode in a diamond formation over the ridge. The sound absorbed in the icy snow as they made their way toward the narrow path. She ran for the lay-line, but the gap was closing. She hesitated knowing it would not be long.

Mitch stood his gaze held on the riders. She peered up at the sky and it was still clear. They were on the edge of the heartland, yet the sky remained clear of the dragons. It made no sense. She glanced around for a vantage point and her foot went through the soft layer of snow. She cried out as her arms flailed, clinging onto the ice cold layer as it chilled her hands. Mitch leaned over to help and the fragile layer gave way. She stifled a scream as the air whooshed out her lungs and she slid along the sodden earth. He jumped down, managing to brace himself along the sides of the tunnel.

The cold seeped in with the melting snow and a numb sensation sent a sharp chill down her spine. Mitch patted her on the back, 'You can get up.'

She opened her eyes, the cave worn with age had carvings of the sacra seals. Decorating the crumbling layer on the walls. 'Don't do that,' she exclaimed.

'You were the one who fell,' he said.

She glared at him and edged her sorcery to the surface. Enough to dry her clothes and steal away the chill. The cave floor revealed a scattering of stone work. Amid the rubble leading down to a gentle stream.

Carved archways marked the entrance and exit at either end. With the water flowing freely. 'Do you think if we...?' She asked while peering underneath the arch.

The horn blew above ground. It gave her a greater chill than the icy snow and she went pale. Mitch shifted a large wooden shell near the water's edge. He placed it in the stream watching as it floated. 'Grab the ores,' he said.

She reached over where the boat had been. The ores were hidden underneath. The rubble shifted as she pulled them free. 'Will it work?' She asked.

The voices carried down from above. 'Do you want to stay?' He asked.

She moved at the edge of the stone floor before it dipped away and held on to the boat. It wobbled and she fell in with a thud. Mitch steadied the small wooden craft as the stream took them in its grip. The low arch was thicker than the length of the boat. The stone was worn at the edges. The flow of water took them away. She tried to move and the boat wobbled. Mitch pulled her back down. He kept a look out with the ores ready to help steer. The stream grew wider and dipped at a gradual angle. As they entered an underground lake, the dark engulfed them and she made a soft light. It shone above the boat, yet the air around them remained in a heavy black shadow.

A movement caught her eye. Mitch raised the ores and neither of them dared to speak. After a while she said, 'Should I dim the light?'

'No,' he whispered in concentration.

'What is it?' She asked

He did not answer as the ripples broke the surface once more. They remained in silence waiting as the next ripple broke the surface. Then a dull grey tail followed. The width spread along the tip of the water then vanished. 'Quadmar,' she whispered.

The massive underwater beast had a grey thick skin and two fins that morphed into arms. The head and neck appeared partially human. The creatures were far longer than their tiny boat. Mitch pulled the ores close and they stayed low. She had encountered the Quadmar once before. When they had blocked her only way of escape. The lake had become calm. Mitch dipped the ores into the water keeping the movement shallow. The boat crept forward toward the centre of the lake. She peered up at the hollow of the cavern rising into the darkness. Tunnels wrapped around the edges offering a possible way out. One at the far side rose to a low embankment.

The ores creaked as they rubbed against the side of the boat. Mitch kept the strokes steady as they made their way along. She fought the urge to speak, not wanting to do anything that would draw attention. A cold chill sank through her cloak. Every time she thought to speak Mitch gave her a knowing glare. Her muscles ached as she lied close to the hard wooden shell. A tall long spiky edge swam through the water from a large tunnel. It was unrecognisable from a distance and she pointed. Mitch rowed hard creating ripples through the surface. She sat up gazing at the water as the spiky edge disappeared into the depths.

She fought back the urge to use her sorcery. The boat tilted to the side as a large quadmar was flung high into the air. A spray of water thrashed over them as the tail whipped around. It hit the surface at a flat angle and drenched them as they clung to the wavering boat. The quadmar rose again. She spotted the dragon's great jaws gripping it with blood streaming down. 'Kat!' She shouted as the claws came out holding his prey close.

The great beast ate while floating on his back, showing off his prize to her horror. She took the ores and began steering the boat toward the shore. The movement was hard on her arms. She was not about to be a captive audience. While the dragon munched down on his magnificent prize.

'What did you think he ate?' Mitch spoke with a hint

of amusement.

'That's not funny,' she retorted.

'Would you like me to row,' he said.

'No,' she replied.

Saranon hurried as she rowed toward the shore, Mitch jumped out and she followed. The ice cold water sent a chill through her. She clasped the boat with her numb fingers. Helping to drag it along the rocky embankment.

Katholomu moved through the water with the last of his morsel in his jaws. He reached the shore and glanced their way. Then shook the water out, it sprayed everywhere. The dragon waited then threw the remains of the quadmar away. He bowed his head managing to round them up and pushed them into a tunnel. The great beast proceeded to curl up at the opening to lake and began to purr. Sunlight streamed from above marking the way out. She glanced around at the worn carvings and the uneven stone stairs. 'Where are we?' She asked out loud.

'The Ridge,' Mitch said.

Her heart sank, she had hoped to bypass the stronghold of the Mercidian.

She turned to him, 'If you want to leave...'

'After last time,' he said.

The encounter with the Corathy wizards had not been a pleasant one. She gave a reluctant nod and they moved on. Her clothes dried with her sorcery, but the memory of the chill remained. A breeze swept from the open hillside. The afternoon sun gave the last of its glow as it began to ease its way toward the ground. 'Have we travelled that long?' She asked.

Her weary muscles answered for her and she wondered how Mitch was fairing.

The thought of staying near the quadmar made her uneasy. She glanced around, finding another alcove with columns partially visible along the walls. She set the sacra seals around and created a small glow for warmth. Then rested against the wall. They were both exhausted and she closed her eyes as the shadows grew in the fading light. The wind picked up and she stirred not realising she had fallen asleep. The sky was dark and Mitch watched as he stood. 'I was going to wake you earlier,' he said.

She used her sorcery to search out in the darkness. A slow sensation reached her, it was the Shalough. She thought she had lost them.

The wind whirred around the hillside bellowing along the edges of her cloak. She removed it and the chill fell through the gaps in her coat. She breathed in the sharp chill air. 'I'm going out to meet them,' she said and ran up the rocky slope.

She sensed her way underneath the glinting stars. The wind whipped across her face and she made her way to the path. The night clouded her vision. Yet she could make out the dark forms heading toward her on horseback. She watched as a small group stayed close to the path. Her sorcery rose just underneath. Keeping her warm from the howling chill echoing down the valley.

She could make out six riders, yet she was certain there had been more. The faint sound of the horses reached her through the cold clear air. A shadow on the hillside moved out of the corner her eye. 'Down,' shouted Mitch as he ran past her.

The air knocked out of her before she hit the ground and rolled. The wizard had taken the brunt and it reverberated through her senses. She glanced around and he was gone. Panic rose and caught in her throat as faded shapes shifted around the periphery. She had lost Mitch. Her sorcery broke through the surface pulsing out in waves. Bouncing off the Shalough where they stood. She unsheathed Tellembre the pearl white blade forged at the temple of Ollanthia.

The bond-breaker shone at the centre from the heart stone embedded in the hilt. She began to wield it, but the bond-breaker trembled and refused to swing. In frustration she slammed the hilt against the closest Shalough. The sorcery protecting the Shalough flared and she screamed. If the blade would not wield then she would use the hilt. Slamming it against another sorcerer. This time the sorcery flared outward into the dark. In horizontal sparks leaving a trail that played with her sight. She used her senses to hone in on the group and slammed the hilt hard. The third time met with a clap of thunder from the release of energy. It threw her back to the hillside with a thud. The cracks of energy shattered through the air. The group of sorcerers were exposed.

The resistance in the bond-breaker faded as the Shalough scattered, fleeing the site. She held Tellembre and waited, yet this time the Shalough fled. Saranon glanced around, there was no sign of Mitch. She reached out her senses and found a trace leading below the path. She made her way down and saw him. He lied still against the rocky alcove. She called his name and he glanced up. 'Don't do that,' she said with relief.

He gazed at Tellembre. 'How did you break the bond?' He asked.

'The what?' She asked.

'You used the blade to break the bond,' he answered.

'Isn't that what it's for,' she asked.

'I've only seen it used as a sword,' he said.

She eyed him with suspicion. The night was still dark and she was hoping to get some sleep. They strode further on and found a location a short distance off the path. She hoped it would be enough as she laid the sacra seals out again. The warmth from her sorcery kept the cold away. Mitch stayed close and put his arm around her. It was comforting to know the wizard was with her as she fell asleep. Her dreams were filled with the remnants of the old Keep Galdamore. The once great city had rivalled Indarin in Serenphel, the home of the Prophet.

The winter sun caught her off-guard as it streamed into the valley floor. She rubbed the sleep from her eyes. The Ridge stood strong and silent. Turrets rose giving a glimpse of the building that hid beneath. She wrapped her cloak tight as they made their way down the slope. In the fallen snow it was difficult to tell where they had been. The thought of encountering the ockren in a long dead Keep left her with a sense of unease. They stayed along the low part of the hill. It gave less visibility, but she did not want to take the risk. The valley floor evened out into a well-trodden pebble road that trailed off. The lower Ridge opened up into a narrow band of structures and columns. Jutting out to emphasise the Keep that lay covered underneath.

Saranon gathered her thoughts before noticing the outskirts were absent of Mercidian. When every detail suggested they should be there. 'It's very quiet,' she said.

Mitch stood behind her. She hesitated then walked forward taking care to look around. A movement came from the outer wall then disappeared. She wondered if the Mercidian would choose to protect the false Oracle. There was only one way to find out. She approached the outer rim of the Keep and a faint sound became audible. It emanated from the ground, but was not from the central core. Saranon hesitated close to the boundary. She could sense the end nodes and the energy shielding the perimeter.

A battle cry rang out and Saranon grabbed Mitch, breaking out of phase with the real world. The first line of sorcerers became visible as they ran. Then there was silence. The sky was black and the ground pale. As distance and time moved in a disproportionate fashion. They made their way up the stairs carved into the hill. Saranon was halfway there. Up ahead a group of Mercidian waited. Standing still in the courtyard that wrapped around. Her concentration slipped and they fell back into the real world. The Mercidian were pulled through with them and sunlight fell where they stood. Commander Sedgewick lost his footing. He glared at her, 'State your business Vandragamond.'

The words were hollow after the Mercidian had blocked her way. Dragons flew into view, circling in the sky. The wizards of Adeyorn charged across the open field. While the Mercidian barricaded their Keep. 'Let me pass,' she said.

'Is this your doing?' He asked.

She wanted to yes, but shook her head. 'I will deal with you later,' he said and made his way across the Ridge. Taralynn stood keeping guard. 'Did I just get fobbed off?' She asked aloud. 'Don't try anything,' Taralynn said.

She gazed down watching Captain Lydia Grace lead the charge. At the last moment the Athgar veered to the side running parallel to the shield. The energy in the Keep wavered and dimmed.

The Commander shouted to the sorcerers below as the shield pulsed. Captain Grace spurred onward with the Athgar wizards in close formation. Ignoring the blasts of the Mercidian as the wizards formed one group. Mitch tapped her on the shoulder, 'They cannot hold out for long.'

She understood as the Mercidian began another attack. The blows began to hit the shield and the wizard group was starting to break apart. She had kept the power of the Angeon close after the faint marks surfaced on her hands. If she did not permit the Angeon to rise, the Athgar wizards would be lost. The scene below them began to merge into chaos.

The burning sensation creased across her skin. As the energy of the Angeon rose to the surface. It surged outward crumbling the shield around the Ridge. Commander Sedgewick turned with a look of horror set deep in his eyes. She raised her arms and the energy flowed forward. The ground began to tremble. A crevasse opened, it ran back to the hill and branched out over the hillside. The mound of earth crumbled from the top. Both sorcerers and wizards alike ran from the site. The rubble fell into the open crevasse. Until an entire vertical section had fallen, creating an artificial pass. She reached out to the Keep mending the great walls on either side. At its centre formed a giant archway high above linking the building and the Keep.

Saranon made her way down to the newly formed pass. Sorcerers stone covered the floor with a smooth hard edge. The markings whirled in a majestic spiral. Captain Grace approached, 'I can't go with you.'

'How do you know?' She asked.

'I wouldn't be much of wizard if I didn't,' she said as she glanced at Mitch.

'What about Commander Sedgewick?' She asked.

Captain Grace smiled, 'He's used to me turning up.'

The energy of the Angeon faded away. She heard the Commander's voice boom across the void. 'Angeon, I hope you know what you're doing.'

'Ignore the old prat,' Captain Grace said as she waved them goodbye.

She glanced back to see the Commander speaking with the Captain. As though they were old friends. A puzzled look crossed her face. 'They know each other,' Mitch answered her unspoken question.

'How did the Captain know where we're going?' She asked.

'It's been obvious for a while,' he said.

'You told her,' she accused.

He did not answer. 'You did,' she exclaimed.

Again he said nothing. She had no idea how Mitch had managed to contact Captain Grace, but she was sure he had. The Ridge dropped at a steep angle to meet the rolling fields. That swept around a scattering of buildings. When they had made a good distance away she turned back to gaze at the Ridge. 'Wow!' The word slipped from her lips as she stood in awe.

The large gateway dividing the Keep above ground reminded her of Odana Temple. Its great columns and archway was truly Zyanthian, harking back to the fallen empire.

'I wonder what it would have been like,' she spoke.

Mitch met her with a calm gaze, 'That is where my ancestors would travel to meet the Angeon.'

'I am not staying there,' she said.

A forest along the lower hills from the Menna Range arced around the edge of the plain. The well-trodden path strayed toward the barren trees. That provided protection from the wind as it gathered speed. The sun lowered in the afternoon, but she wanted to keep going. Her body was weary and she walked through the pain.

Mitch placed a hand on her shoulder and pointed to a hut in the woods. He went ahead and invited her in. The wooden hut was simple with a large stone fireplace.

It had been built for wanderers with the royal crest carved into the frame around the door. She dropped the long iron handle holding the door in place. The floor was made of rough stone. With low wooden benches wrapping around the walls. A warm fire in the hearth spread the heat around the room. As night fell and the wind bellowed outside. She stood listening unsure, a sensation reached her that made her uneasy. A noise crept out from behind the door and the long iron handle rose.

She froze as the door creaked open. Adeen lifted the thick hood of her dark cloak as she entered. The Otturin sorceress warmed her hands by the fire and Mitch stepped out of her way. Silence clung in the air as the wind howled outside.

'Where is the Oracle?' Adeen asked.

Saranon glanced at Mitch, 'I do not know.'

'I asked you to bring the Oracle,' Adeen spoke in a firm tone.

'Do you know what happens to people who hunt the Oracle?' She asked.

'You do not know what you are talking about?' Adeen said.

'What happened to the sorcerers who harmed Christine?' She asked.

Adeen drew a sharp breath and Saranon took a step back. She had taken a guess from her conversations with the Prophet in Serenphel. She hoped there was not much difference between the two. 'I will give you one more chance,' Adeen said.

Before she could respond the sorceress vanished. She thought the Otturin had understood that she did not want to be part of their game. 'She's gone,' Mitch said.

Saranon tried to relax, but her heart was thudding in her ears. The scowl remained as she seethed. Mitch held up part of a cooked rabbit skewered on a stick.

She sat down and ate, not wanting to admit defeat. 'I found a lay-line, but the glow had turned green,' he said.

'What do you mean?' She exclaimed.

'It doesn't work,' he said.

At first it was a sense of relief then the true meaning sank in. 'I'm going to take a look,' she said. Mitch followed as the chill wind whipped through his cloak. It was freezing compared to the warm hut, but she had to see for herself. They trudged through the snow staying close to the path. The bright stars shone giving a faint light. She was about to call on her sorcery then recognised the faint green glow.

Her numb fingers reached out and there was nothing. The lay-line remained silent. She let her mind roam using her sorcery around the edges. The rough surface of the green glow appeared. She extended her energy further. The sorcery strangling the lay-line dropped down toward the Pearl Castle. She lost her balance and fell. Mitch helped her up and they went inside. She warmed her hands by the fire and snuggled down to sleep. 'You need a plan,' he said after waiting a while.

'I need a whole lot more,' she replied, gazing into the open fire.

CHAPTER FIFTEEN

A key to enter

The hut had grown cold as they packed their belongings and shrank the sova bags. They fitted well inside the leather pouch that hung on her belt. The forest gave no sign of the Otturin, but Saranon knew they would be watching. The thought annoyed her as they made their way to the Pearl Castle. She could make out the flags along the turrets fluttering in the breeze. A crystal clear sky greeted them as the sun shone across the pale layer of snow. The path came to an abrupt end close to the lay-line and they made their way down to the open field. A silence hung in the air as a lone falcon flew overhead.

The path widened as it met with the cobble road leading toward the buildings. A thin trail of smoke wafted from a stone cottage on the outskirts. As they neared Mitch hesitated. She glanced around and the buildings appeared to be deserted. The side of the barn made a thunk as a hard object hit and they ran from it. A shadow began to block out the light. As the air around grew hazy with sorcery seeping from the Mercidian. She ran through the unnatural fog, yet the only person she could find was Mitch. He became uneasy as the shadows grew.

A storm gathered along the ground. As the shards of sorcery broke through, crackling deeper into the fog. Snow pummelled into them and she held out her arms. Saranon skidded backward. As her sorcery hit the wall of ice splaying through the air. The wind from the blast loosened her cloak letting the chill take hold. Movement caught her eye near the building and she ran after the sorcerers. 'Wait,' Mitch yelled out.

She darted around the corner and slipped as the impact from the blast hit. The sorcery bellowed in a ferocious blaze melting away the unnatural fog.

She turned as the energy rose. It catapulted in a blinding arc cutting the air apart. A scream pierced her ears and she glanced up. Clara ran toward her. 'Stop! Please Stop!' Clara cried out.

Flynn stumbled, the blaze had hit along his side. Saranon hesitated, but in that moment he signalled to the Mercidian and they attacked. She held out against them, blocking each blow as they came. Each time the force knocked her back taking away the ground she had made. She fell back into Mitch and he stood strong. The sorcerers were closing in and all she could do was react. Mitch reached out creating a barrier with his wizardry. She raised her arms as the energy rose from within. This time she held the blast strong aiming it straight into the middle of the group.

The impact shook the buildings and dust whirled along the edges. It was enough to clear the way as two sorcerers fell. She could not tell if they were injured, but that was not her target. She strode toward Flynn standing so close she could feel his breath. As his unwavering gaze followed her. 'I told you the next time we met...' She left the last words unsaid.

'Go on then,' he dared her.

She lunged forward gripping his chest as the sorcery ran through and he fell. It was enough to wound him. Clara ran screaming at her, and a blast of sorcery pelted through the air.

Saranon blocked it and Clara continued until the two met. Flynn reached out, but there was nothing he could do. 'This is not about you,' she said.

'Don't you dare,' Clara shouted. 'Don't you dare say that. How could you? I wish we'd never met.'

The words cut through Saranon and she hesitated. 'I didn't want this,' she said.

Flynn let out a groan and they both turned. An icy chill ran along the ground and a silence clung in the air. 'Ulrich is after the Pearl Castle and you would let him have it,' she said. 'What deal did you make?'

The question was directed to Flynn. Yet Clara answered, 'He has access to the imbenik chambers.'

'You gave him the Keep,' Saranon spoke to Flynn.

There was no angry tone, the energy that held her frustration was gone. 'Wait,' Flynn called out. 'You won't get inside the Castle on your own.' He held out his hand, 'Take this.'

She hesitated before accepting the small sacra seal. It had a pearl finish that matched the flawless surface of the Castle. The thin circle glowed in the light as it lay in her hand. She saw the catch, it was only made for sorcery to pass. Mitch saw her expression change and she explained, 'You will have to stay here.'

For a wizard he conveyed no hint of dismay at being left behind. She glanced around them and could see why. If there had been a threat it had faded as the sky cleared. The Mercidian gathering around the building. Letting down their guard in admission that the fight was over. She hesitated, not wanting to leave the wizard behind. Clara waited expecting her to speak. Saranon wondered if she would regret her words before they were spoken. 'Look after Mitch,' she said.

Clara beamed with delight.

The flags atop the Pearl Castle rippled in the distance. She braced herself for what she would find. The path trailed along the hillside and she gazed toward it. The great marmoz dragons of the Menna Range stared down. On the opposite side the dragons of the Heartland gathered. The dark unwavering eyes followed her every step as she left the field far behind. The narrow path opened to meet a lay-line and she remembered Mitch's warning. The opening looked well enough, but she hesitated and took the long way.

The dragons watched on. As the morning vanished into a low light covering the valley floor. The trees thickened into a forest that spread across the hills with their branches. Letting the harsh unbroken wind howl through. She gripped her cloak tight and the hood flew back. An icy chill whipped through her hair and she drew the hood close. The path met another turn. As her boots stepped across the cobble road hidden underneath the snow. It was growing dark and soon there would be no place to hide. The attack from the day had made her weary and her muscles ached.

If she went any further the danger of encountering the Mercidian would be great. There would be no rest if that happened. She held the white pearl seal in her hand. Then with reluctance found a place hidden in the woods to rest. She kept her sorcery close not wanting to draw attention. The chill settled and she managed to use the sacra seal to hide the heat. The sorcery was enough to warm the edges as the wind travelled past. She drifted into an uneven sleep waking during the night. Each time she heard the rustle from the dragons in the distance.

The light had yet to appear over the hillside. Her muscles had stopped their constant ache. A dragon flew over and she gazed up into the darkness of the early morning sky. Its great wings spread whooshing with a hollow drone into the wind. A voice shouted in the distance. A light glowed from the outer boundary of the Pearl Castle. She packed the long cloak away into a sova bag, it shrank down and she hid it. Her sleeves let the harsh edge of the wind trickle in. Yet this time she let her energy rise below the surface. It kept the ice in the wind at bay.

More than once she questioned herself flipping the white sacra seal in her hand. The stone emblem was no bigger than a coin and cool to the touch. An owl hooted above in the branches and she made her way down the hillside. The end nodes were hidden with the fresh snow. The sorcerers stone marking them gave a faint hum. The edge of the Keep would not be far away, yet she hesitated. The darkness stirred and she clung to the hilt of Tellembre. The owl fluttered into the sky and a voice spoke close by. She froze, not knowing what to do and waited as the footsteps trudged away.

It was too soon. If she encountered the Mercidian at the boundary they would have fair warning. Ulrich could not know she was here, not yet. She crept around staying close to the edge of the boundary. Careful not to pass through. She almost stepped on the end node hidden at the edge of the snow. The sacra seal was warm recognising the energy from the Keep. She leaned down taking great care not to touch the surface of the sorcerers stone. She held the sacra seal above the surface, her heart pounding in her chest. There would be no going back.

The energy flooded inside and the small pearl seal made contact with the Keep. Her sorcery moved through the seal tracing the swirling pattern carved atop the stone. It glowed underneath the layer of snow as the sorcery spread out. The surface gave way as a thin crease appeared, then it widened to expose a staircase. A voice called out and she ran down the stairs as the opening closed behind. A dull glow lit in a trail along the edge of the stairs carved in the ground. The narrow entrance transformed, as it widened to meet the stone outer walls of the foundations.

The bulk of the great columns holding the weight of the Castle above, formed a maze as they merged with the rough cut walls. A grey pattern embedded in the stone gave it a dull ashen colour. In stark contrast to the pearl finish that shone across the land. Saranon called to the Keep and it did not answer. She could feel the hum as she glided her finger tips over the cool surface of the stone. It gave a calm sensation, yet as her hand lifted a faint green tinge remained. It rippled along the wall before it disappeared. Not a sound changed in the Keep and a shiver ran up her spine.

The outer paths circled around forming an underground labyrinth. Taking her deeper toward the main building. Steps wrapped close to the thick stone column many times wider than she. Tiny decorations glinted from the light trimming the lower wall. A low howl came from the distance and she hesitated, steadying her thoughts. If the Keep was trapped she could not falter. Saranon ran as the path doubled back and hit a dead end. She almost slammed into the wall and stopped short. A load grunt echoed, she was not alone.

She held her hand against the stone wall and attempted to meld through. Nothing happened. Saranon would have to go back. The place went silent once more as she followed the curved edges of the columns and walls. The corridors wrapped around and she went further toward the indolin Chambers. It was all that stood between her and the habitable area above. The walls carried no sign of the faint green glow as she brushed past them. The hum of the Keep was almost gone in a place where it should have been strong.

She peered upward at the crack running across the seal above the door. Saranon placed the tip of her boot on a narrow ledge and leaned up. Her energy ran through the seal and it healed. The energy ebbed toward the ground then dissipated. A shadow moved in the distance from the doorway. She lost her footing and slammed into the floor. When she reached out with her senses there was nothing. The imbenik chambers were well laid out. Yet the corridors created a maze of uncertainty.

Saranon kept an open gaze watching for movement. A gruff low grumble came from close by and she hesitated. There was still no sign of sorcery, but someone was there. She moved her hand along the cool surface of the stone. Not a peep came from the depths of the Keep. It was not until the darkness moved that she noticed the shadow waiting. It glinted in the soft light behind the column at the far end. As it moved saranon could see the outline of a figure taller than she. It disappeared and she ran after it as fear set it. There was something wrong about the outline, it niggled at the edge of her mind.

She slowed down letting caution dictate her moves, keeping a safe distance. Saranon veered to the left and moved away from the centre. Soon she would have to return. Silence fell as she came closer to the seals bordering the main building. The columns thickened spreading out into long stone walls. Holding the beautiful pearl stone above. She reached out and the image emerged from the shadows. The minotaur stood almost twice her height. His dark shoulders covered in the hide of a bull.

She was so close and hesitated as the minotaur charged. It came to an abrupt stop as it stood level with the sealed entrance. Saranon's heart thudded so hard she could feel it beat in her ears. She caught her breath as she hid behind a column. The minotaur gave a snort and she hesitated. The beast made a move and she bolted back into the labyrinth. Her heart thudding in her ears. All the corridors appeared the same and she stood not knowing which one to take. The minotaur rammed into the wall with too much speed. It jolted with a thud, its deep black eyes glared at her.

She ran through the nearest doorway without thinking. It opened up into an array of columns offering a refuge to escape. She breathed a sigh of relief, but the sound of the angry minotaur reached her. Saranon took off, regaining her senses. Her energy flowed along the walls guiding the way. She could see the way out and ran for the narrow stairway. The minotaur ran behind storming through the great columns. She hastened up the stairs and the beast rammed into the narrow entrance at speed. Its head made it through the threshold of the stairway, then it stopped.

For a moment she wondered if it would squeeze into the narrow space. Instead it relaxed and turned away. She leaned against the stone wall catching her breath, her lungs hurt. 'So much for an easy way in,' she said.

The cold air rushed around the sorcerers stone marking the end node. As she made her way to the surface. Mitch hauled her out of sight before she could ask what he was doing. He held a finger to his lips for silence. They waited near the forest covering the low hillside. She wanted to speak, but her lungs hurt. She crouched down as Mitch peered overhead. When he gave the signal she followed him to a hideaway in the hillside that led to an old ruin. The walls stood and part of the roof, the inside opened into an alcove. Before she could speak Clara appeared.

It was not the person she wanted to see after being chased by a minotaur. 'Wait. I didn't know,' Clara said. 'Did you meet Haig?'

'Yes, I did,' Saranon spoke too loud. Then whispered, 'It would have been nice if someone warned me.'

'I thought you were going through the Castle, not underneath,' Clara replied.

'The green haze is there,' she said. 'I need to get in.'

She peered at the Keep through the remnants of the old building. The outer wall was still intact, but the windows and doors had long gone. The end crumbled where the roof dipped down into the broken structure. Snow covered the edges of the rubble floor.

Clara asked, 'How was he?'

Saranon glared at her in disbelief, 'You want to know how the minotaur is?'

'You probably scared him,' Clara said.

She tried to comprehend how a beast twice the size

would fear her. 'It was running at me,' she exclaimed.

'You scared him,' Clara said.

Mitch kept a look out as the guards made their rounds. They were some distance away from the Pearl Castle, but it was too close if they were found. She could not rest, 'We have to get in,' she said.

Clara responded, 'Now it's "we" is it?'

'You know... Haig,' she said.

'Oh no. I am not going in there with you,' Clara glared at her.

'I'll go,' Mitch said.

Silence fell on the small group. It was not what she had expected, but he knew the danger. 'All right, I'll go,' Clara said.

They waited as the wind hurled flecks of ice and snow in swirls along the ground. The warmth provided by the sacra seal was enough to keep out the chill in the air. Anything more could give them away. Mitch stayed watch while she rested. There was no sign that the Mercidian knew she was close, but a sensation kept niggling at her. It was too late to turn back and if the Pearl Castle was in danger then she had to find Ulrich.

The memory of the minotaur sent shivers down her spine. She listened as the guards made their way along the path through the forest. Mitch shook her and she woke, not realising she had been asleep. He rested while she crouched against the old stone wall. The gaping whole that had once held a window. Somehow she had to make it past the minotaur. Clara stirred from her rest as the low afternoon light fell over the valley. 'Why did you come back?' She asked.

'You aren't the only one that wants Ulrich gone,' Clara replied. 'You should have handed Christine over.'

She remained silent. 'Fine, don't talk to me,' Clara said.

'I didn't want to find the Oracle... Not like that,' she said. 'An Oracle will rise when ready, if not...'

She left the last words unspoken as she watched the guards making their rounds. 'If not then what?' Clara asked.

'No good will come from forcing the hand of an Oracle,' she said.

She glanced down at the palm of her hand, there was only a faint trace. Yet she hid it from view. 'Christine would have been safe,' Clara explained.

'With three clans wanting the same thing? She would have been better alone,' Saranon said.

'Like you at Antavagon,' Clara responded.

There was silence and Clara backed away. The lights of the Keep began to glow along the outer rim. Marking the fading sky as the winter sun set below the hills. The chill deepened in the air breaching her thick coat, yet she had to wait. 'We have to go now,' Clara said.

'What?' She asked.

'That only works until the sun sets,' Clara explained.

'Now you tell me,' she remarked.

They followed Mitch, the wizard had impeccable timing. He moved to the edge of the boundary between the movement of the guards. She stayed close and he waited crouching low. He gave her a gentle nudge forward and she ran toward the end node. The sacra seal fell in place. A hiss of escaping air broke the surface as the narrow stair case opened. Mitch ran ahead into the darkness. She and Clara made their way down. As the sorcerers stone forming the entrance sealed them in the labyrinth.

Mitch was amid the columns spread along the outer section of the Keep. The minotaur was nowhere and Clara ran ahead. An uneasy feeling welled at the pit of her stomach and she hesitated. The minotaur, Haig, was out in the darkness amid the great columns. Try as she might she could not catch up. The frustration showed as she gazed around glimpsing at shadows. Clara called from up ahead. She ran to catch up forgetting where she was and tripped, sliding along the floor.

A figure moved from behind the column. She caught sight of the large shoulders and called out to Mitch. A gruff snort bellowed from the shadows. She jumped up to face the minotaur. Her heart thudding in her ears. 'Haig,' she whispered.

The beast moved into the soft light of the Keep emanating from the walls. His expression impossible to read as his eyes focused on her. 'Saranon,' he spoke the word in a gruff tone and she froze.

'You can speak,' she gasped.

Haig gave a deep chuckle that made her spine tingle. 'You can do magic,' he said.

'Yes,' she answered.

'You can do magic for me,' he said.

Before she could reply Haig held out his hands. Each wrist was bound by a band with a seal. 'Break them magic user,' he said.

She hesitated. 'Break them,' he told her.

Clara came running. 'Don't,' she cried out.

It was too late. The bands crumbled and the minotaur was free. Haig rubbed his wrists, 'I have waited a long time Angeon. You may pass.'

No one was about to argue as the beast towered over them. She ran toward the centre hoping to find a way in. 'You freed a minotaur,' Clara said in amazement.

She took no notice. 'You freed a minotaur,' Clara repeated. 'How did you do that?'

Saranon had not thought about how and the expression showed on her face. Clara shook her head in disbelief, 'This way.'

'But...' She said.

'The guards are that way,' Clara said.

She wondered if Haig had stopped her from going in the wrong direction. The corridors were silent, but something nagged at the back of her mind. It was emanating from deep underground. 'The Keep,' she spoke aloud.

A tapping echoed up the walls, it barely audible. 'What's happening?' Clara asked.

She wished she knew, 'We have to help the Keep.'

'This way,' Clara rushed toward a sealed door.

They stopped in the archway. The two heavy doors were carved with a seal over the entire frame. Clara stepped back to let her pass, 'It's the central chamber.'

Saranon placed a hand on the door, it was warm to the touch. The stallic energy from the Keep emanated through and a green glow flared. 'Stand back,' she said.

She steadied herself unsure of what would be behind the heavy doors. Her sorcery rose and she hesitated as the green glow ran along the carvings in wood. It linked up with the detail surrounding the frame and engulfed the entire archway. Time was running out as the sorcery built up inside. It hit the frame with a thud and the glow faltered. It was not enough. She rammed the door with the energy from her outstretched hands. The glow halted, but still it was not enough. She gathered her strength and held on. Keeping the blast steady and unrelenting. She held on as the blast continued. A great rush of air shot back as she hit the floor. 'You did it,' Clara cried out.

She glanced up to see the charred remains of the heavy wooden doors. The seal had broken and all she could hear was the Pearl Castle screaming out.

CHAPTER SIXTEEN

The raging Keep

The voice of the Keep struck through Saranon's mind and she struggled to hold it back. The energy raging inside cascaded down the walls. Flooding the lower area and seeping across the floor. 'Wait,' Clara shouted through the noise.

She halted at the lower step watching the stallic energy cross the floor. Heading toward them. 'There is sheal under there,' Clara said.

'I know,' she answered.

The pale glow of stallic energy moved closer. A slim fluid line making its way along the smooth cold surface. Somewhere underneath lay the toxins of the Keep embedded in the sheal. The glowing liquid sparkled as it splattered underfoot. Clara ran along the balcony wrapping around the outer wall. The surface underneath disappeared.

Saranon twisted back holding onto the edge hidden below the liquid. 'Hold on,' Mitch shouted.

He lowered a rope. The stallic energy lapped around her and she tried to concentrate. Her foot hit something hard, 'I found the floor.'

She waded through sensing the outline of the conduit and stopped. There was no way around it, she would have to go in. The liquid wrapped around her arms and prickled along her senses. Her energy held it back, but she had to find the conduit. She dived under and the shock made it hard to think. The pain seared across her arms. She scrambled to break free of the surface. Sending a spray of stallic energy through the air. She gasped for air, 'Sheal.'

The pain numbed and she dived again, ready for the shock of the sheal against her skin. Her energy guided her as she relied on her senses. Making out the line of holes running along the conduit. Her energy waned under the pressure, yet she held on. The weight wrapped around her limbs. Gripping her strength as the energy rippled through her mind. The rough surface of the broken conduit stopped her and she clung on. Her energy spread around the weakened outer wall. Saranon had to concentrate as the sheal closed around. Trapping her in the depths beneath the surface.

The conduit heated with her energy and she could sense the gap closing. Her head broke the surface as the liquid caved away dragging her down. She slipped and reached out finding her grip on the conduit. Clara called out and the energy rushed in her head blocking the words.

The stallic energy disappeared as Keep sealed the opening. She glanced down, still hanging on to the conduit. The liquid sheal swirled well below, leaving her hanging in mid-air. Saranon tried to pull herself up, but there was nothing to hang onto. A thudding sound ran along the surface and a rope swayed close to her shoulders. Mitch lowered himself with the rope using his feet to kick off the side.

He took hold off her and they made it the balcony. Saranon dropped on the floor to catch her breath. Her head was spinning so fast and all she could hear was the Pearl Castle thundering in her mind. Mitch stayed by her side as the Keep rumbled. Clara panicked and ran toward the archway. The Keep closed it, melding the wall into the gap. 'No,' she shouted in a hoarse voice.

Clara was caught between rushing for the opening as it closed and staying. The Keep made the decision for them as the wall solidified. The central core was thudding from deep beneath and it called out. Mitch shouted and she gazed up to see them both. 'You passed out,' Clara said.

'What?' She asked, trying to get up.

Her head spun. Mitch caught her before she fell again, his steady arms wrapped around her. 'You need to lie down,' he said.

'I'm fine,' she said while making another attempt to stand.

The floor went sideways. 'I don't feel so good,' she said.

Mitch stopped her before she hit the hard surface. 'I'll check on the conduit,' Clara spoke in a firm voice.

She was about to argue, but the look on Clara's face was so stern she did not dare. Saranon leaned back in Mitch's arms as they rested. He held on tight in the silence. While her mind raced between the rumbling of the central core hidden in the depths. The energy creased up through the walls and pulsed along the conduit below them. The balcony opened into the upper level revealing a control room. Soft rays of light glowed across a screen matching the patterns of the Keep. She tried to move and Mitch refused to let go. 'It's her Keep,' he whispered.

She watched with a great reluctance for not being able to help. Yet it was Clara to whom the Pearl Castle responded.

'It's not always about you,' Mitch said.

She glared at him, the wizard could be infuriating. Saranon's head spun as she rested against him. 'What are you doing?' She asked.

'We thought we lost you,' he said.

His answer made no sense, but she was too exhausted and drifted in and out of sleep. She could sense the Keep moving. Reaching out to the connections that still held it. The frustration broke through in a hollow thudding clambering throughout the building. The faint noise became audible above the control room. Clara hesitated, 'If I increase the power everyone will know.'

'How long will it take?' She asked.

'I can delay the last stage until morning,' Clara replied.

Her muscles were sore when she moved, 'That will do'

Clara made the preparations adjusting the controls as

the Keep responded. Saranon drew the blade Tellembre. The light pearl bond-breaker gave a soft glow in the dim light from the walls. She had created the blade from Ollanthia in her homeland. It seemed so long ago. The Keep was older than the Pearl Castle from a time Zyanthia had long forgotten. Clara hesitated. Yet the bond-breaker Odayour she had given as a gift stayed by Clara's side. 'I will not follow,' Mitch said breaking the silence.

'I would not expect you to,' she replied.

Saranon tried to hide the fact that she had overlooked the wizard. He did not appear to be amused.

The control room wrapped around into several corridors. She found a small room and began to change. A faint banging noise echoed into the chamber as she emerged. Yet the Keep remained calm. 'It's the guards,' Clara said.

She stumbled hitting the bench and Clara glared at her. 'I need you to distract them. I'm not ready.'

Saranon brushed herself off and strode toward the edge of the chamber. Heat radiated off the walls. The columns of the corridors encircled a colourful mosaic embedded in the floor.

Sorcery pulsated in creases through the sealed archway as the doors began to give. The surge trickled in small flashes flowing out along the corridor. A crack let off a thunderous sound as a broken line edged its way diagonally across the seal. The doors still held, but it would not be long. Saranon steadied herself on the mosaic circle at the centre of the columns. A fine spray of shards flew across the space and she blocked it with her shield. The break line in the door widened and she heard muffled shouts through the gap. The Mercidians pounded at the doorway and she waited. Her heart thudding in her ears. Every blow to the seal reverberated through the Keep. The air heated around her, yet still she waited.

A jarring crack hit the archway and the doors flung open in a hail of dust and fumes. The sorcery struck through the air. Her energy surged, she could feel it rise to the surface shielding her from the blow. The explosion hit the shield with a deafening force. The air cleared revealing the Mercidian guards. Commander Felina stood firm as her guards hesitated. An awkward silence hung in the air and Saranon drew the blade Tellembre. She waited to see what the Commander would do.

Behind her the open passage led to the control room. The Commander's eyes shifted and stayed on the bond-breaker. A haze rippled in waves through the air sweeping around the room as the dust scattered. The stone in Tellembre's hilt shone. The Keep sealed in the passageway behind her. Closing off her only link to the control room. The haze evaporated as the Mercidian guards surrounded her. 'I am here for Ulrich,' she said holding the blade firm.

'This is my Keep,' the Commander responded.

It was the only warning Saranon had as the first blow struck. Tellembre swung as it glided in the air sinking deep into the guard. She let the blade slide free and in one swift blow carried the sword around to meet the next guard. The blade plunged and the guard stumbled back.

Ormond grasped his wound as the blood fell. A silence fell as the guards stood back. He healed the open wound and staggered to his feet. 'You don't know what you do,' Ormond said.

'The Pearl Castle is being bled dry, soon you won't have Keep to protect. All I want is Ulrich,' she said.

'What do you mean?' Ormond asked.

The pain of the Keep surrounded her as it broke through the connections. There were many woven around the building. She held the blade down and the stone at the centre of the hilt shone bright. The sword slammed into the mosaic floor as she let her energy ripple into the Keep. The screams emanating from central core seeped into the space flowing up the columns. An awful low sound filtered through. She gazed upon the guards watching their expressions.

A voice came through from the depths, a voice meant for her. Break them, break them all. The Pearl Castle stirred underneath, Break the Fires of Chaos.

Saranon forgot they had an audience. 'As you wish,' she said.

Felina, the Keep said.

She was stunned, realising the Keep had spoken to the Commander. 'The Pearl Castle is speaking to you,' she said.

'I told you, this is my Keep,' the Commander said.

It was a sharp tone that sent chills down her spine yet she did not show it. 'Then protect it from the real threat,' her words lingered as no one spoke.

The central core rumbled beneath her feet as a warning.

The walls reverberated the deep sound upward. For a moment all stood still, waiting. She could hear Ormond's heavy breathing from the wound. It was still troubling him after he had tried to heal it. She held his shoulder and he relented. As she used her energy to complete the healing process. Her eyes stayed transfixed to the body on the floor. Yet there was only emptiness where her emotions should have been. One more thread from the Fires of Chaos fell and the Keep cried out.

It was enough to send a panic through the Mercidian in the Keep. Edolyn rushed into the room and set eyes upon the body of the fallen soldier. She let out a howl of rage and threw up her arms as the seal opened to the control room. Clara shouted out, but she did not answer. Saranon dared not take her gaze from Edolyn. Ormond reached out to grab her and she elbowed him in the freshly healed wound. He let out a yelp from the pain. The air began to creep in a tidal flow toward Edolyn. Clara appeared at the other end from the corridor. She saw the flicker in Edolyn's eyes. Before the air electrified in an array of sorcery culminating in a great ball.

Clara's scream hit the void. Saranon had no time to wonder why. As the Angeon rose from deep within breaking through the creases in her skin. Her eyes glowed as the energy of old took hold. With every effort she pulled the ball of sorcery toward her. It flexed in the air as time slowed. A rush of energy caught her off-guard and Clara's screaming hit her ears. It was Saranon who fell. The weight of hauling the sorcery out midstream knocked her across the floor. A cackle broke from Edolyn's lips. 'Next time you will think before breaking into the Pearl Castle. I do not know what the Shalough thought you were.'

The words cut deep as Saranon glanced toward her friend.

Edolyn spoke to Commander Felina, 'Take them out of here.'

'Your eminence,' the Commander hesitated.

'You heard me,' Edolyn reiterated.

Before Ormond could move Saranon had melded through the floor. Clara gave a smile before she disappeared into the structure of the Keep. It guided her through to a secret passage and let go. She lost her balance and sprawled across the floor. It was not the graceful movement she had expected, but it gave her a way out. The passage had two doors. One led back the way she came and the other would take her closer to the great hall. It was so tempting to head further into the Keep, her legs moved before she realised. She came to a stand still as the thought of her friends niggled away at the edge of her mind. She could not leave Clara and Mitch.

With a heavy heart she strode toward the door that would take her back. Light gleamed along the crease as the door swung with a soft movement. The polished tiles glinted. As the low winter sun shone from the tall narrow windows. The walls reflected the light with a warm glow. It was not the place she expected to be. Saranon glanced around in a daze. Footsteps approached and it brought her back to reality. As an aged sorcerer with long greying hair entered. 'What has the world come to when it chooses a Vandragamond?'

'Pardon?' She asked.

'Permitting one from the strongest clan to walk the land,' he continued. 'And the most reckless. I suppose you are pleased with what you have done?'

Saranon stood in open astonishment. 'The Oracle...'

'It is not your place...' He interrupted.

'Can destroy world!' She shouted at him.

The words thundered in the open space. 'Can destroy the region,' she corrected. 'Christine is my equal, not Ulrich.'

Her rage boiled beneath the surface, she had to find Ulrich and stop him. Commander Felina spoke in the silence, 'The Fires of Chaos are linked to the Keep.'

The sorcerer's face went a livid red, 'Abominations of treachery.'

'Thurlow,' the Commander said, waiting for the sorcerer to settle.

'You know what to do,' he said and left without any further acknowledgement.

'Did I just get dismissed?' She asked.

'Think yourself lucky,' Commander Felina answered. 'He only has time for those who stray from the Code.'

She had almost forgotten about the Uvalen Code. That governed sorcery in the world of Tordoren. 'Follow me,' the Commander said as she began to leave.

'Where?' She asked.

'To find Ulrich,' the Commander replied.

A smile creased across her face, finally she would meet the false oracle. A wave of relief swept through as the anticipation built underneath. Every step leading her closer as she stayed behind the Commander. 'Don't get any ideas back there,' Commander Felina glanced her way.

They reached a hollow alcove in the central building. She hesitated as a thin vapour of sorcery trickled along the walls. A crack thundered in a stark bold sound hurting her ears. She shouted out to the Mercidian guards. The sorcery blasted through escaping as the remnants shattered. She answered the pulsing blasts that ricocheted outward. Raising her energy and wrapping it around the guards. She skidded against the outer wall with the sudden impact crushing into the shield. The pulse rippled again and she staggered forward under the weight. Before the next blast hit, shattering against the frame of the arch. The pain seared through webbing its way closer with each impact. She glanced at the devastation inside, there was no trace of Ulrich.

A rage swept over her, cascading down the edges of her vision. The blasts evaporated in a hollow silence. A howl escaped her lips filled with all the frustration welling beneath. Her fists slammed down on the charred table and it crumpled under the pressure. 'I will tear him apart and send the pieces to the far reaches of Tordoren.'

A hush met her as the Mercidian guards fell into silence. 'Spoken like at true Vandragamond,' the Commander said in flat tone.

She could not tell if the remark was serious or sarcasm

and let go of the energy of the Angeon. 'He tapped straight into the conduit,' she said.

A flash of fear swept over the Commander. The sorceress stepped back, 'I would hate to be Ulrich when you find him.'

She gazed around the damage, the smoke still rising from the charred furniture. 'Take care of the Keep,' was all she could say.

Commander Felina nodded in agreement. The Pearl Castle hummed. It was tiny, but this time the tune was different. It was one of contentment. In stark contrast to the seething anger framing her mind.

CHAPTER SEVENTEEN

The artefact

A cold chill hit in the open courtyard, it failed to calm Saranon's temper. The dragon Katholomu raised his giant head over the stone perimeter. The beast's eyes pierced through her and came almost level with her gaze. He was waiting, waiting for her to make the call. Fight or Flee? This time she gave into the dragon's wish and a wicked smile creased along his jaw. His belly rumbled under the dark thick layer of leathery skin and scales. She raised her hand and whispered, 'If you do not want a coward find me Ulrich.'

The rumble turned into a low growl of delight as she clambered up his shoulders. She could feel the warmth through his thick skin. Mitch ran out and climbed up beside her. 'Are you sure?' She asked.

Knowing that where ever the dragon took them it lead

to danger. The wizard waited for the dragon to rise into the stirring gale, 'I am coming with you.'

She did not understand, but as the great beast swerved in a tight arc all she could do was cling on. The howling winds wrapped around them. As they toward the empty valley that held the remnants of an ancient empire. The mountain ridge that held the last of the long fallen Keep Galdamore rushed by. The white snow hid any sign from below the icy clouds. The wind whipped across her face and she stayed close. The bellowing streams of air turned into a gale. That brought with it the flecks of snow scattering across the dragon. They melted against the heat of Katholomu's skin. The stench of wet dragon filled her lungs. She gagged on the smell.

Mitch drew a deep breath in, but said nothing. A gust blew the great beast off course and he hastened back to the direction. He was flying straight and true for Sturanin. She held on tight. Hoping with every passing moment that Ulrich was somewhere still out in the valley. If they headed to Sturanin Keep she would have to face the Shalough. Yet she had asked the dragon to find Ulrich. The slope of the hillside steepened as they flew up the valley. Along the same path she had taken to reach the Pearl Castle. The gale passed as the sun set and Kat lowered his wings dropping from the sky in a fluid motion. Swooping low as his belly skimmed the ground. He came to a sudden stop and Saranon lost her grip. She hurtled onto the dragon's head and stared down at his deep black eyes.

He moved his brow and rested on the ground as

she fell. Mitch caught her before she hit the cold layer of snow. The last of the light dimmed as night fell and she began to set up camp. The wizard hesitated with a hint of amusement creasing across his smile. 'What's so funny?' She asked.

'There is a camp up ahead,' he answered.

'I can't see it,' she spoke as she gazed upon nothing but the snow covered valley.

'Turn around,' he took her shoulder and pointed.

A tiny seal glowed marking the entrance to an alcove, it was so faint. He let go and it disappeared. 'Why can't I see it,' she asked.

'It's for wizards,' he said as he led her through the invisible shield.

A chorus of out of sync voices flooded through the air and a warmth that took the chill from her bones. A pain seared up her arms as feeling returned from the cold. Before she could ask, Anthony spotted her with a keen eye. She cringed at the sight of the guard from Qwezkin Fort. There was a nodding glance between wizards as Mitch left her. 'What are you doing here?' She asked as she eyed him with suspicion.

'I might ask you that,' he said in a gruff tone.

He was almost the same age as Mitch, but he missed nothing. 'I seek Ulrich,' she said.

'Then our goal is the same,' he replied.

'Why would you seek out a sorcerer?' She asked.

'Why do you think?' he said.

'Uh...' Her expression carried so much doubt.

'He endangered the trade line,' Anthony said. 'You haven't changed.'

She could feel her cheeks go hot and crimson. 'Now...' She stumbled for words and fumed at the wizard.

The warm glow of wizard lights threw shadows across the open space. A remnant of an old Keep long gone. Yet the stone outline and heavy columns remained. Worn with time and filled with modifications made by the Athgar wizards. She strode near the troops bustling around the space with Anthony following behind. His hair was filled with grit from a long travel. One hand touched the hilt of a blade as he moved with ease. The sun had tanned his olive skin, yet he blended in well with Athgar who roamed the borders. It was odd to see them again. Riddley and Jameson nodded as they saw her. Each wizard had a task and she felt out of place.

Low voices emanated up ahead and she went to made her way closer. Anthony placed a heavy hand on her shoulder and shook his head. It was polite, but she knew what it meant. Jane lifted the hood from her cloak. As she entered from the shield bringing a damp chill inside. The lights wavered in an unseen breeze bringing a deep silence over the troops. 'It's done,' Jane said.

'What is?' She asked.

The wizards went about their work ignoring the question. She glared at Anthony who pretended not to notice as he sat near Riddley.

She was about to leave and Anthony pulled her back with too much strength. She knocked over a barrel and fell to floor with a clatter. The short swords sprawled across the ground as she rolled out of the way. A hush tone fell, as she glanced around there were nervous stares. A lone cough broke through. Anthony steadied the barrel, 'This is not for you.'

Saranon gazed up into his dark eyes, 'You don't have to go after Ulrich.'

'You haven't seen wizards hunt a sorcerer have you?' He said in a cold tone.

She thought back to the time. Captain Mirshendy and Mitch had chased her through the streets of Rededere. The wizards had cornered her with ease, even though she did not like to admit it.

CHAPTER EIGHTEEN

The battle awaits

Saranon wrapped the thick cloak around her shoulder. Yet the winter's chill crept through steeling the warmth from within. The wizards blended into the frost laden landscape. With an ease that scorned her clumsiness. Mitch was nowhere to be seen. 'Where are you?' She yelled.

A flicker crossed her vision, but nothing more. There was a reason why she detested wizards when they showed off. Dragons flocked high along the far ridge line across the valley. She gazed as they watched, but what were they waiting for? She did not have time to think. As the light glistened into the heart of the long valley whisking the shadows away.

The sky cleared and movement caught her eye. A small group in the distance ventured toward the Keep Sturanin. She freed the hilt of her bond-breaker as the blade sung.

Her numb fingers fumbled over the dagger. A whoosh of air sped past. 'They've gone,' she said.

As the crowded feeling left. 'Yes,' whispered Mitch.

The voice from nowhere made her jump as he remained hidden from view. He was no help and she scrambled to keep up. The snow covered ground slowed her down. She was falling even further behind. She stumbled onto a rocky path and gained pace over the hillside. She was catching up when a thin dark line appeared along the horizon.

The horses and their riders made a tight formation. With the flags of the Shalough bellowing in the wind. An eerie silence fell as she gazed at them. The line of riders marched toward the group of sorcerers swarming onto the plateau. 'No,' she cried out into the wind. 'No,' she said again.

Almost willing them to stop. It was too much to bear as the Shalough closed the gap to the sorcerer group and Ulrich with them. His heavy cape bellowing in the wind.

A horn blew out in the crisp chill air and the horses followed gathering speed. Their hooves kicking up flecks of ice creating a white cloudy haze. He rode high and his tall stature with greying hair made him stand out. From the gleaming metal helmets worn by the soldiers. They flanked around in a tight circle as the first line moved forward. Forming a barricade with their shields. As the wizards hedged closer with a wide buffer in between.

There fell a momentary silence on the land. As Ulrich disappeared behind a wall of safety. Concealed by the ever growing numbers. Aas the Shalough swarmed onto the pale snow covering the terrain. The sun shone glinting off their armour and shouts rang out across the plain. Captain Trevell led the Athgar wizards riding from the heartland. They rode hard and the Shalough closed the distance with a sweeping ease. The first blaze let loose from the sorcerer clan. It flared across the shield protecting the wizard riders. The Shalough sorcerers edged in. Forming an arc wrapping around each end, swords and spears ready.

As the first blade plunged its way through the shield. A whooshing noise came from overhead. Faint dots outlining the bright clear sky merged. First from the south as the dragon riders came into sight. Then the east coming in hard and low to the ground. Then from the north the dragons without riders gathered across the ridge line. Waiting in anticipation. The wizards from the sky struck down with a force that shed the snow from the land. The sodden muddy earth squelched beneath the horses hooves. As chaos ensued across the plain. Devaughn held his rank at the lead. Narrowing in on Captain Trevell as the shield lay in tatters.

The Captain outstretched his arms to the sky before he fell. Blood ran where his body hit the ground. A cry went up through the ranks of Shalough soldiers and they spurred on. The wizards rode their dragons circling in with a continuous attack from the air. It was enough to splinter a few from the tight formation of the Shalough. A sorcerer screamed in agony as the blast hit true. A merging line flew into the sky from the Keep Sturanin. As the sorcerers joined the dragon riders. They were but a faint line and the distance was soon closing when they could take aim. A silence drew in the skies above as the wizards angled their dragons ready for the attack. Both troops hesitated. As the rush of swooping wings filled the air with a harrowing sound.

A cry rang out from above as the largest dragon of them all took to the sky. His wings spread the full length casting a shadow wide along the weeping ground. The deep whoosh droned lower than the other dragons circling through the air. The great underbelly was thick and hard with age. As his head faced straight for the Shalough his big cunning eyes honed in. The jaw dropped to show the jagged line of teeth and a gush of air rushed in to fill his belly. Cries rang out as the wizards made quick work to retreat. Before the sight of the fire breather. A crackling spray gushed out of its gaping mouth down upon the sorcerer soldiers. Their screams just audible above the hurtling flames.

Atop the Angeon rode and what the dragon did not finish she came for. Katholomu dug his claws in deep as the earth spewed forth with a heavy landing. Saranon circled in on Devaughn. Before he could flee with the soldiers who were edging back. The dragon riders from Sturanin were almost in reach. It would not be long before they could join the fight. The two faced off as their bond-breakers struck. The echo of the swords spread across the open plain. The great dragon kept the area around them clear. His glaring eyes enough to stir a primal fear in the most foolhardy. A crack, as metal and bone split deep, filled the air and it was Devaughn who lowered to his knees.

The dragon riders from Sturanin were in sight, yet no blast hit the ground. They landed with grace between the Angeon and the troops of the Shalough. Only a few remained on contested ground. Lord Halleron lowered his dragon. Strategically placing it beside Katholomu the dragon of the Angeon. To a hush of silent awe. Commander Regner of the Shalough clan met the wizard Lord on the bloody field. While the Angeon stayed near the great dragon.

Saranon cleaned her blade on the dragon's claw. The unwanted burden fell to the ground. She had meant to wound her opponent. A tiny flicker of movement caught her eye. She sensed Ulrich disappearing behind the ranks of soldiers. 'He's gone,' she said.

Lord Halleron scratched his chin as he took a steady glance at the surroundings. 'You wouldn't want to disappoint me. By losing your bargaining chip?' The Lord spoke in a soothing tone.

Commander Regner did not take the bait, 'We will find him.'

'It would seem your sorcerers have a habit of losing things,' Lord Halleron said.

'Where is the Oracle?' the Commander asked.

The Lord grinned showing his jagged teeth in a heavy set jaw, 'Wouldn't you like to know.'

'You know where the Oracle is?' Saranon interupted.

'Of course I do,' he said.

'Hand her over,' the Commander said.

'You have no idea…' she said.

Lord Halleron glanced at her. Saranon continued, 'She can absorb your darkest secrets and use them against you. She is better off with the Athgar.'

'Perhaps I should have brought her,' the Lord mused.

'I'm serious,' she said. '...And when she grows up the Fires of Chaos will have nothing hidden from her.'

Saranon thought back to when she had rescued the Christine. It would be a pleasant day when the little Oracle could manipulate the Fires of Chaos. Commander Regner gazed down at the Angeon's blade in thought, 'I will find Ulrich.'

'We will find Ulrich,' Lord Halleron said. 'He damaged our trade line.'

Saranon fought the urge to leave as the sorcerer and wizard spoke. The sky was growing dark and she should have been gone. Instead the wizard made it clear she had to stay. It riled her, but the numbers were so many. If she left the fighting might break out again. It was a sore compromise and her frustration was plain to see. Fires were lit to keep the troops warm. The wizards created dome shields to trap the warmth in and the snow out. The dragons formed a perimeter as they rested. With their tails curling around each other' adding another break from the cold. Song filled the air and Saranon found herself standing alone. She was the only one who seemed to notice that earlier there had been a battle on the open plain.

The shrill of energy ran through her from the fight. It buzzed around her head and clouded her mind. Devaughn had been a pleasant accident. She meant to blast him before the blade had struck. The conversation between Lord Halleron and the Commander drawled on. Saranon itched to leap on Katholomu and take to the sky. She let out a deep sigh and stepped back to rest on the dragon. Mitch tapped her on the shoulder, she had almost forgotten about him. She waited for a lull in the conversation. When no one was looking and sneaked off with the wizard. 'Took you long enough,' said Anthony, waiting for them.

'What's going on?' She asked.

'Stay out of sight,' Anthony said.

He led them in a wide arc. Stretching out into the ranks of wizards huddled around the bonfires. 'I know someone who can get you to Ulrich,' he said.

Without any further explanation. They weaved around the edges of the Athgar clan. Before heading south toward the last group of wizards. Meredith greeted them. She was so shocked to see Corathy that she gaped in astonishment. Captain Harkin sat near the open fire, his face was bruised and he did not stand. 'This is your pass to the south, Angeon,' Anthony said.

He waited with the group issuing instructions in a low voice. Meredith nodded, but Saranon could not make out what they were saying. There was an uneasy edge to the group and she stayed close to Mitch. 'When do we leave?' She asked.

'Patience,' Anthony said as he joined them by the fire. 'You need to clear that head of yours.'

The wizard was a few years older than she, but his words carried the weight of experience. 'If you leave now you will be greeted by every Shalough other than the one you seek,' he said.

His words did not sit easy and her frustration showed as she kicked up the dirt at the fire's edge. Meredith spoke, 'Temper. You are not only one who is disappointed.'

She watched as the fire burned into the late evening. Keeping away from the direct heat. Too many sounds emanated from the far edges of the plain denying her sleep. Every muscle ached, part of her wanted to go back and the other wanted to find the false prophet. Mitch was fast asleep curled up in a cloak behind her. He lay close to the other wizards resting beneath the starry sky. Anthony caught her glancing in the direction of Lord Halleron. 'We can deal with the sorcerer clan,' he said.

'I should have gone after Ulrich,' she thought aloud.

'That one's hard to catch,' Captain Harkin said.

As he sat by the fire mesmerised by the flames. 'I should be searching for him,' she said.

'And bring the entire Shalough clan after you,' Anthony said. 'Get some rest and be patient.'

'Sorcerers always provide an opportunity, they are too quick to stir,' the Captain added.

'What?' Saranon asked.

'You'll see,' Anthony replied. 'It's all about patience.'

She hated mind games, and it felt like the wizards were using the moment to annoy her. If they were it was working. 'How can you be so sure?' She asked.

'For an Angeon you are no different to the other sorcerers,' he grinned.

'Now you're mocking me,' she said.

'He has a point,' the Captain said. 'Ulrich will be harder to find if you rush in.'

Her flickering shadow sprawled across the sleeping wizards. As she stood in the warmth of the fire. Calm spread across the open ground and she made her way in the dark. Mitch grabbed her leg and she froze. 'Don't do that,' she whispered.

He had laid out a makeshift bed and she tucked herself in peering up at the stars. She fought sleep until it took the wafting voices away into a distant dream. One filled with a creeping dread seeping silently through the land. Deep beneath the surface. A whisper edged its way from below. The voice was too soft, but it repeated the same message over and over again. Her palms itched as the voice filtered up from Tordoren. In her dreams she opened her hands. She gasped at the shadowy marks visible to the eye. The camp was resting yet there was movement in the distance. The Shalough were coming. She had to wake up, but the dream held her fast. Mitch was sleeping and she called out, shouting his name. Hoping that he could hear her thoughts.

'Wake up,' a voice shouted overhead.

She tried to break free and light creased through her waking mind. The energy of the Angeon flooded along the surface. She did not remember calling it. The Athgar wizards were standing around, yet no one spoke. She looked up into Mitch's eyes, 'The Shalough.'

'We have to leave,' Anthony said.

Saranon cried out, 'Wait.'

'It's time to leave,' he said and helped her atop a magnificent marmoz dragon. 'This is Striker.'

'You have a dragon?' She asked.

'I do now,' he said.

They lifted into the dark morning sky with a graceful whoosh. Before the light creased along the horizon. She clung onto the base of the dragon's neck. As Anthony guided the beast toward the heartland.

A crimson hue broke across the land carving shadows deep into the hillside. The ground sparked with a wave of sorcery cascading along the ground. She gazed in horror, but the wave stopped short as it hit the shield protecting the Athgar. 'I pity anyone who takes on Lord Halleron,' Anthony spoke.

She remembered the bruises on the Captain, 'Is that what happened to Captain Harkin?'

'That is not for you to ask,' he said in a firm tone, ending the subject.

The hillside swept into a vast valley. Teaming with wildlife roaming the pockets of warm springs breaking through the ice. There were few signs of the dragons, but the lack of snow gave their presence away. Their warm underbellies heating the ground beneath. Patches of grass filled the valley floor. Ensuring an ideal place for dragons to hunt. The sun glistened off the melted snow as they flew past. 'Where are we headed?' She asked.

'Ragnorda,' he answered.

The Keep belonged to the Corathy and she wondered

how they would be greeted. 'Do you think we will really find Ulrich?'

'If Captain Harkin has anything to do with it. The damage to the trade line hurt them,' he said.

The dragons glided through the clear winter's day over the rolling hills and valleys. They veered south from the Summer House. The home of Lady Alvere shone, the garden was beautiful even from the sky. It was not long before Striker eased her pace. The great beast slowed and made a soft landing in the field surrounding Ragnorda. The Keep had a simple elegance with fine lines and curved trimmings. Marking the gates and main entrance. The buttresses rose up to meet an ornamental finish with carved gargoyles. They were the last to arrive and were greeted inside the warmth of the dragon pens. 'Welcome to my home,' said Meredith.

'Where is the Captain?' She asked, glancing around.

'He has business to attend to,' Meredith said.

'Lady Muir?' Anthony asked.

'Yes,' Meredith said.

Saranon had the distinct feeling she had been left out of an unspoken conversation. She went to find Mitch. He was grooming Katholomu who had curled up to rest in the pens. 'How?' She asked in astonishment.

The great beast had his paws and legs sticking out of the pen. He had somehow managed to squeeze the rest of his body in the space. 'He knows something,' Mitch said. 'Show me your hands.'

She was speechless as she held out her palms and froze.

The faint marks were visible with the same shadowy outline that had been in her dream. She could hardly breathe and went pale. Mitch leaned close, 'Don't tell anyone.'

She wanted to crumple onto the floor, but instead nodded in agreement. Rolling down the edges of her sleeves to hide the evidence. 'You didn't know,' he said.

'I...' she stammered.

'It's okay,' he said.

Mitch joined the gathering as though nothing had happened. Her stomach was queasy and she rested beside the dragon. 'How did you know?' She whispered.

Kat peered at her through a small slit as he continued to rest. He chose to ignore her as he watched on and she wondered what the great beast was thinking. The great beast had not been his usual grumpy self. When she reached out to pat his thick leathery skin. Ash covered her hand as she pulled it away. 'What have you done?' She asked, but the dragon remained silent.

Music played rummaging down the corridor from above. It was a joyful tune in contrast to the recent events. 'The supplies made it through,' Meredith answered her puzzled gaze.

'Ulrich is still out there,' she said.

'Do you want to give him a clue?' Meredith asked.

'No,' she answered.

'Then as far as anyone knows we are staying here,' Meredith replied.

'Is this about being patient?' She asked.

Meredith smiled as she led them below the main hall.

'We do not allow many sorcerers at Ragnorda.'

'I'll show you the best part,' Anthony said.

As he entered a chamber with slender columns. The stony walls fell away into an underground stream. A channel that ran around two sides for the room, then disappeared from view. The sound of running water trickled in the background. At the end of the room stood a pale altar. Carved with small replicas of the gargoyles that watched over the Keep. The veins of the stone swirled in a dark pattern breaking up the lighter tone. She stood at the centre of the chamber kneeling down as the pattern on the floor moved. Ragnorda was calling out. Saranon placed her hands on the smooth surface. The water began to seep along the floor being pulled from the open stream. The delicate lines weaved along the surface until they reached her hands.

Her heart thudded in her chest. As she concentrated on the Keep's energy rising up from the floor. A fine dust sprayed off the stone from the Keep. It rose with the stallic energy from the central core. The water and air all combining in the heat beneath her palms. The two bond-breakers began to form as she listened to the rise and fall of the rumbling. That emanated from the central core hidden far below. The blades formed with a deep burgundy wine heart stone. As each hilt shone she held them still caught in a trance with the Keep. The blades sparkled with the light reflecting off the pools of water on the floor. She held her arms steady until the blades were complete.

'You should not have done that,' Meredith gasped.

'It was the Keep who willed it,' she said, her voice sounding hollow.

Ragnorda let go and she held out one of the blades for Meredith. 'It is for you,' she said and held out the other for Anthony. 'Ragnorda wants the false oracle found.'

'I only meant you to meet the Keep,' Meredith said.

Saranon smiled. She had to remember that bond-breakers were uncommon even more so for wizards. The music became louder as they made their way to the great hall. The blades tucked away in dagger form. Tellembre stayed hidden beneath the fold of her coat as they entered. She glanced around and gaped as Mitch sat next to Lady Muir at the head of the table. His goblet was rested too close to hers. She followed Anthony to a table close to the door. It would provide an easy way to slip out unnoticed if they had to leave early. She gazed at Mitch as he whispered in Lady Muir's ear and they laughed. 'You look like a scorned woman,' Meredith said.

She blushed trying hide it, but it was no use. She did not think of herself as a woman, yet she was seventeen. 'Get entangled with a wizard and you'll know about it,' Meredith continued.

'That's half true,' said Anthony as he glanced across the table. 'The reason why wizards…'

Captain Harkin interrupted before she could find out more. 'We have the go ahead,' he said.

The conversation changed to finding Ulrich and for once she was not interested. She glared at Mitch intently at the other end of the great hall. He continued to ignore her and it annoyed her even more.

'You have changed since I last saw you,' Anthony said. 'Have you finished reading the books you copied from Qwezkin Fort,' he asked.

'No,' her cheeks felt hot as she spoke.

'Shame,' he said. 'I was wondering what you thought of the one about connecting with your wizardry.'

She threw a chunk of potato at him and he stifled a chuckle. 'I thought it was quite a good read,' the Captain added.

She glared at all three of them while she finished her meal. 'We don't often get sorcerers in these parts,' Anthony said.

'What about the Shalough?' She asked.

'That would involve work,' he said and she gave him a puzzled look. 'When they come this close to the border your friends in Darkonia get excited. The Shalough would be forced to defend themselves.'

'They are not my friends,' she said.

'I thought you were on good terms with the Vandragamond,' he said.

'They don't come down here,' she said.

The wizards burst out laughing. Saranon could not figure it out. She had understood the Vandragamond to be trapped by their own sorcery. She was one of them, but she was also the Angeon. 'When the Shalough are close to the border. The Vandragamond can greet them,' Meredith said.

'With an axe, a sword, or anything else they can get

their hands on,' Captain Harkin said.

'They wait for the Shalough to use their sorcery. Then they can strike,' Anthony said.

She had not known the Vandragamond could travel, yet she was able to. Captain Harkin rose from the table. 'Sleep well, it may be an early start tomorrow.'

She was left to endure the laughter emanating from Lady Muir's table. With Mitch fawning over the wizardess. It was not the first time, but he usually made an attempt to be discreet and hide it from her.

CHAPTER NINETEEN

Chasing the runaway

The fire burned low into the evening and the warmth from the Keep added to the heat. The air became hot. Although Saranon was reluctant to leave the evening was getting late. Anthony led her to a quiet guest area on the third level overlooking the valley. Several sparse sleeping rooms led off from the sitting area. Her room was large enough to hold two narrow beds, but not much more. She took care to unpack leaning the staff and equipment against the wall. She had no idea what would be needed to track down Ulrich. The sorcerer had a habit of finding a way to escape. The damage at the Pearl Castle had been brutal. If it were not for the size of the Keep the impact would have been far more.

She was too drained to think and curled up on the bed. It sank under her weight as she snuggled down. An element of excitement ran through Ragnorda keeping her from sleep. The door bustled open and Mitch staggered through tripping over her bed. The jolt brought her upright and she pushed him away, 'You're drunk.'

He ignored her and made a clumsy attempt to change in the dark. There was a loud thud as he fell backwards into the bags. The staff clattered on the floor and a soft glow from the orb lit the room. She went to help Mitch and he stepped back. 'You never made me a bond-breaker,' he said.

'You already have one,' she explained.

'It would have been nice if you remembered me,' he said. Mitch fought with the blankets as he tried to lie down on the bed. It was only just able to fit him.

She reached into the bag and brought out a bond-breaker in the form of a dagger. It was sheathed in an elegant pattern. With the dark navy heart stone in the hilt still showing. She leaned over and handed it to him, 'I was going to wait until we were in Normisia.'

He took it and silence filled the room as she slumped into bed. 'Where did you make it?' He asked.

'Greddin Fort. The last time I checked you were Normisian,' she replied. 'Why did you have to drool all over Lady Muir?'

'When you're older you will understand,' he said.

'I'm seventeen,' she said, glaring at him.

'Thanks for the bond-breaker,' he said, placing his hand on the hilt.

'Don't take it out. You just wrecked half the room,'

she said.

Mitch put it down beside the bed. 'Lady Muir was going to execute Captain Harkin,' he whispered.

The response sent a chill down her spine. It had not occurred to her that the Captain had risked everything. The heavy sound of snoring came from the wizard and she crammed her head close to the pillow. There was little chance of sleep. Yet she managed to drift off into dreams filled of nothing.

Movement woke her as Anthony tapped her on her shoulder, 'We have a leave.'

It was still dark and her head ached, 'It isn't morning.'

He had disappeared from the room while she rubbed her eyes. Her muscles were stiff and it took a while to get ready. Mitch packed up the rest. Shrinking the sova bags down to their tiny size before tucking them away. He moved at a clumsy pace down the stairs and she ran ahead. The small band of wizards waited for their arrival. Mitch sat down, head in his hands. His face was pale. Saranon's head was still thumping with a dull ache, but it was beginning to ease. Captain Harkin spoke, 'Stay close, I'll give the signal when you can move in.'

He was staring straight at her and she nodded. They moved out and Mitch did not budge. 'Why do you get to stay behind?' She shouted.

The Captain glared at her and she realised, 'Oh.'

The whistling wind sent a chill through the courtyard as the last of winter clung on. A white layer covered the hills through the valley. Only this time they were headed away from Keep Sturanin. The wizards knew the hillside well and they need not worry about her taking the lead. She could barely keep pace. A tiny glow shone up from the snow marking a faint lay-line and she smiled. The land was full of secrets that only the wizards knew. Anthony waited for her as she struggled. There was no sign of any sorcery other than her own, but she had to trust the Athgar. They had reason enough to seek out Ulrich.

The darkness eased with the rising sun. Revealing the entire valley and the forest below. The heavy frost was broken by patches of green. Marking the land as dragon territory. A few trees had blossomed early giving a magical appearance amid the snow. They had reached the end of the lay-line. All she wanted to do was run into the grass covered valley. Anthony held the hood of her cloak and whispered, 'No.'

She was about to speak. 'He's here,' the wizard said.

She glanced across the hills as the sun sparkled off the ridge line. There was no sign and she gazed longer in search of anything that might give Ulrich away.

Captain Harkin glanced her way, 'I will give the sign.'

She was beginning to get annoyed and almost wished to have gone on her own.

The well trodden path lay bare showing the pebbles below. The hardened ground allowed them to make good distance. Serensa loomed up ahead, the resting giant of a Keep in the hill. A hand full of sentinel dragons watched from above. The great beasts relaxed their wings in a half spread ready at any moment to take flight. Ulrich broke away from a small group. He was riding to Serensa and paying no heed of anyone. She glanced along the hillside where the dragons were forming a line. More gathered maintaining a casual glance down into the valley. Ulrich was mid-way along the winding path when the row of winged beasts increased. They were waiting and she could feel the tension.

The great beasts began to gather in the valley. Melting the snow that fell around the perimeter. Ulrich was gaining speed, soon he would be at Serensa. His horse reared and flung him to the wet muddy ground. The horse ran off, but it was not a person that had sent the steed into a spin. A dragon swooped lower still taunting the horse, it circled back wings spread wide. The animal shrieked galloping in a frightened frenzy for the nearest refuge. Saranon made her move breaking out of phase as light turned into a murky dark. The Angeon crept in with every step, seeping through her thoughts. Then the sun glistened as the real world welcomed her and the dragons watched. She stood on the path ahead, her cloak bellowing in the wind. The hot white glow of her yellow eyes glared at the false oracle and she dropped her hood. Ulrich was facing the Angeon.

He had trouble hiding his surprise and cursed the wizards. A rush of energy began pulling the false oracle into the void. It streamed toward the Angeon. Yet he held on, the Shalough were close. Saranon could feel the hooves of galloping horses hitting the hard ground. Ulrich built up his energy, a smile creased across his wrinkled face. The blasts of sorcery from the Shalough erupted through the air. Shattering the trees and scorching the earth. The Angeon still stood. A blaze of cold fire broke in a wide haze splitting the crisp morning air.

Ulrich shuddered as the shield held. Pelting blasts with bold precision straight for the Angeon. Each Shalough waiting with perfect timing, to keep the sorcery strong as it struck with a hollow drone. Sparks flew in a spray as the Angeon held the blasts back. Ulrich was gaining ground at a slow pace. As she stepped back with each blast that hit true thundering into the shield. It had decreased, but still protected her. Ulrich moved forward keeping pace with the Shalough. He was steadying himself and waited for the sorcerers to attack, but it never came.

He glanced behind him and a moment of panic struck him. The minotaur from the Pearl Castle had escaped. Ulrich turned to face the Angeon. She had regained her original position on the path. He continued to fall in line as blast after blast hit. He was not waiting anymore. A horrible howl emerged as the minotaur attacked and left only Ulrich standing.

The Angeon came closer, there was no gap between each attack. Ulrich held on, but as the sorcery cycled, his strength dimmed and Angeon closed in. He gave the blasts everything he had. The Angeon was nearing the edge of the shield, once that fell it was over. A giant thunderous crack pounded and he plunged backward. The ground met him with a thud.

The Angeon stood over him. He was rasping for every breath. 'You don't know what you've done,' he shouted. 'I was protecting your predecessor. Fool!'

Ulrich coughed up blood. 'You are not the only Angeon in this world,' his last words were faint.

He leaned back, the gurgle of death taking the air from his lungs. 'I was never the only Angeon,' Saranon said.

A cold rage ran through her. Somewhere among the Shalough hid an Angeon. Ulrich had been headed toward Serensa. When she had been there it had offered no sign. Yet Ulrich had made a deal with the Fires of Chaos. Perhaps the Angeon was truly hidden. Haig, the minotaur, was twice her height. Yet in the heartland amid the dragons he appeared small. They both did. 'Thank you,' she said.

'It is you I thank, Ulrich was no friend,' Haig said.

She gazed over the valley, there was no sign of the Shalough.

The wizards held no fear of the minotaur as they gathered around. Anthony patted her on the shoulder, 'Ulrich brought it on himself.'

A mix of feelings welled up within her. She could not speak. They waited in the cold fresh air as Captain Harkin and the wizards wrapped the body. To take it back to Ragnorda. It was the proof the wizards had been wanting. The death marked the end of years of hardship with the trade line. The link between north and south would make the Athgar great once more. Her stomach churned. If there was another Angeon out there, she had to find who it was. 'I have to go,' she told Anthony.

He peered into her eyes, 'We can deal with this.'

'There is something else,' she exclaimed.

Saranon had no doubt the wizards would secure the trade line. 'Do not fall for the Fires of Chaos,' he said.

'I won't,' she had no intention of allowing the Fires of Chaos to win, not this time.

Defeating Ulrich had taken much of her strength. She stayed close to the dragons of the heartland. Hiding in their shadows. The journey took her deeper into Shalough territory. The stream trickled by as she followed along its edge. The warm bellies of the great beast kept the harsh frost of winter at bay. Birds sang on the branches taunting her of spring as the sun began to fall below the ridge line.

The shadows darkened along the ground reaching farther as night fell. Yet she did not stop. The tiny white glow of a lay-line lured her in. She checked letting her energy sense its way along the path. It had not been used for some time. Saranon entered and she could tell why it remained unused. The lay-line took her close to the dragon dens. The great scales and thick skin moved within a fraction of the energy that let her pass at speed. A tail flicked and missed. The fear did not sink in, she had to make it to Serensa and find the Angeon before the Fires of Chaos did. What if they already knew? She was more determined than ever to head straight for the Keep.

Thunder cracked through the sky, it was not safe to be in the lay-line yet the end was in sight. The wind whipped through and she pulled her cloak tight just as the rain drenched her. She could sense the Keep up ahead as the rain pelted from the blackened sky. Saranon waited as the troops rode by making their way to the building rising from the hill. The Shalough sorcerers were a distance away and she watched wondering if they knew. It would be a long night as the howling wind ran through her cloak. There was no sign of the Fires of Chaos yet she could not be sure. She trudged, pacing herself along the muddy ground. What would make a sorcerer ruin the trade line? The question ate away at her mind.

The end nodes marking the boundary of Serensa were but a few steps away. As soon as she crossed the line the Shalough would know. If they did not already. She let the ends of the cloak fly free in the wind as the rain poured on her face. One hand gripped the hilt of Tellembre. The cream pearl blade stayed in its sheath at her side. She was Vandragamond, she did not run from a fight. She was the Angeon. She passed the end nodes and the Keep remained quiet. As the wind bellowed around the building. Lights shone from the energy of the central core and she headed to the brightest one. Steps led to the main entrance and the two heavy doors flung open as she made it to the landing.

Thunder struck along the hillside. Lighting the building as it edged close to the ground. The Shalough were caught off guard. Her eyes blazing with a determination that made her forget the icy chill. As a gush of wind droned through the entrance. 'Where is the Angeon?' She shouted.

Commander Meghan addressed her, 'Stand down Vandragamond.'

'Don't play coy with me. Where is the Angeon?' She demanded.

'Have you lost your mind? Perhaps Veridan should've

dealt with you,' the Commander said.

'Veridan ran away,' she said in an even tone scanning the troops that had come in from the cold.

A 'group of Shalough were gathering in the main entrance. She caught sight of Ranger Korban, but chose to ignore him. Dargon stepped forward blocking her path. 'Where are you hiding the Angeon?' She asked.

'Believe me, we would know if there was an Angeon,' his voice was firm and he did not back down.

She was tempted to take him on, she had to find who it was. Lindford stood beside him, his features similar to Ulrich. His hair greying with age. He stared at her unwavering. She held his gaze and grabbed his right hand turning it over. The grey mark was there, it matched hers.

He forced his arm free of her grip and she revealed the mark on her hands. 'I should have known,' she said.

It was Ulrich's brother who wore the mark of the Angeon. It was not enough to harm her, but to hide her predecessor as well. Her head was filled with a cascade of emotions. She had to leave even with the rain beating down. Serensa 'had become unbearable and the Keep would have known. She strode out to the landing as the wind caught at the edges of her cloak.

'Wait! I didn't know. No one did,' Commander Meghan called out.

She glanced back to find the sorcerers in a state of shock. 'Ulrich did,' she said.

'We didn't know. You cannot blame everyone for what one sorcerer's deeds,' the Commander said.

She hated to admit the Commander had a point. The secret had been concealed well. If she left the Fires of Chaos may show. She strode up to Lindford, 'Come with me.'

She did not wait to see if he followed and made her way toward the centre of Serensa. If the Keep was going to hide an Angeon the least it could do was help train him. The stadium for the soldiers had thick walls close to a main conduit. Leading down to the central core. It offered protection and now it would be an ideal training space. The soldiers practising stopped and silence fell around the two-storey room. A balcony ran along the side above her and benches, in rows lay underneath. She made her way down the isle to the threshold of the stadium.

Lindford spoke behind her, 'Practice is over.'

The Shalough filed out into the benches all eyes were on her. She let her sodden cloak fall on the floor. 'Enter,' she said, when it was clear Lindford would not follow.

'No,' he replied.

She gazed at him and he stood firm. She did not have time for games. 'I killed Ulrich,' she said.

She caught the change in his expression. He entered the stadium as the Shalough sorcerers looked on. Lindford steadied himself at the opposite end of stadium. It was only for a brief moment then the blast came. She was ready, the fight with Ulrich had heightened her senses. Her energy lay below the surface, but this was not about defeat. She had to call the Angeon to the surface or he would be vulnerable. She spread her attack wide with little effort. Yet it vanquished Lindford's attempt with ease. He staggered back and fired again. She kept her attack wide. The energy spreading around the edges rather than in a direct line. It was not enough for the Angeon locked within to rise.

Lindford strengthened his attack increasing the flow of energy every time. She maintained her strategy with a firm patience. The Angeon had to rise to the surface. That was her aim. Serensa absorbed the sorcery in the thick walls as sparks flew. She could make out the glowing crease along his arms, the Angeon was about to rise. She could sense it and kept up the attack. Sweeping her energy around both sides, making him rely on the sorcery of old. She was so close, then came the glow in his eyes and she gave a shout of victory. The Angeon had risen to the surface. The Shalough crowded around the arena in silent awe. She waited for Lindford to return the energy inside, but it stayed on the surface. Dargon rushed into the arena and she held up her hand for him to stop.

Time slowed and it felt as though they waited too long. Then the glow dissipated. The relief on Dargon was visible and he rushed in as Lindford fell to his knees. 'In the morning we spar.' She said.

His face was drained with exhaustion. 'Ulrich was protecting you from something.' She explained.

Saranon picked up her cloak and used her energy to dry it. Instead of returning through the crowd she waited for Commander Meghan. 'I need to speak with Serensa,' she said.

'I don't think…' The Commander began.

A sealed entrance behind them opened onto the

stadium. She took her leave, her head was filled with so many thoughts. Including the Keep that had hidden Lindford from her. She travelled down to the chamber. The dark liquid shaol ran in a slow stream to one side. At the end lay an altar, yet she had no need of it. She expanded a sova bag making a small bed on the floor and rested. Clearing her head of the mess that raged inside. 'What did you think I would do?' She spoke the words aloud.

Serensa answered in her mind, you are Vandragamand always. 'I am the Angeon always. Lindford is my kin, you could have told me,' she said.

Serensa answered, he stays here.

'I was not going to take him. He is too weak,' she said.

There was silence. Perhaps she could have been a bit less blunt with her choice of words. Serensa entered her mind once more, You agree he stays. 'I agree, he should remain,' she said.

Senensa responded, typical Vandragamond. Saranon smiled, 'Typical Keep, always hiding secrets.'

Serensa answered, I am not the only one. Then the Keep fell silent. The chamber was warm and dry. She drifted off to a peaceful sleep filled of nothing. As the central core hummed away in the depths below.

Serensa broke her thoughts. It was early morning and the Shalough were preparing for the day. She made her way to the arena, her muscles were tired and sore. The arena was almost empty. She spotted Lindford who appeared well rested. 'Are you ready to spar?' He asked.

He appeared concerned at her appearance. She was

waking up, but she could still spar. 'I'm ready when you are,' she replied.

'Typical Vandragamond,' he said.

She hesitated, 'Do you hear the Keep?'

'No,' he said.

'She can hear you,' Saranon said.

They entered the arena and Dargon stayed. This time he sat in anticipation and she smiled, 'I think your friend wants a show.'

Lindford shook his head in dismay. It did not stop him from leading as the first blast rang out. She concentrated keeping the same steady pace. Moving ever so slightly to practice what she knew. She could only hope it would be enough. At times the blasts hit their mark, she absorbed the blows just as the Keep did. This was about practice, not the fight.

Bridget entered and they stopped. It had been a long morning and the sun was nearing midday. Dargon spoke, 'Caddell wants to speak with the Angeon at Serensa.'

The Fires of Chaos were here already. She replied, 'Well, then I had better go.'

'He wants to see Lindford,' Dargon explained.

'I am the Angeon at Serensa,' she said in a firm tone.

Dargon bowed, 'Indeed.'

She glanced around the room, 'Shall we go?'

They made their way toward the main entrance. As they did Saranon let the energy of the Angeon rise to the surface. She may be Vandragamond, but she was also the Angeon. It was time to meet the Fires of Chaos. The

Shalough bowed and stepped away letting her pass as she moved ahead. A hush of silent awe fell on the sorcerers gathered in the entrance as all eyes turned to her. For a moment everyone ignored the Fires of Chaos as she entered. Her voice boomed across the great height as light shone through the open doors. Illuminating the pale walls, in stark contrast to her heavy dark cloak. 'I am the Angeon,' she shouted into the silence.

CHAPTER TWENTY

Taking on the Fires of Chaos

Saranon strode with a determined march to face the Fires of Chaos. The sorcerers stayed in a close group near the threshold of the entrance. She grabbed the hilt of the bond-breaker Tellembre. The blade sang as it was released, glowing in the light. It was not the blade that mattered as the sorcerers eyes followed its move. 'You are not the one we seek,' Caddell said.

'I could say the same,' she said.

Her eyes caught on the shadowy movement. Across the skin of the sorcerer behind Caddell. The sign of forbidden sorcery. She spread her energy wide as she had done when sparring Lindford. All bar one of of the group fell in agony. She steadied herself, not wanting to reveal her surprise.

Dark shadows crept across the skin of the Fires of Chaos. Her stomach ached as she realised they had stolen wizardry. She stayed firm as the Shalough gathered in a silent vigil. No one stepped in to help. A long moment passed, before the sorcerers from the Fires of Chaos began to realise they would live. Giselbert distanced himself from the group. 'At least one of you had sense,' she said.

Dargon gave a menacing expression and stood by her side. 'I can either hand them over to the Athgar or you can deal with them. What say you?' Saranon asked him.

Dargon gave a terrifying grin that sent a chill down her spine. 'We can deal with them,' he said. 'What of that one?' he pointed to Giselbert.

The tall gaunt sorcerer trembled. 'I have no interest in that one,' she said.

'Be gone,' Dargon had no need to say more.

The sorcerer vanished from sight as he darted across the open courtyard. It did not take long for order to be restored to Serensa. She did not want to know what would happen to the Fires of Chaos that had become razen. Dark sorcery was universally detested, even among the Shalough.

The sky darkened and she glanced upward. To see the wingspan of Katholomu as he landed with a great thud near the stairs. He poked his nose through the doorway and she patted him. 'You missed the action,' she told him.

The magnificent beast eyed her and let out a sound of disgruntlement. Mitch ran up the stairs to greet her and she fought the urge to run into his arms. 'If you ever need someone to spar with I would be more than happy to,' she spoke to Lindford.

'Stay out of trouble,' he said.

She smiled and waved. Then followed Mitch, clambering up to the great dragon's shoulder. She waited for him to give the signal and Kat whooshed into the air. His wings spread their full width taking them higher.

'You made some friends,' he said in her ear as the wind rushed past.

'Maybe,' she answered. 'How did you escape Lady Muir?'

'She only had eyes for another,' he said.

She laughed and hugged the dragon tight. It was good to be back in the air. She watched as they flew over the heartland. Dragons joined them at brief intervals darting through the sky. 'Has anyone heard from the battle?' She asked.

'Lord Halleron had an entire league, what do you think happened?' he said.

'Umm...' She said.

'The Shalough retreated,' he answered.

The great beast flew in one direction, the last she had ever expected. 'What are you doing?' She asked.

'I am taking you where you need to go,' Mitch said.

The sun set low on the horizon when Katholomu glided the last distance. The Keep shone golden as the last rays of light beamed off the building. The dragon circled down with a jolt as he hit the ground, still moving. The grass had grown over the fields surrounding Antavagon. The stone markers along with the camps were gone. A wind swept past and she hesitated. 'Why did you bring me here?' Saranon asked.

This time Katholomu answered, 'Home.'

'This is not my home,' she replied.

The great dragon nudged her toward the Keep. Antavagon remained silent as she stood in Darkonia, her homeland. She took a deep breath and ventured in. The place was clean and the morning light swept over the plain walls. She reached out and hesitated. Mitch made a noise as he strode toward her and she jumped. 'You need to let go,' he said and she turned away.

There was so much pain hidden within the Keep. She made her way down to the pale room where the altar lay in the middle. Light streamed through from above. She could still see the blood on the floor and her hands. Tasha's blood. The memory of not being able to save her friend remained etched in her mind.

She touched the altar and a voice spoke. ' I have been waiting,' the lady said.

The lady was taller than Tasha, but she had the same fawn coloured hair. 'Who are you? Saranon asked.

'You know who I am,' the lady answered. 'I am Antavagon.'

'But I thought you were…' She began.

'Your friend. That, I have always been,' the lady answered. 'It is time.'

She pulled her hand away from the altar. 'Katholomu brought you home.'

'But this isn't…' She said.

'I have guided you from the moment you left,' the lady responded. 'Look at your hands, tell me what you see?'

The marks on her palms were stronger, there was no way she could hide them.

CHAPTER TWENTY-ONE

Home eternal

One choice was all it took, the ground trembled from below. Saranon glanced back at Antavagon rising over the land. It remained silent as she left. The Keep that held so much anguish. Yet where there had been pain the memory of her friend Tasha remained. The riding cat took her to the glow of the lay-line. She slid off and the misquew bowed its head. The path led to a rumbling deep within Tordoren, one she could not ignore. Each step took her into the territory of the Arthrose. Once she may have hesitated. Yet she was no longer the child that had grown in the shadows of Darkonia. A breeze hinted the end of winter as it fled along the steep valley carved into the earth.

Keep Kedorenn stood partly visible along the steep cliff. The closer Saranon stepped the more certain she became. That the Arthrose knew she was there. A flicker ran near the edge of her vision, as she made the final step movement caught her eye. The flanks of the Darkonian Army spread across both sides of the terrain. Major Shenoff eyed her, his hand resting on the hilt of his blade.

Two years had passed, yet the Major looked not a day older. His broad shoulders carried the weight of a mask of calm. Greying hair kept neat under the rim of the helmet. A faint noise could be heard and to her dismay Mitch emerged from the lay-line. The wizard had a habit of showing up at the wrong time. Her cringe did not go unnoticed. Barely a word was spoken as they followed toward the Keep.

Glimpses of fresh grass and moss wedged between the rocks gave a hint of the warmer days to come. She stayed close to the Major who had little to say. Yet there was something about his eager stride that set her at ease. It was not long before the path veered into the cliff. Opening into a deep void filled with many outlooks across the land. Pennie stood out with her blonde hair and sparkling eyes. She had been so long away and hesitated in the grip of her friend. 'You are here to find the Prince,' Pennie said.

Whispered into her ear while darting around. Her old friend had always been able to think of a plan. The problem was seeing it through, Saranon had been the one to do that. She smiled and took a deep breath while buying time. A Prince? 'What happened?' She blurted it out, but Pennie beamed with delight.

It felt like old times, Pennie had grown and changed. Her hair was longer and tied neatly back. Saranon realised she was being led away as the door closed behind Mitch. Pennie returned to the friend she knew well, the one that had a greater temper than her. 'Are you mad? This is the largest stronghold the Arthrose has within the Army. If one of the Captain's wants you dead there will be little anyone can do.'

'You are here,' Saranon said.

'I am not the one who destroyed the camps. The only reason why you are here. Is because the deaths of the Arthrose Councillors were investigated. It wasn't you,' Pennie snapped.

She was speechless, the Eye of Escora had been in her hands. Saranon had wanted it so badly. She always thought she had willed it to happen. 'You have to find Prince Demarkos, his companions returned without him. They are shaken, but the details are vague,' Pennie became insistent. 'If he isn't found soon the Arthrose will be looking for someone to blame.'

That glare hid so much fear. Saranon nodded, she could not believe she had returned. To run straight into one of Pennie's schemes. A smile crept across her face. It did not take long for Mitch to merge into the background, she wished it was so easy for her. The Major made himself busy, but she could tell he was finding any excuse to stay nearby. The control room had commanding views that swept along the great ravine. Saranon caressed the wall with her finger tips. A faint movement rumbled from beneath. 'You will not find Kedorenn responsive,' the Major said as he watched her.

She paid him little heed as the Keep sang. It was well loved and hummed away with a vibrant tone through the walls. She lifted her hand and the space fell silent. Except for the officers maintaining the Keep.

No sooner than she gazed back toward the control room, when the door burst open revealing a weary Captain Assinden. Pennie's hylizen drew up short of speaking, staring at her and then the Major. The Major nodded and Captain Jacob Assinden relaxed his guard. At least there were a few familiar faces in Darkonia. 'The trail ends at Lepithia,' he said.

A hushed tone fell over the small group as Major Shenoff stared straight at her. Saranon had no idea what it meant and the Major filled in the silence. 'Lepithia is on its way out. The Keep has been abandoned and we stay well clear. Looks like you bought your ticket home.' There was no joy in the Major's voice.

Captain Assinden spoke, 'We can take you as far as the end node.'

He guided her out of the room. 'Bring the Prince back alive,' the edge in his tone sent a chill down her spine.

Pennie rushed to greet her in the chaos that followed. Everyone wanted the Prince to return regardless of how they felt about her. The wind whipped around the base of the Keep with a terrible drone. It played havoc with the dragons who were grounded. 'We take the misquew,' Captain Assinden said.

No one was prepared to argue. Saranon could sense the change in the flow of energy seeping through the ground.

Before they reached the edge of the Keep. The riding cats would travel no closer and she had to disembark. The wizards remained where they were. Captain Assinden had taken her as far as he was prepared to go. Pennie strode toward the building and she followed. It took them into the hillside and the air prickled. 'Are you sure we should be looking here?' She asked.

Pennie nodded, but waited for Saranon to take the lead. It had always been that way for as long as they had been friends. An echo rang out from within. No hum ran along the walls, but odd sounds drifted up from the depths. Stairs led upward and the sounds grew faint as she glanced around. The place was dust ridden and a cold breeze emanated from the broken windows. There was no sign that anyone had been here, yet she felt the need to check if only for her friend. Saranon made her way down and Pennie volunteered to stay behind. The occasional jarring clunk filtered through the old Keep.

The indolin chambers were mostly intact, but the conduits had been left to decay. Pools of sheal liquid dripped along the floor. She moved further away from the stairs and any sign of the outside world. A faint sound travelled up from below. Merging with the last gasps of the central core hidden deep in Tordoren. A voice reached her ears then it was gone. Her heart pounded as she glanced around. There was no sign of life, but Saranon swore she heard it.

The path to the imbenik chambers was blocked with a myriad of fallen rubble. Doubt filled her mind, but she pressed on. A great rumbling echoed through the walls and she called out. This time the voice was clear. She stood near an open conduit, its contents long gone. Saranon called down into the darkness and a reply sent a chill down her spine. 'I have been waiting for you,' he said in a calm and confident tone.

'I doubt that,' she retorted.

As she climbed into the broken conduit and made her way down. Gloom filled the void with one tiny light shimmering against the darkness. It was not the Prince that waited to greet her. The Host was part wizard and part Keep. He rested on the floor, barely moving. He pointed to a sleeping sorcerer down the corridor and a gaping void in between. 'How long do you have?' Saranon asked.

'Hours, minutes, they are the same,' the Host replied. 'The energy is gone.'

The hairs on the back of her neck stood on end. The Host was calm, he knew his life would end and there was nothing she could do. She made her way into the darkness letting her energy flow. Melding with what remained of the Keep. A ledge extended out to where the Prince slept. At a closer glance he was tall and his frame strong. He woke with a start, he had short curls of fawn brown colour. There was no mistaking his eyes, they were Tasha's.

Saranon held out her hand and the Prince hesitated. 'Now would be a good time to leave,' she said.

He did not move. 'Major Shenoff sent me,' she explained.

'The Major would not send a Vandragamond,' he

rasped.

Saranon handed him a flask and he took gulps of water, letting it drip down his chin. 'I will wait,' Prince Demarkos replied.

She had to fight the urge to thump him. 'You can wait above ground, it will be easier to evacuate,' she suggested in a firm tone.

The Prince gazed around, as though taking in the surroundings for the first time. He was unsteady on his feet and almost fell. Saranon was not impressed, but there was an uneasy sense as she watched him. There was no explanation for the Prince's state, at least none that she could see. She guided him away from the dying Host who lay motionless in the rubble. He leaned against her for support and they glanced at each other. As Prince Demarkos became more aware he grew anxious. Pennie greeted them as light streamed through. The fields outside were empty of life, overgrown and untouched. She slipped back down to where the Host remained. His forehead was cool and he still breathed. He spoke in a whisper, 'You are looking for this.'

The Host clasped her hand and images flooded through. The colour drained from his face and the images faded with his last dying breath. The Prince left behind was no accident.

A terrible clambering climbed up the walls. The Host was gone and no energy remained. A great rumbling moved through the building, roaring up from the cavities. As she entered the broken conduit the sound haunted her from the depths. The sound of the central core straining under the weight. Saranon clambered up, willing her limbs to move faster. As she reached out over the jagged opening. A sound filled her with such dread that she hesitated. The eruption rumbled deep beneath the ground. Making its way up the empty conduits through the walls. She ran to find Pennie, 'Get out!'

Pennie stood there for a moment, not comprehending the danger. 'It collapsed, run!'

Pennie waited. 'Why aren't you going?' Saranon asked.

'I'm not leaving without you,' Pennie replied.

She wanted to shake her friend. 'You have to go now. I will be behind you, but you have to leave now,' She was running out of patience.

A terrible roar emerged from deep below. It steadily grew louder. Pennie hesitated then went with the Prince who was still struggling. The rumble from beneath drowned out all other noise. They were not going to make it. She was in a dying Keep and her friend was not going to make it. Saranon turned to face what remained of Lepithia. She glanced down at the faint marks on her hands. The noise became so loud it almost hurt her ears. Then a silence followed as she reached out to the Angeon. The sorcery of old and the Vandragamond that she knew she was. The others had been Shalough, except for her. Except the one who could break the world, and break Tordoren. The thought filled her with a deep horror and understanding. The blast was erupting deep beneath the surface, heading closer with every passing moment.

Saranon had lost one friend, she was not about to lose another. The Angeon enveloped her very essence. Tordoren had chosen her. It had chosen her above the Shalough, it had chosen a different path. She reached out with the energy of the Angeon letting it flow freely, filling the void. The rumbling from the deep was so loud, yet so far away. She let the energy sink deep. Ripping an opening in the ground that pierced deep into Tordoren. The rumbling swept into the void as it opened beneath. Crashing into the darkness as the building crumbled around her. She held on, keeping the great crevasse open. Tordoren rumbled deep below forcing the void to close.

She held on as the pressure increased, hoping it would be enough. The hollow void filled with a deep warning as it shook. The sides began to give way and finally Saranon let it crumble. The earth swallowed the last of the dying Keep. A shudder sent a fine spray of dirt and dust hurtling through the air. Saranon waited in the shield as the air became thick. She made her way through the haze and a breeze began to creep in. The fine mist dissipated as she made her way to the lay-line. Her hands were sore and the marks were real. This time Tordoren had chosen someone else. Someone the rest of the world had not been expecting. Someone with the strength to choose a different path.

ACKNOWLEDGEMENTS

Life has been a journey filled with many challenges, and the people I would like to thank would not fit on this page. To everyone out there who has been part of this incredible journey thank you, your support has been appreciated.

– Please Leave a Review –

For all the wonderful people who have read the book it would be fantastic if you can leave a review, this helps other readers find it. Thank you.

BOOKS

The Legacy of Zyanthia series:
Made in the Image of the Goddess
Running through the Rising Tide
Deep in the Shadow of the Fallen
Challenging the Fires of Chaos

AUTHOR

If you love fantasy with adventure and a hint of the unexpected the quest is about to begin. Escape into fantasy, and the mystical world of magic mixed with adventure. You are in good company although chose your company wisely. There are anti-heroes, wizards, and a range of chaotic characters ahead. Not to mention dragons. A fantasy world set in an ancient mythical world has to have dragons. Tales of sword and sorcery captivated Chantelle from a young age. Reading until all hours of the night to find out what would happen to the characters. There was just one problem the story would finish far too soon.

Hidden away in the distant past the life of a fantasy writer began. The real life struggles have been a saga all of their own for author Chantelle Griffin born in Tasmania, Australia. Her dreams haunted her from an early age. Vivid tumultuous dreams carrying adventure and danger. It took the author into a fantasy world filled with sorcery and treachery. The story continues to captivate her writing. If you love fantasy with adventure follow the Legacy of Zyanthia series.

www.chantellegriffin.com

GLOSSARY

ANGEON: 'The Angeon is Darkonia's answer to the Oracle, a sorcerer born with the ability to break down all defences and render a civilisation powerless.' There had been no Angeon since shortly after the Dreshan Occupation ended over 200 years ago with Zeralden Hadenvar the last Angeon who ruled Darkonia (as Queen) by marriage to the King's second son.

BOND-BREAKER: A weapon made by sorcery when dormant resembles a dagger, when activated resembles a sword it acts as a catalyst to magnify and aim the user's energy and can be used equally well by wizards as well as sorcerers. 'The most feared swords a sorcerer could use made of heart stone a melding of the elements to form a solid material that resembled crystal and sharp enough to cut through stone.'

CENTRAL CORE: The working core mechanism which powers the Keep, usually hidden away deep within the earth. It is a large engine created by sorcery which then continues to thrive on a combination of energy drawn from deep within the earth and sorcery. The combination creates a very raw and powerful energy which is difficult to manipulate.

DEAD ZONE: This is created when part of the Keep is not receiving energy from the central core or when energy has been diverted.

END NODE: Last outpost of a Keep's main energy source located at semi-regular intervals around the perimeter.

FERMADICIDE: Dark skeletal creatures.

FIRE MARK: A mark on the right shoulder to, the symbol of the fires of chaos given to the Issola in the camps.

HILAZEN: Bonded wizard.

HOST: Wizard joined with a Keep, it takes 60 hours to complete a union.

HYRIK: Restraint on sorcery, like a collar.

IMBENIK CHAMBER: Near the central core within the Keep, in between the indolin chamber and the central core it contains alters where a sorcerer can meld with the Keep.

INDOLIN CHAMBER: Inside the Keep, in between the habitable area and the central core.

KEDRIL(S): Tools to fix a Keep.

KEEP: A building protected by a central core powered by sorcery and energy from the earth. The tunnels led down to the primary systems and the central core that transferred energy from far below the ground into the core and turned into a usable energy source. Most central cores were located deep in the ground where the temperature was constantly warm…'

KULTIER: Long giant cockroaches.

LAY-LINE: Fast method of travel.

MAZETTE: Small (bird size) dragons.

MISQUEW: Riding cat.

NEFRELLE: Small creature (cat size), part human with very sharp teeth and claws.

OCKREN: Big cat, the soul of the Keep.

PALAFON: Tiny dragon.

QUADMAR: Aquatic creature from the murky depths, larger than a mermaid.

SACRA SEAL: Small, can hold it on your hand.

SHEAL: Liquid inside the Keep, very potent compressed raw energy.

SKADA: Small mechanical creatures that help maintain the Keep, they resemble a large spider.

SOVA BAG: A deceptive small light pouch that can become an enormous bag and hold a lot of objects, it will not hold living things.

STALLIC ENERGY: Energy from the Keep.

TALIK: Communication device. 'The sorceress held up her talik a small round disc that could open small enough to fit in the palm of her hand and placed her thumb on the centre of the outside…'

TRIDEN: Giant crab/spider, dark brown.

UVALEN CODE: '…A complex masterpiece describing the natural laws that governed sorcery.'

ZENNIGH: A large cat that normally lives within a Keep, they are too big to fit in a house but that has not stopped the occasional one from trying and getting their head jammed in the doorway.

ZYANTHIAN REGION: Armedicia, Taria, Normisia, Darkonia and Alveron were formed from one country called Zyanthia.